the Beauty of Lies

of

Lies

a stand by me novel

BRINDA BERRY

Published by Sweet Biscuit Publishing LLC
Edited by Nancy Cassidy of
www.redpencoach.com

Acknowledgments

Undying gratitude to Audrey Estes and Mandy Dismang for their candid first readings of this novel. Many times, they read what were merely the seeds I'd planted and needed to tend. Their excitement about reading helped me to remember why I do this.

My constant critique partner Abbie Roads gave me the best comments. The good, bad, and the ugly—she left no stone unturned and helped me to pull all the weeds.

The devil is surely in the details. Thank you, Nancy Cassidy, for diligent editing. You cared as much as I did about making this the best novel possible.

I'm drawn to great cover art. I love the cover for this book. Thank you Najla Qamber, for cover design magic; Scott Hoover, for memorable photography; Ellie of Lovenbooks.com, for awesome photo matchmaking; and model/actor Hollis Chambers, for bringing a book boyfriend to life.

As always, the READerlicious.com writers supported me with an endless and much appreciated offering of opinions, critiques, and belly laughs.

A special thank you to my husband Brent, who has never asked me to quit chasing my dreams. To him, I say, "145. Always."

And to you reader, thank you. I strive to take you away from your troubles for a few hours. I hope I succeeded.

Truth is beautiful, without doubt; but so are lies.

~Ralph Waldo Emerson

Toe the Line

Leo Jensen

I SCROLL DOWN THE LIST of unopened emails and wonder why bat-shit crazy seems to follow me.

"SUBJECT: You must like getting your toes sucked." The subject line alone forces me to grimace. I can guess what's coming next. I'll open the email and find some misguided blog follower who wants to rant at me for my latest post. Or maybe the sender is making an offer.

At least my toes would be getting some action.

Yesterday, I wrote a blog post about a teacher who was fired for inappropriate behavior. Why did she lose her job? She'd chronicled about toe *affection* on her personal, yet public, blog. A fetish post for certain, but pretty tame by internet standards.

I wrote that her romantic preferences were her business, and certainly didn't merit getting canned. It's not like she fondled a student's little piggies. Teachers certainly don't deserve scarlet letters for admitting they have a love life.

Love and romance.

These are topics I have no business talking about, since I'm officially on strike when it comes to women. My *A Torrid Toe Affair* post garnered over two hundred comments, some more snarky than others. Blog traffic spikes with sex-related topics.

Last week, I exposed a restaurant owner taking advantage of underage employees. The week before, I featured a postcard submission from a woman who'd been fired by her employer for not letting him give her dictation. Naked. Him, not her.

I seem to be a regular employee advocate this month. The month before, my posts were all about politics.

Don't get me wrong. I'm not a masked marauder for justice. No cape in my closet. My talent for revealing truth seems to be accidental. It's not what I really want out of life. I want to write books that entertain and thrill and keep you awake at night, turning pages.

I spend all my daytime hours working on my paying gig using my pseudonym, Mr. Expose. In the middle of the night, I hammer out my latest manuscript called *The Incident,* a political thriller on its third rewrite.

I click the boxes of at least twenty emails. Delete, delete, delete. I have more pressing things to do than read this shit.

The postcards on my desk pull at my attention. I pick up the top one. It's a plain, white postcard with a picture of a crow on the front. I flip the card over to study the back. The sender's handwriting tells me that he or she was in a hurry. The connective strokes between each letter are broken and thready. Barely there. The breaks between the letters indicate the person is impatient.

Handwriting analysis experts say our writing is like a fingerprint. The lines and curlicues can reveal the personality of the sender—whether they are open and honest or if they're hiding something.

I took a class on graphology, because writers are like that. We like to know what makes people tick.

Some people don't like my requirement for a postcard submission. They say my rule is archaic. That an online columnist shouldn't act like a Luddite. The requirement does stop most impulsive people who would send an electronic submission in the same way they post a Facebook status—without taking time to think about repercussions.

The world is full of crazies.

Case in point. My cursor hovers over a new email in a thread of messages from one particular woman over the course of the past month. Even though I should delete these as quickly as I do the other spammy emails in my box, I don't. I can't help myself. Sometimes, it's good to read one or two to remind myself of the reason I stay anonymous.

From: angelgirl@me.com
To: mrexposeblog@gmail.com

Mr. Expose,

I submitted a postcard to your blog. After sending it, I realized I shouldn't have. May I request that you return the submission to me? I'll be sending a self-addressed envelope to your postal box where you can send the postcard back. I believe I signed my name as 'Betrayed Woman,' or 'Angry Woman.'

I apologize for my error and hope I've written you in time.

Thank you,

Angel

***

From: mrexposeblog@gmail.com
To: angelgirl@me.com

Dear Angel,

Thanks for following my blog and sending in a submission. I regret it's against my policy to return any items sent in. I get frequent requests similar to yours. As you know, I have no real way of identifying you, since submissions don't contain real names.

You can rest assured that no one will know you submitted the postcard. I am very serious about the privacy of my sources.

I'm happy to say I've received over 500 postcards already this year. Chances are yours will not be selected for a blog post on Mr. Expose. I hope this allays your fears.

Sincerely,

Mr. Expose

***

From: angelgirl@me.com
To: mrexposeblog@gmail.com

Mr. Expose,

I don't think you understand. It's important to

me that I get the postcard back. Its return is crucial to my well-being. I couldn't sign my name since your guidelines tell us not to, but you can easily pick my card out of a pile. It's pink with some flowery things on the back. I'm putting a self-addressed envelope in the mail to your box. Please return my postcard.

Many lives will be damaged by my thoughtless and selfish submission if it is selected for a blog. Consider this more of a plea than a simple request.

Angel

***

From: mrexposeblog@gmail.com
To: angelgirl@me.com

Angel,

I do understand there is a measure of urgency to your request. Still, I cannot break policy. I could spend all my time with administrative tasks such as this.

In the future, I suggest you think through your actions more carefully. Impulsiveness is the downfall of many.

Please do not email again.

Mr. Expose

***

From: angelgirl@me.com
To: mrexposeblog@gmail.com

It's not like I'm going to prison if I don't get my card back, but I absolutely need to take care of destroying the postcard myself. Hindsight is 20/20 multiplied by a million. I completely see my mistake now. My thoughts were a jumbled mess when I wrote the postcard and revenge was my only goal. But I have no quarrel with the person my postcard will affect and I need to stop the publication. I am really, really sorry, but I must demand that you respond to my request.

***

From: angelgirl@me.com
To: mrexposeblog@gmail.com

Mr. Expose,

Did you receive my last email? I think you must

have lost it or it's in your spam folder. Please reply.

Angel

***

From: angelgirl@me.com
To: mrexposeblog@gmail.com

Mr. Expose???!!!

I've sent the envelope so you can return my postcard. I am begging you to be human. I realize you must think I'm irrational to want something you obviously consider unimportant, but come on. I know from reading your blog that you attempt to correct the wrongs of the world by exposing those who would be dishonest.

This postcard and information will only do harm at this point. You will *destroy* lives.

Angel

***

From: angelgirl@me.com
To: mrexposeblog@gmail.com

16

Mr. Expose,

I can't keep writing you. You keep blogging and posting pics from random postcards, so I know you are in your stash of postcards often enough to do me the courtesy of a reply.

You are a postcard hoarding a-hole.

Yours truly,

Angel

***

My cell phone pings with an incoming message. I glance at the cell's display and tap the message from my ex-girlfriend.

Tori: *Don't be King of the Assholes. Answer my calls. If you don't, I will come in person.*

King? I'm honored. Between the crazy woman texting me, and the one emailing about her postcard, there's a consensus.

I've gone my entire life being known as the nice guy. Not anymore. I've wandered to the dark side. Maybe this is where I'll find solitude, a place to get my manuscript finished for the agent who requested it.

Tori isn't going to harass me into calling,

and Angel Girl isn't going to force me to dig out her postcard. I don't hesitate this time when my cursor hovers over the email message.

Delete.

Waiting for the Other Shoe to Drop

Harper Angel Wade

LETTING MYSELF INTO A STRANGER'S apartment isn't the worst of sins. Mr. Expose has something that belongs to me, and I intend to get it. I'm not a real criminal. I committed my last illegal act in grade school when I shoplifted a My Little Pony for a friend. Later, regret set in and I imagined being hauled away and thrown into the slammer. I took the toy back to the store and slipped it onto the shelf. Incarceration didn't scare me as much as a tongue-lashing from my daddy, the town pastor.

Breaking and entering is my first official crime of adulthood. My decisions these days have returned to the devil-made-me-do-it variety.

I push a desk drawer closed and continue to search through the paperwork in a box on his desk. A water bill, a flyer, a grocery list.

There's a pamphlet for renter's insurance. Boy, does he ever need some. There are all kinds of nut jobs in this world who would rob him blind. If I could advise the guy on how to avoid this situation in the future, I'd be sure to tell him that his apartment was a break-in waiting to happen. He conveniently left a key for me right under the welcome mat; as if that isn't the first place a burglar would look.

And, while I'm handing out advice, I'd caution him not to be so assholey. His recent emails to me were downright rude and as short as my attention span during Sunday sermons.

In fact, his replies weren't at all like his introspective musings on the Mr. Expose blog. No. Those are poetic masterpieces that dig into the psyche and pull back the curtain on evil.

But Mr. Expose blogger, also known as Leo Jensen, refuses to return my postcard. He recited all this baloney about policy and not mailing things back when people change their minds. Yada yada.

I blame him for my foray into the dark world of thievery. Harper Angel Wade—one account of felony, stealing a postcard.

The scraping sound of a key in the door lock has me frantically searching for a place to hide. My heart thrashes around in my chest like a trapped animal. I slip around a corner and slide underneath Leo's bed like a runner into home base, a slight friction burn setting my left leg on fire.

The space underneath is shallow and barely covered by the cream comforter. In my limited vantage point, I make out movement near the apartment entrance. It will be a miracle if he doesn't notice me. My head skims the bottom of the bed frame. My weight loss this year is the only thing saving me from being wedged under this bed like a piece of barbecue in your back molars.

Minutes tick by and a teeny drop of sweat escapes my hairline. It tickles against my hot face while taking its sweet time to meander centimeter by centimeter, eventually dripping into my eye. I strain to catch a glimpse of Leo. He's walking around in the next room, each step squeaking as if his soles are too clean against the spit-shined floor.

Does Mr. Perfect sense something is amiss in his judgmental, I'm-too-spectacular-for-myself world?

The disturbing protests of his noisy shoes end, but he's still moving around the apartment.

A dreaded June bug scuttles along the baseboard at my eye level. Just kill me now. I can handle anything but a June bug. I squeeze my eyes shut for a second and try to forget about the Starship Troopers movie—the one that convinced me bugs are evil.

His feet linger at the side of the bed. There's

a clattering noise as he drops some stuff onto the nightstand. I lose a little dignity and concentration as I stare at Leo's ankles. The squeaky shoes have been discarded somewhere.

His feet aren't bad. Not bad at all. Usually a guy's feet give me the heebie jeebies—a residual phobia from the summer I worked in a men's shoe store. But his bare feet are actually nice. No callused, cracked heels or Bigfoot hairy toes.

After our email exchange, I pictured him as some cranky old fart who lived with twenty cats and stacks old newspapers in the corner. The newspapers would, of course, be hiding the stacks of postcards.

On the contrary, it appears Mr. Expose has good grooming habits and a very tidy apartment. No errant socks or dust bunnies share my hiding place. The June bug scuttles along the baseboard, daring me to look away. I can't blame him for the June bug. They have a mind of their own.

But this guy isn't perfect or predictable. Although he's stuck to the same schedule every day this week, today he failed to eat lunch at the bar on Printer's Avenue.

One would think he knew I was going to show up.

I suppress a sigh and crane my neck from side to side, looking for a comfortable position.

The June bug has disappeared to the opposite side of the room. Leo's feet move out of view, but he's still in the bedroom. I inhale deeply, the scent of his woodsy cologne reaching my nose. Nice.

The bed sags a little over my head. No way. He's going to take a nap?

Resting my forehead on the floor, I allow myself a bit of self-pity and picture my rap sheet. It's a bad hair day for a mug shot. The humid Nashville weather will make me appear a likely felon.

Clickety-clickety-tap-tap. He's pounding the keys on his laptop and I imagine the worst. Prayer is not out of the question here. If he's working from his bed instead of the fantastic desk in the other room, I'm going to scream. He works for hours straight. Why did he skip lunch to work on his computer?

The tapping stops. There's some movement on the bed as he gets comfortable.

The television clicks on. I need to cough. It's as if my mouth has dried and been filled cotton balls. Dry, tickly cotton balls. The sounds of a soap opera meet my ears. It's unbelievable, but also a little amusing that he deviated from routine so he could watch daytime drama. Perhaps this is where he learned his poetic, yet dramatic writing style for his blog.

Ruining lives by exposing one postcard at a

time.

My muscles ache from holding still as a two-by-four for an entire hour. Checking my watch, I try not to panic. Finally, the television clicks off and Leo leaves. I take my time extracting my stiff body from underneath his bed.

If he decides to do what he normally does at this time, I'll have less than an hour to finish rifling through his apartment. At 1:00 in the afternoon on every Tuesday and Thursday, Leo visits the Nashville Library. I haven't followed him inside, but he always goes in with a handful of paperwork and leaves empty handed. This excursion ranks high on his list of puzzling routines, but no more mysterious than most of the facts about him.

His apartment reminds me of a library. Everything has an organized spot, which makes the location of his blogging material sort of mind-boggling. Postcards for his Mr. Expose blog should certainly be beside his desk, an area I've already searched.

I look around the bedroom, partitioned off from the living room in his loft apartment. This place totally lacks storage space. One armoire sits in the corner, and a trunk lies underneath a long set of windows. The guy doesn't have much stuff. This should be easy.

I open the double doors of the armoire to find the wooden space packed with jeans, one black suit, and some long sleeved shirts. Shoes are piled at the bottom. I close the doors and move on to the trunk.

"If I were a postcard, where would I be? Yes. Here." I lift the lid. Crapola. The trunk is filled with t-shirts folded neatly into perfect squares of the same diameter. Did Leo get his training at The Gap? I squish my hands down into the spaces between shirts to make sure there isn't anything else hidden.

I slam the lid and bump against a side table. A coffee mug tips over and liquid drizzles over the surface and onto the edge of a magazine. My heart taps double-time in my throat.

Oh, come on, Mr. Tidy. You couldn't have put your mug in the sink? I grab the edge of my T-shirt and wipe at it before coffee can soak into the magazine.

I look down at the once white material. Ruined. Oh, Leo Jensen, you are truly a pain in the patootie. I like this shirt and living out of a suitcase doesn't allow me one to spare.

I walk once more back through the open living area and kitchen. One wall has a bookshelf filled completely with hardbacks. I search the cabinets beside the refrigerator and another set built into the bottom of the island bar.

He has little food and only a few appliances, pots, and pans. No wonder he eats lunch most days in the bar.

No postcards hidden in the kitchen.

I catch a glimpse of someone in the large window lining one wall. A bolt of fear zings my heart like I've been electrocuted.

I've been caught.

Then I recognize the image. Wild hair that's escaped my usual ponytail during the excursion under the bed. Frazzled expression. It's only me, my crazy, mug shot-ready reflection. There is no way I'm getting trapped in here again. With a sigh, I let myself out, lock up, and return the shiny gold key to its place under the mat.

***

The next morning, I'm up later than usual. My cell alarm flashes 10:30 am. I push damp hair from my forehead. The hotel building lacks modern heating and air conditioning. Finally, cool air pushes up from the floor unit. I pull the string on the light-blocking curtains. A film of condensation obstructs my view momentarily, and I wipe my palm across the glass. The unit blows frigid air into the bottom of my oversized T-shirt and forces the fabric to billow bell-shaped around my thighs. I shudder.

Cold. I hate being cold. My mind flashes to another city. I detested Tacoma with its never-changing, dark horizons. My entire life turned blue and gray last winter. But I can't blame everything on the weather.

Tacoma's climate and people matched my life with Wesley—cold, distant, and lonely. A person on the outside, looking in with my nose pressed to the window. Tacoma was the perfect place to hide a wife and keep her estranged from family, far away in Texas.

Her family and his.

The view through my window isn't the greatest, but it's one I've studied for days—one rooftop below my fifth floor window, a busy street with lots of noisy traffic, and a row of restaurants and bars on the opposite side of the street.

Movement across the street reels my attention back to the present. Leo Jensen opens the coffee shop door and allows a girl to exit. She stops and spends several seconds smiling and talking to him. His classic All-American profile shines from all the way over there.

"Leo, you seem nice. Why were you so mean in the emails?" I step back and grab my binoculars from the nightstand before returning to the window. The two of them pull into focus.

The girl, a cute, twentyish brunette, shifts subtly closer to Leo. He backs away. I shake my head. Body language doesn't lie. Lady, are you blind? The girl across the street obviously is, and keeps inching toward him.

Leo points toward the west, gives her a smile, and enters the coffee shop. The girl walks away, but I can still see her smiling long after he disappears inside.

I quickly get dressed and find my phone. Evidently, I slept like the dead, because I've missed several calls. My mother's voicemail urges me to call my daddy. She doesn't say what he wants, but I know he's going to try to persuade me to move home.

The second voicemail is the one I dread listening to even more than my mother's. I stare at the number that belongs to Isabella Warren— Wesley's legal wife and the mother of his beautiful daughter, Charley.

Wesley. Dead, but still reaching out from the grave to affect us.

"Harper? I wanted to talk when you have time. You're the only one who understands what I'm going through. Charley and I have a museum visit today, but you can call back anytime after nine. Hope you are doing well."

I swallow the lump I get every time I imagine Charley missing her dad. Wesley.

It's still hard to reconcile the Wesley who kept me in Tacoma with the Wesley that seven-year-old Charley knew—a kind, caring father. Trying to make the mental picture work is like squashing a one-foot-square block into an ant-sized pinhole.

First, I need to visit Dog Ears Bookstore, a cute little place only a couple of blocks from my hotel. The hotel concierge said Dog Ears stocks the best resources for books about the neighborhoods and places to live in Nashville.

I take my time, enjoying the scenery as I stroll the five blocks. Nashville feels like home. The city's not exactly like Austin, but a close cousin. A cousin with more of a swagger—louder and more worried about getting your attention. Still, the music and the people are of the same family.

Colorful objects fill the bookstore window. There's an elaborate tea set with hardback books stacked under various colorful cups. On closer inspection, it's clear that all the books deal with tea.

Taking a deep breath, I enter and look around for an employee. There's only one, apparently, and she's with a customer, so I turn to the nearest shelf and pick up a book. The bookstore opened an hour ago and most aisles appear empty.

A buoyant voice startles me. "I see you've found Fifty Ways to Please Your Lover," the girl says, the same girl I spotted talking to Leo a day ago at the bar. Lucky coincidence? She gives me a cheerleader smile to match her voice.

"Excuse me?" I shift uncomfortably.

She cocks her head to the side and looks at

the book in my hands. "Wrong book?"

"Oh," I flip the book to the front. The cover, a naked couple locked in an incredibly acrobatic embrace, causes me to avert my eyes. "I...um...picked it up by mistake." I shove the book back onto the shelf.

"What brings you in today? By the way," she gives a devious smirk, "that book you picked up is a New York Times bestseller. I sell at least a copy a day."

"I don't want to please a lover." I lower my voice to right above a whisper. Is my declaration a Freudian slip buried deep in my heart? Can the other customer hear this conversation?

She grins.

I want to crawl behind a shelf. "I don't have a lover." I am not helping the situation, but cannot seem to stop myself. "I don't need a book for that."

She bobs her head in agreement as if she deals with awkward customers every day. "OK then. Wonderful. My name is Josie. Can I help you find a great read today?"

The only other customer in the store exits and I refocus on Josie. "I'm browsing."

"Sure. Let me point out some sections of the store. We have self-help in front of you. Popular fiction books on all these stands near the front middle. Popular non-fiction near the back. Fiction organized by genres and then author on the walls." Josie points to a poster mounted behind the counter. "There's a map of the store. Or ask me."

"Non-Fiction. Is there a book about Nashville?"

"Too many to list. Follow me." She leads the way to the left wall of the store. "Are you looking for a travelogue? Or a historical?"

I lift my shoulders, attempting a casual shrug. "I'm visiting. It's my first time."

She glances over at me before striding to the end of the shelf. "A Nashville virgin. You'll want tourist stuff then. There's so much to do that you'll have to be selective."

"I'm thinking about sticking around. Moving here, if I can find a job and a place to live."

"Really? We must've made some impression on you. You aren't a musician, are you?"

"No." I pause for a minute. "I think I've seen you before. Were you eating lunch at Dastardly Bastards the other day?" I deliver my words slow enough to sound uncertain.

"Oh yeah. I eat there all the time. Good burgers."

"You were at a table near me. I think you might've been with your boyfriend."

She snorts. "Leo? No. He's my brother. But you just reminded me of something. Are you looking for a house? Or an apartment?" Josie pulls a book about Nashville restaurants from the shelf and hands it to me.

"What?" I'm confused.

"You said you need a place to live. There's an apartment in Leo's building that's empty. It's for rent if you're interested. The rental has these amazing high ceilings. Leo's been hoping it doesn't rent because the last renters were partiers and drove him insane. But you don't seem the type to swing from the—"

"Can you give me the info? I'll check it out. That would be amazing." I pull out my phone. Some things are meant to be and I know without any doubt, I've been handed a plan.

"Let me see what info I've got." She leaves to search on her laptop.

"I'm so glad I stopped in here." I walk to stand in front of the counter and pick up a brochure that I have no intention of reading.

"I found the number. There's a couple of guys who own a bakery and the apartments. Here's you go." She flips a Dog Ears Bookstore business card over and writes on the back, then hands it to me. "The apartment is above the bakery. I thought about renting it myself, but I don't want to live so close to my brother. I love him and all, but...you know. I need some privacy. But he's great," she adds. "You'll love him for a neighbor."

"Is your brother a singer? I mean, he looked familiar. Maybe I've heard him play." I'm reaching for anything to keep the conversation going about Leo.

"No. He's a writer."

"Oh." I take a minute to grab a book from the shelf. "So, what kind of stuff does he write?"

I'm waiting for her to tell me all about the blog. Suddenly I'm not sure this is going to be easy. It's not likely that she'll just outright tell me where he stores his writing inspiration.

"Oh, he wants to write the next great American novel. We'll see. He's actually pretty good."

She's not answering my question. I want to talk about Mr. Expose, but I can see it isn't going to happen. I slip the card into my pocket. "I'll call as soon as I leave here. Thanks. And I'll take this book." I slide the hardback across the counter.

"So, the apartment's small. It's just you? No husband or kids?" Josie asks.

My pulse quickens at the thought of Wesley and how I begged him for a baby. No wonder he didn't want a child. He already had one and a wife to spare. I shift and look at my left hand. "No husband. I'm a widow."

"I'm so sorry." She has a funny expression on her face. That awkward look people get when they wish they could suck back the words they've said earlier. I know the feeling. Explicitly.

She concentrates on her register and rings up the book. "That's $24.99."

I hand her my credit card. "It's only me, starting a new life."

A life without regrets and with my eyes wide open.

Worse Comes to Worst

Leo

"WHERE'S YOUR STALKER TODAY?" Dane slides a plate of burger and fries across the bar. The pendant light above his head glints off his shit-eating grin. He grabs my cola and refills the empty glass without breaking eye contact.

I ignore his razzing and glance toward the stage as a guy taps the mic and perches on a stool, ready to croon to the diners. Dane teasing me about a stalker makes me think about my pain-in-the-ass ex, Tori, who turns up like a bad penny. The thought of her could ruin my meal. I'd rather talk about anything else. "Since when do you have lunch entertainment?"

Dane gives the guy on stage his attention for all of a second before looking at me. "Yesterday. So you're interested in the music lineup now? Quit changing the subject. I'm talking about your personal fan club. The chic who watches you like you're the last donut in the case. I told you man, she quizzed me about you yesterday after you left. But I didn't divulge confidential information. My lips are sealed. I'm like an attorney. Or a bartender or a therapist."

Dane's stalker comment isn't too far off. Not that I'm actually worried about the blonde who seems to be everywhere I go. Still, it's weird, and my run-ins with Tori have me on edge. The first time, it was the eerie feeling of being watched that made me notice her. I was checking my post office box and the blonde was at Letters Express, where I check my mail for the Mr. Expose blog. I smiled at her and she looked away.

The second day she was there again. And every day that week. I shake my head. Shit. Soon, I'll be thinking my entire life is a conspiracy theory and women are the archenemy.

"Earth to Leo. Come in, Leo," Dane says. "If you want me to introduce you, I can. That's if she comes in again."

"Not interested." I wish my words were the truth. I am interested, but there's something about her that's too intense. Too knowing. Her moss green eyes seem to look straight into my soul.

And I need a breather from intense.

Dane glances toward the door. "Yup, there she is. Just a little late today," he says in his drawling Southern accent that charms all his customers. He wipes the very clean bar in front of him and watches one of his waitresses walk a menu and the girl over to a table in the corner.

My shoulders tense. I resist turning to look at the blonde. I've watched her plenty over the past two weeks and maybe she's thinking *I'm* the creepy one. "Poker at your place this week?"

"Eight o'clock. Bring some pretzels or something."

"Sounds great."

Dane lowers his head, pretending to read a newspaper he picks up from the counter. "Don't look now, but the stalker hasn't taken her eyes off you since the minute she walked in."

"Quit looking at her and stop with the stalker talk," I mutter and take a bite of my burger.

He chuckles. "She's hot. She can stalk me anytime she wants."

I finish swallowing before I answer. "If you're so into her, why don't you give her your number?"

"Because she's all about you, you dumb shit." Dane's eyebrows draw together. "But you're going to let one bad relationship hold you back."

"No." I wipe my hands on a napkin. "We're not going there. I'm not discussing my dating life with a dude who thinks speed dating is a way of life. You could be with the girl you really want, if you'd quit chasing skirt."

Dane's mouth opens as if he's going to say something, then stops. His eyes narrow and he shakes his head. Luckily, the sound of acoustic guitar prevents us from continuing the conversation. He shifts his attention to the musician.

I glance from the small stage near the windows back to Dane and nod approvingly. "Dang. He's good."

"Thought I'd try some live music for the lunch crowd," Dane says. He looks over his shoulder at the waitress to his right. "What you need, hon?"

She holds out a sheet of paper. "The delivery guy is at the back door unloading. Sign the ticket."

Dane takes the delivery slip from her, signs it, and hands it back. She doesn't move. "Need something else?" he asks.

Now, I realize she's smiling at me. "Leo, I was just wondering...want to go to a concert with me tomorrow night?"

I give her a regretful smile. "Sorry. Poker night."

"Come on. You can play poker anytime." She tilts her head and raises her eyebrows in a beseeching pose. "I have a friend who can come along. She's really freaky, if you know what I mean."

Freaky. I must be waving a freak flag lately.

"Well, that's sweet and all, but I have to pass."

"I'm anything but sweet," she answers with a glint in her eye.

Dane's lips quirk at the corner and he points toward the back. "Delivery is waiting." After the waitress leaves, he leans on the bar. "You turned down a threesome. Are you insane? There's something seriously wrong with you."

I take an extra-large bite of burger and turn to watch the musician on stage.

Dane's not deterred by my lack of interest. "Leah's never asked me to get it on with her and a friend. You have that whole sensitive thing going on. Girls love that shit. You probably read them poetry while you—"

"Ignoring you now." I grab my plate in one hand and my drink in the other. "I came in to eat, not be lectured by the guy who woke up last week without his wallet and keys and called me to pick him up at a strange girl's house."

"Touché." He says. Then he adds, "You need to get laid. Obviously."

"Whatever, man. See you tomorrow night. I won't be in for lunch." Then I turn and scan the room for an empty table. There's a table for two far from the blonde, so I make my way to it.

From the corner of my eye, I'm aware that she watches me. I can feel her gaze prickling along my skin like a sunburn. I'm tempted to look at her and raise a confronting eyebrow.

I make sure I'm seated facing the door where I won't miss my sister when she arrives. She finally enters at half-past noon. I'm taking the last bite of my burger when she plops into the seat across from me and grabs a few french fries from my plate and dredges them through my ketchup.

"What's up, brother o' mine?" Josie says around a mouthful of food.

"Are you on time anywhere?" I push my plate to the middle of the table so she'll stop reaching across to grab more fries.

"Customer kept chatting me up at the store. Couldn't get away."

"I don't believe that for a minute." Josie's the most talkative person I know. Her customer at the bookstore was probably trying to get away from her.

As far as twins go, we couldn't be more different physically or socially. Her hair is dark and mine light. She makes friends with strangers everywhere, and I don't like people much. Josie's life is one happy ride with the wind blowing through her hair.

Mine's been filled with the wind knocking me down.

"What do you have to do to get a waitress around here?" Josie frowns as she grabs my glass and takes a drink. "Be right back. I guess it's self-serve."

Josie makes her way over to Dane, who's standing behind the bar. I watch them flirt with each other in the comfortable way they've been playing at all year.

The place has filled with lunch customers and I wonder about the girl in the corner. I casually turn to see if I can catch her in my peripheral view, and see the table is empty. She's always popping up and then disappearing when I look for her.

***

A week later, I've given up on seeing the girl again. It's odd that I've found myself looking for one particular blonde in this city's sea of beautiful women. But really, it's only curiosity because I like to figure out people's motives.

Did she want a one-night stand? Do I look like her last boyfriend? Is she planning to stab me in a dark alley and harvest my organs for a black market price?

I walk into the Letter Express store where I rent a post office box and there she is. I stare at her as she turns the key to her box. She's wearing shorts today. My gaze slides from her legs up to her hair pulled into a little perky ponytail.

The door opens again and a little boy runs inside with his mother chasing him. The toddler squeals and smacks into the back of the blonde's legs, pushing her against the metal mailbox wall.

Her stack of mail avalanches to the floor. The mother pulls her kid away. "Sorry about that." She drags her kid away by the arm without even offering to help pick up the mess.

My box is on the opposite side of the store, but I make my way over to her before I can question my own motives.

Curiosity has always been my strongest and worst personality trait. "I've got it." I bend to pick up the envelopes. There are at least twenty bills strewn around her feet.

She tucks a strand behind her ear and kneels to pick up the nearest mail. "Oh, thanks. This is crazy. I just moved here and all my mail must've forwarded at once."

I reach for a large manila envelope and she's grabbed for the same package. We don't say anything for a second.

She hasn't looked up at me yet, and when she does, there's a blush to her cheeks.

I glance at the name on the envelope as I pass it to her. Mrs. Wesley Wade. "Here you go."

"Thanks." Her voice is low and husky and shy.

"Anytime." We're both still kneeling even though we've picked up the mail. At this close proximity, I notice all the things I couldn't see from across a room. Amazing eyes, full bottom lower lip, creamy skin. Too bad she's married.

What an asinine thought. It's a good thing she's married. In fact, the Mrs. in front of her name is a stabbing reminder that I'll be staying far away from her.

I get to my feet after staring into her eyes far longer than acceptable. I blame it on the incredible flecks of green in her eyes that make me think of cool water running over the rocks of a spring creek. I hold out my hand to help her to her feet and give her a friendly smile.

She takes my hand and rises. Her touch is silky but her grip firm. "Thank you. Have we met before?"

Is that a pickup line? Because she's been stalking me. Or watching me, maybe. "I don't think so."

"Oh." She hugs the envelopes to her chest. "Are you sure?"

I get an uneasy feeling in my gut. The kind of intuition private investigators must have when something isn't quite jiving. "I'm sure. Have a good one." I turn and leave without even checking my box or offering my name. She's married and might be interested, since she seems to be wherever I turn. In my book, married is equivalent to carrying the black plague.

My apartment building is a good mile from Letters Express. I could have mail delivered to my building, but I keep the box for business purposes. The walk always starts my workday with a way to clear the morning fog in my head. My routine gives me the illusion that I've walked to work when I return to my home office.

I skip the coffee this morning. The married blonde has wrecked my routine.

My loft apartment is located in what was once the old fire station. It's a historic renovation, part of an initiative to keep buildings alive through the decades.

The outside of the fire station looks much the same as it did a hundred years ago. Weathered red bricks on the outside have been carefully restored instead of replaced. I know from talking with the contractor that restoring costs a lot more than replacing. The bottom floor houses a pastry shop owned by a couple of guys who moved from Rhode Island earlier this year.

I enter the back stairs that lead to the two apartments on the upper floor. The heavy metal door to the apartment squeaks as I open it, and I make a mental note to add WD-40 to my shopping list for the week. The smells of vanilla and cinnamon waft up through the vents and I'm glad I don't have a sweet tooth. Otherwise, living here would be insane.

Tossing my phone onto one of my few pieces of furniture, an antique architect's desk, I walk to the kitchen to make a drink. Since I've missed my mandatory coffee run, I grumpily search through a cabinet to find my coffee press and a tin of coffee.

I'm so wrapped up in putting a tea kettle of water on to boil and measuring out coffee that I almost miss the sound at my door. The door literally dings like a bell when anyone raps on the steel surface, the acoustics sending sound high into the hallway ceiling.

"Coming." I stride over and open the door, hoping my new stereo speakers have arrived. Instead of the delivery person I expect, it's the woman from this morning.

I stand speechless as I take her in. Did she actually follow me home?

"Can I help you?" My automatic response is a stupid thing to say, like I'm offering her customer service.

The blonde licks her bottom lip and smiles nervously. "You're Leo Jensen."

"Yes." An unpleasant feeling jabs me in the gut. Dane probably gave her my name after all. I can't really be upset at him since he doesn't actually think she's stalking me. But showing up at my place crosses the line. Of course, stalking does too.

She looks past me into my apartment. "Can I come in?"

"I'm sorry." I cock my head to the side and

squint at her. She's a piece of work. I step outside into the corridor and close my door behind me. "I don't mean to seem unfriendly, but is there a reason you're here?"

"Oh, I'm...well..." Her cheeks flush a deep pink. "James and Erik told me your name. I'm Harper." She holds out her hand.

I stare for a second, but good manners prevail. "Nice to meet you," I say and give her hand a quick shake. "What can I do for you?"

"I wanted to meet you before I move in." She tucks the same strand of hair behind her ear and points across the corridor to the door opposite mine. "Here."

"I didn't realize they intended to rent it. So, you..." Actually, I'd assumed my bakery owner landlords wouldn't rent to anyone after the year of complaints they'd had about the thugs who lived in the apartment across the hall. They'd even mentioned using it for storage.

There's a good ten seconds of holy shit silence while I wonder what to do about this situation.

She gives me a tight-lipped smile. "Well, I should let you get back to work. Just wanted to say hey to my neighbor."

"Oh yeah. Neighbors." I nod. The teapot on the stove begins to whistle and my cell phone rings in a duet of interruption. "Sorry, I—"

She raises a hand in a wave. "No, it's fine.

I'll talk to you later. I'll be right," she points across the hall, "there."

Harper pivots and takes four steps across the hallway. Throwing one glance over her shoulder before she twists the knob, she beams at me. Like she has my number and can tell she's freaking me.

She's attractive and scary as hell at the same time.

Fuck my life.

Catching a Tailwind

Harper

AFTER INTRODUCING MYSELF TO LEO, I walk across the hall, and throw a glance over my shoulder. I beam at him in an encouraging way. A trust-me-I'm-harmless face. This is no time to fall prey to paranoia. He can't know I've been in his apartment.

He's watching me with these cute wrinkles marring his forehead. If I didn't know better, I'd swear he's absolutely terrified of me—a comical thought. When I pilfered through his belongings, I left everything in place, but maybe...just maybe, he's noticed me watching him.

I'll have to back off from the overly friendly thing if I ever want to get a hold of my postcard.

Thoughts of my postcard are quickly replaced with what I admit is a gleeful thrill.

I enter my apartment and tread softly, as if I'm going to disturb the real owner. Because I still can't believe this is my new home.

Not only is this apartment the most

beautiful empty space I've ever seen, it has the sunniest windows on God's green earth. And there's the perk of its location, right next to Leo.

My happiness is marred by the knowledge of how I'm able to pay for this place. I get a hollow feeling when I think of the money that Wesley left me. Not even his real wife, I nevertheless inherited money he earmarked for me. I puzzle over why he bothered.

I shake off the ghosts as I always do when the negative thoughts spill into my consciousness.

Instead, I spin slowly in the center of the room before I sit cross-legged on the hardwood floor. Sunshine streams in, forming a circle exactly around me. My cell rings, breaking into the stillness and helping me feel less alone.

Daddy.

I hesitate, but only for an instant since I know he'll call back if I don't answer. He's not one for leaving voicemail.

"Hi Daddy."

"Angel?"

"Someone else calling you Daddy?"

"Funny. Of course not. You don't sound like yourself. Are you doing OK?"

"Sure. I've moved into my new apartment." I wait for the impending argument with a leaden feeling in my stomach.

"So you are staying." He speaks the words

slowly, in a way that invites discussion. This is new. Although I'm twenty-two years old, he and Mama have questioned all my decisions since I ran off with Wesley.

"For a while. I like the weather here. The people are nice."

"You thought you liked it in Tacoma, too," he says.

Daddy wouldn't say this if he knew I actually wanted to move back to Texas for most of my time with Wesley. I never voiced those thoughts to my parents. They were already unhappy Wesley had moved me across the country, away from my family and friends.

"Well, I like Nashville better," I say.

"You're all alone, Angel. It's not right. A girl your age needs family nearby."

I give a long-suffering sigh. "I'm not a girl. I'm a woman. I can live on my own."

"We know that. But you would be happy here. You could meet a nice young man."

I rub my forehead. "Daddy, I know you mean well, but you have to quit. You have to accept that I can make smart decisions that work for me. Do you think I can't take care of myself? That I need some 'nice young man' to take care of me?" He can't see the air quotes, but I still do them with my free hand.

Of course, I've made horrible, impulsive choices. Running off to marry Wesley when we'd only dated a few weeks ruined their opinion of me forever.

There's silence and the seconds tick by as I wait for him to respond. "Daddy?"

"Your mother and I worry about you. We want you to be happy. We pray for you every day."

"I know." I can only imagine the sermons Daddy's given, alluding to his prodigal daughter.

"Will you make me a promise?"

"Sure."

"That if you change your mind and want to move home, you'll call us. We'll rent a truck and move all your things for you. You can stay in your old room. And there's a group of singles at the church that you can join. We have a new member of our congregation that has a lot in common with you. She's a little older, but she lost her husband after twenty-two years of marriage."

I'm silent, my eyes closed, and my heart cold.

"Angel?"

"I'm here." If only they knew the truth. I hadn't been legally married for the past four years. It was all a farce and the joke was on me. "Listen, I have to go. Someone's waiting for me," I say, hoping he can't hear the lie in my voice. Mama believes everything I say, but Daddy always knows. I visualize his narrowed eyes though the phone line.

He doesn't call me on the lie. "OK. Call tomorrow?" he asks.

"If I get a chance." I get to my feet. "Bye Daddy. I love you. Tell Mama I love her, too." I end the call and stick my phone into my back pocket.

I make my way to the parking lot behind the building. My vehicle is filled with everything I've hauled from Tacoma. Anything I couldn't bring ended up in a donation bin at the local Goodwill store. I unhook the tarp that covers the cardboard boxes in the truck bed. There are only five boxes of various sizes and shapes, a suitcase, and one duffel bag.

One medium-sized box contains the lightest items, so I grab it first. It takes only minutes to walk the flight of stairs at the back of the building and store my belongings inside. I return and do the same with the second and third box, each one slightly heavier than the last.

I struggle with the fourth box. The awkward shape only lets me put my arms around three-fourths of it. This box should've been the first to go upstairs while I still had lots of energy. Planning ahead has never been my forte.

I creep up the steps blindly, since the box blocks my view. Ten more steps, maybe? My foot hits the edge of the step and slides off. "Ah!" I grab the box tight, an error in judgment on my part since the box isn't going to save me from free falling down the remaining steps.

"Wait," a female voice behind me demands. Footsteps pound on the metal stairs as she ascends. Two hands rest on the center of my back to brace me. "What do you think you're doing?"

I twist to see Josie behind me. "Trying to make it up these stairs before I drop this box like a Donkey Kong barrel."

She laughs. "So you decided to go for the apartment. I'm so glad. Have you met my brother yet?"

"Can we talk after you push me to the top?"

She chuckles and pushes lightly on my back. "Go, woman. You have to work with me here. Don't go fast and knock me down. If I fall, I'm taking you with me."

I step cautiously to the top of the stairs and put the box down at the landing. "Made it."

"My brother should be helping you. I'll get him. He should be home if he isn't doing his volunteer tutoring at the library. He's teaching a guy how to read."

Ah. It takes all my willpower not to quiz her about this. "No, really. I only have a couple more."

But she's already walked around me and

opened the door at the top of the stairs. "I'm going to get him," she says without turning. "Don't lift anything heavy. Leave this," she says, nodding to the box at my feet.

"I don't think he'll want to—"

She pauses and gives me a quizzical look. "What? Leo will rush out here. He's old-fashioned like that."

Josie races through the door without another word, and I'm left waiting. I glance to my vehicle. The rest of my belongings are light, so I travel down the steps carefully. I'm aware of a faint soreness in my back that will set in by tomorrow from all physical movement I've done today.

The duffel is stored in the cab along with a shopping bag. I grab both and return to the stairs. Halfway up, I hear a faint argument coming from the hallway inside.

"Josie," the deep voice says. "I'm sure she doesn't need us butting in."

How embarrassing. He doesn't want to help. Josie's probably dragging Leo, his heels scuffing up the wood floor of the hallway.

I knew there was something off about Leo's face when I said hello earlier. He thinks I'm going to be loud or needy or nosy. Mr. Expose is wrong. I'm going to be the best neighbor he's ever had.

I only wish Leo would look happier to see

me. He studies me as if I'm a dangerous animal at the zoo, and he's glad to be on the other side of the cage. He's such an enigma and too young to be a curmudgeon. Too cute. Too clever.

Also, he volunteers at the library. How many people my age do that? He's practically ready for sainthood.

My mouth twitches at the corner as I walk the rest of the way up. Not only am I going to retrieve my postcard from his stash, I'm going to get to know him—the guy who volunteers his time. Maybe he's so crabby because he needs a friend.

The door pops open and Leo nods at me. "Harper." He says my name with a clipped tone.

"Leo." I only say his name and forego conversation, since he didn't like the small talk earlier. I smile at him with only a partial parting of the lips. No need to scare him. At his startled look, I attempt a more genuine smile in case I look like a fox eyeing the lone chicken.

"Don't pick anything else up," he says, echoing his sister's words from earlier. "I'll be back." His thoughtful words are the complete opposite of his gruff tone. He lifts the heavy box.

"He'll be back," Josie says in a Terminator voice and opens the stairwell door for Leo to go through. She holds it for me, so I follow Leo. He's not a tall guy. But he's not short either. He's average height with a lean frame, but his biceps bulge from the effort of holding my heavy box.

Josie catches up to walk beside me in the hallway. "I peeked in your apartment. Where's the rest of your stuff? Your furniture?" she asks. She runs ahead so she can open my apartment door.

I shake my head. "I don't have any. I lived in a furnished apartment before. I'll have to get some."

"Oh. That's too bad. It'll be expensive to get all new stuff," she says. Josie steps aside to allow Leo and the big box through first. I follow and try to stop staring at his toned arms and tantalizing biceps. *My, what nice arms you have.* I smack the wolfish voice down inside my head.

Ogling the unfriendly neighbor is wrong.

"Where do you want this?" Leo raises one eyebrow.

Did he see me looking at him? At his arms? And now I'm staring at his face. A really nice face. And he's waiting for me to snap out of it and answer him.

"Anywhere," I say, my voice a little squeaky.

"Harper? You get too hot out there?" Josie presses fingertips lightly to my shoulder and my mind leaps to the present.

"Oh yeah. I'm fine. Just resting for a second."

Josie looks at me with concern. She glances around the sparse room and then at Leo. "You look like you could pass out. Let's go over to Leo's. You can sit at his place for a bit, since you don't have furniture."

"I think she just needs a minute." Leo gives her a hard stare.

"Leo," she says, her mouth dropping open a bit at the end of his name.

He's silent, and looking at her like they have some sort of telepathy. "Look. She said she's fine."

Josie smacks her brother's arm. "What is wrong with you?" She pivots to me. "Come on. Leo will fix us both a cold drink."

"Um...I'm good, Thanks." My embarrassed laugh draws Leo's gaze to mine.

He shakes his head slightly. "Ladies." He waves a hand forward, sweeping in the general direction of his apartment. The hard line of his mouth says he'd rather be flogged than serve me a cola.

"I really don't want to." I especially don't want to give Leo the impression that I'm going to be an unwanted guest hanging out at his apartment all the time. "I have stuff I stuck in the refrigerator here. Want something?"

My place is identical to Leo's in layout. There's an open living area and kitchen with high ceilings and exposed black ductwork. The kitchen boasts the usual furnishings—refrigerator and stove. At least I have those things.

I make my way across the room before Josie can protest further and open the stainless steel door. "I have bottled water, sodas, and I can make tea if you want. I have a teapot and kitchen things in the heavy box Leo brought in."

"Well, if you don't have anything else heavy…" Leo trails off, waiting for my response. His statement doesn't surprise me. It's like he can't wait to get out of the room.

Josie doesn't respond, but glares at Leo. I grab a bottled water for me and one to offer her. "I've got it from here. Thanks."

I barely have the last word out when he turns on his heel and exits. He closes the door behind him. My throat tightens at the outright hostility.

"What the frick?" Josie's eyes are wide and confused. "I am so sorry. He's not usually so anti-social. I have no idea what his problem is today." She takes the water from my outstretched hand.

I lift my shoulders in a careless shrug. "Men. Who knows what they think."

Turning my back on her is the best way to hide the hurt I feel at his hostility. I make my way over to a spot near the window and sit on the floor.

"I know him better than anyone. We're twins," she states, like I'll get the extent of their relationship.

My only child status leaves me lacking any knowledge of sibling relationships. "So you're close."

"Very. We are uncomfortably aware of how the other thinks. Something is going on with him, but I guess I'll find out the details later," she says and sits near me with her back against the wall. She glances back at the closed door, as if she can see through it to read his thoughts across the hall. "He's had some drama this year that put him in a funk. That's all. His attitude doesn't have a thing to do with you."

Now she's got me curious about Leo. He can't have problems. He lives in a beautiful apartment, he's gorgeous, and he seems to have lots of friends. In fact, I'm slightly peeved that Mr. Expose thinks he's got anything to be unhappy about.

We need a new topic that doesn't involve her rude brother. "Where can I get some furniture? Inexpensive. Maybe just a sofa or a bed for starters."

I take a swig from my water bottle and let my head fall back on the wall.

Josie tilts her head while she thinks. After a moment of comfortable silence, she nods to herself. "IKEA or something like that, maybe. I saw you have a truck. Want me to help? I'm free today. And my brother's attitude stinks at the moment, so I think I'll wait a while to visit."

"Oh. Well, I can't imagine you'd want to spend your Saturday doing this." I wave a hand at my bare room.

"No problem. It'll give us a chance to visit. I need to get to know the girl Leo will have the hots for soon."

I laugh, a little too high-pitched and short. She's trying to make up for the horrible way he treated me. "I doubt that will happen."

"Why not? Listen, don't judge him on today. He's a sweetheart. Quiet sometimes. A little on the suffering-writer, broody side, but always sweet to women. Gets him in trouble, actually."

"I'm not looking to date anyone."

Josie glances down at my left hand. "Oh, gosh. That was totally insensitive of me. I'm so sorry."

My ring finger is empty. Empty like my life. Last night, I took out the wedding set from where I keep it as a reminder of my mistakes. I don't even have to wear the rings to feel the weight of their impact on everything I am now. The invisible circles might as well be tattooed on my finger. An unpleasant heaviness has settled deep in my chest, an anchor from four years based on lies.

I smile at her. "Nothing to be sorry about. I

think I will take you up on your offer. But only if you'll let me buy you lunch. Deal?"

"Works for me. Cool." She stands and screws the lid on her water bottle.

I get to my feet and grab her empty bottle so I can put them both in the trash. My back is to her when she clears her throat.

"Do you mind if I ask what happened? Your husband, I mean? You're really young, so I'm guessing it was something bad."

"Wesley—that's my husband. Was my husband. He was killed in a car accident."

"Oh God. That's horrible."

I almost wish I could cry at this moment. I feel the numbness settling in more and more lately when anyone asks about Wesley.

My past is all a lie that doesn't make sense.

But I don't deserve to be detached from all that's happened. I need to remember how easily a person can be fooled. My life before Wesley was all sunshine and rainbows and unicorns. A true fantasy where my parents sheltered me and friends were who they appeared on the surface.

Now I understand that a person's character can run as deep as an ocean.

"Yeah. Well, death is not an un-horrible thing." I pause and inhale deeply.

Josie waits for me to say more. When I don't, she glances at her phone. "It's getting late and it's going to be really hot by lunchtime. Let's get this shopping trip started. I get to pick where we eat afterward, right? I know just the spot. They serve carnitas to die for and huge margaritas the size of melons."

"Sounds like the perfect lunch." I grab my purse and throw the strap over my shoulder. As I walk to the door, I rub my itchy ring finger.

***

From: angelgirl@me.com
To: isabellawarren@iconic.net

Dear Isabella,

I'm settled into my new place. It's nice. I'll have the postcard in my possession soon. You don't have to worry. Charley will never know her father is anyone different from the man she loved.

Take care,

Harper

Another Think Coming

Leo

JOSIE STORMS INTO MY APARTMENT without knocking. Her eyes flash with something beyond irritation. She's ready to rumble. "You were a jerk. You know that, right?" She tosses her bright orange purse onto the sofa and then joins it. Next, she grabs a pillow and tosses it at me in case I'm not paying enough attention to her rant.

"No, I was not. I helped carry the heavy box inside." Guilt tickles my conscience. I scratch it by remembering how her appearance in the apartment next door can't be coincidence.

"You know what I mean."

"What do you know about this girl? You just met her."

My sister's eyes narrow. "I know enough to wonder what's making you act like a total douchebag. And for your information, I met her the other day and know a lot about her already."

"Really." I draw out the word and sit in the chair near her. Ah, Josie. She has a heart for strays. She's like the proverbial cat lady, but with people. You have issues? Josie takes you under her protective wing. She and my ex were friends at one time.

I don't blame Josie for what happened, but we were both taken in.

"She's been stalking you, too?"

My question has the desired effect. Josie's eyebrows lower in a confused dip. "Are you kidding me?"

"Not a bit. Stalking, chasing. Whatever. I mean, come on. Girls like her are exactly like Tori. They go after what they want with a vengeance."

Her expression changes from confused back to confrontational, her mouth kicking up at the corner. "And just how has she been stalking you? I have to hear this."

"She eats lunch at Dastardly Bastards when we do."

"So?" She's actually grinning now. "How else?"

"She's has a post office box where I do."

"Uh huh. It's probably the closest mailing center."

My argument feels lame all of a sudden, but I'm not crazy. Dane knows. "Come on. Then she moves in here."

"Because I told her about the empty apartment when she was in the bookstore."

"And how did she happen to go to the store my sister owns? See, stalking."

A delighted bubble of laughter is all I get from Josie. "Gosh. You are an idiot. How does your ego even fit in this room?"

I tamp down the urge to get mad at her amusement. It'll only feed her delight, as she knows how to push all my buttons. "I'm serious. That woman has been watching me."

"Has it occurred to you that she might think you're attractive?"

"Again, stalkers probably think that about the person they stalk."

"Oh, brother." Josie rises and strolls over to my kitchen cabinets to begin her usual pilfering for a snack. "She mentioned seeing us together at Dane's place for lunch one day. She thought you were a famous singer or something like that."

"That's a good reason for following me? Because she thinks I'm a singer?"

"Thinking you are a star is a good excuse for looking at you. I can assure you. She's not a stalker." Josie pulls a box of crackers from my cupboard. "I think she's sweet. You should get to know her. We went shopping and to lunch today."

"Perfect. My sister is now friends with Harper the Stalker."

"Don't call her that. I think she's lonely."

"Common characteristic of a stalker."

"There'd be a lot of stalkers in the world if that's what makes you one. Besides she needed some help." She pauses and pops a cracker into her mouth.

"She has a husband to help her move in. You have to quit getting into people's business."

Josie shakes her head. "Not married."

"She is. I saw her mail at Letters Express the other day." I do know something about Harper. Josie's been blinded by some sort of superficial charm. "She's is a married woman who's been following me and—

"Wrong." Her mouth pinches ruefully at the corners. "She's a widow."

"Widow?"

"Yes. Her husband was killed in some accident."

"Oh." I stare out the window to avoid looking at Josie. Harper shouldn't be trying to carry all that stuff by herself. I'd assumed she had manipulated the situation to get Josie's help. But there is no husband, no parents, friends, or anyone to help her.

She's all alone.

"Yeah. It's sad, huh? Remember how we felt after Mom and Dad died?"

There's a tiny residual clench of my heart, the one that will never go away at the mention of my parents.

"Um hm. What else do you know about her?" My voice is softer now. I picture her pretty features, those eyes that hypnotize me. Her small, high breasts and tight ass. She's so feminine and frail.

I think about her all alone in this city, prey to guys who don't know she's lost a husband, and my feelings shift from suspicion to sympathy.

Josie takes her former position on the sofa and curls her legs underneath her bottom. "She moved here from Tacoma, Washington, but doesn't know anyone. She used to live in Texas."

"So, why Nashville?"

"I guess she just likes it here. She's funny. Leo, I think you'll get along with her. And she needs friends. Do me a favor and be nice to her. She's not stalking you."

I nod at Josie. I'll make it up to Harper. "OK. You win. Seeing her in so many places was kind of freaky, that's all."

"Say I was right."

"You were more informed."

"Say I'm always right. Because it's true. Don't you think she's cute?"

I shoot her a warning look. "Josie."

"It's about time you stopped moping around and move on. Bad breakups happen. It's life."

I gather up my ammunition and shoot with

an unfair advantage. I know how to make her back off. "Let's talk about you and Dane. I think—"

"Shut. Up." She scolds me with comedic flair and a grin, but she's conflicted. It's in the way she's overly dramatic with her response.

We both lock in a stare—a sign of a truce for as long as I can remember.

Then, she nods at me. "I can't stick around, but be nice to Harper. Offer a sort of olive branch, because she thinks you don't like her."

I roll my eyes to the ceiling and lean my head against the back of my chair. "What do you want me to do? I can't just go over there. And if I tell her I thought she was watching me...well, I don't see that as a good start for her as my neighbor."

"No. Definitely don't do that. Just go over and take her something. Like food."

"Like a bag of chips and a six-pack?" I raise my eyebrows.

"Oh, you're a riot. She'd move out if you did that. Go to Fresh Market and grab some cheeses and a put them in a basket with some crackers. Add a bottle of wine to it."

"For Pete's sake, don't you think that sounds a little..." I wave a hand around, searching for the right word. "A little like a romantic gesture? Cheese and wine? I'm not asking her out. I only want to make her think she's OK as my neighbor."

"She might be fooled into thinking you're cultured. I'd love my neighbor if he brought me that."

"Don't need her to love me. Tolerate me? Yes. You've got to do better than the cultured argument. What about chips and dip?"

She huffs at me. Literally huffs. "Why do I even try? Fine. Take her some Fritos and bean dip."

"Sounds great. They sell those at the local gas station."

"You, my idiot brother, do what you want. You don't listen to me anyway." She mutters the entire time she walks to my door. "Always pretending to want my advice and then, when I give it? Deaf."

After Josie leaves, I grab my wallet and keys so I can head out and pick something up for the neighbor.

***

I knock on Harper's door three times. Her truck was parked outside when I returned from the store, so I know she's home. Is she looking through the peephole at me? Have I upset her so much she's not going to answer? I feel like a dork standing here with this basket, since I wouldn't be taking food to a new neighbor under normal circumstances.

This feels like something my mother would've done when she was alive. I can hear her telling me to do exactly what Josie had.

The door finally opens. I take in Harper without knowing what to say. She appears to be harried, her ponytail lopsided with strands of hair falling at her cheeks. She's a hot mess. It's very cute except for one small detail— she holds a steel meat mallet.

For one uncomfortable moment, I remember seeing her watching me in all my usual haunts. Maybe Josie was deathly wrong and this is where I meet my end.

"Harper." I take a step back out of swinging distance.

"Oh. It's you." She blows a strand of hair from her eyes.

"I wanted to bring you a housewarming gift." I hold up the basket by the handle.

"Thanks." She opens the door wider. "Come on in."

"You look busy. I can leave this—"

"No, it's fine," she says. "Sorry to ask, but could you hold something while you're here?" She takes the basket with her free hand and walks to the kitchen area.

I stand in the doorway, not really wanting to come in. But it seems a little rude to back away and run for my life. And I could probably dodge the mallet. I'm amused by my own paranoia. Josie would have a good laugh if she knew.

"So can you hold something for me?" she repeats.

"Sure," I say and step inside. I chuckle to myself at the feeling of stepping into the lair of a dangerous creature.

"What's so funny?"

"Nothing." I hide my grin. "Am I holding a steak down or what?"

"Huh?" Her eyebrows knit and she tilts her head. "I don't understand."

I point to the weapon she holds.

"Oh. I don't have a hammer, and I'm trying to put my bed together. The entire thing came in a box."

Only a woman would move into a place without owning basic tools. "How about I go get my tools?"

"You have a hammer?" She waits a beat. "Of course you do. Yes, please. That'd be great."

She walks around the bar and places the mallet inside a drawer. "I'll put this food away."

Because Josie suggested cheese and crackers, I was determined to steer clear of those items. It's the way of brothers and sisters. You do the opposite of what they want.

Instead, I'd filled the basket with gourmet marinara sauce, whole grain pasta, fresh French bread, and a parmesan cheese. I don't know if she cooks, but spaghetti seemed easy and safe. I figure if you can boil water, you can make pasta.

I leave and return five minutes later with a small metal toolbox. She opens the door on one knock. Her ponytail is fixed now, no stray pieces escaping the hair band.

I grin because I kind of enjoyed the other look. It was wild and uninhibited. Sexy.

"Real hammer, real screws. I assume you need screws for the bed? Unless you wanted to use paperclips or something." My sarcasm makes her smile.

She assumes a serious expression. "I used bread bag twists. That doesn't work?"

I follow Harper into her bedroom where planks spill from the end of a long box. The picture on the side is of a platform bed. "This, right?"

"Um hm." She kneels on one side of the box and grabs a sheet of instructions. "When you knocked earlier, I was reading these. I realized I needed a hammer and a screwdriver."

"Yeah. You always do." I turn my head to nod at the mattress leaning against the wall. "You didn't carry all this up here, did you?"

"Your sister helped me."

I grimace. "Don't do that again. Come and get me. Josie should've yelled when you needed help," I say. Then I realize they didn't, based on my actions the first time they asked. "Sorry about earlier. I was in the middle of something," I lie. "Instructions." I hold out my hand for them. It's not too difficult to figure out what we need. I search for the pouch of screws and locate my Philips screwdriver.

Harper doesn't say much. I spend a few seconds of silence concentrating on lining up two boards of the platform frame. "So. What brings you to Nashville? Hand me one of those washers, please."

She drops the washer into my outstretched hand. "I don't know. I mean, I thought I'd visit here and after I did, I loved it."

"You travel a lot?" I grab the Philips and insert the screw.

Harper hesitates. "No. I grew up in Texas. After I got married, I moved to Washington. I haven't been anywhere else."

I nod, a little uncomfortable that I've taken the conversation to a topic that suddenly feels very personal. "I need a screw. A long screw." I hold out my hand again and press my lips together at my words.

She stares at me. There's a noticeable flush to her cheeks. Good God. I'm not the only one whose thoughts went straight to the gutter. The girl's got a dirty mind, and it didn't take a shortcut for her to travel there.

I dip my head so she can't see my grin. "Can

you hand me another long screw? Same length as the last one?"

Harper's hand shakes a little as she rummages through the bag. She locates the one I need and drops it near my leg. "Here you go." No eye contact now.

For a girl who's been staring at me every time I see her at Dane's bar, she is now painfully shy. "What do you do, Harper?" I ask and continue twisting the screwdriver.

She's silent.

"Do you have a job yet?" I ask.

"I applied for a few. I've only worked one place before, so it's probably going to be tough to get hired."

"How old are you?"

"Twenty-two," she answers and her chin lifts in challenge. "I did some babysitting and dogsitting when I was in high school. But my parents didn't want me to work then, so I didn't. And Wesley thought women should stay...well, I just didn't work."

I nod. Apparently, her dead husband didn't want her to work any more than her parents did.

"What do you do?" she asks.

It makes sense she'd return the question. Still, I always hesitate to tell people much about how I spend my time and make money. "I'm writing the next breakout novel." I give the statement lightly so I almost sound like I'm teasing.

"A writer. That's interesting. Have you written anything I've read?"

"I doubt it. Screw?" I hold out my palm and move to hold the next two pieces of wood together.

She quickly drops the screw into my extended hand. No blushing this time. All this talk must be distracting her.

"Is that how you make a living?"

I'm caught a little off-guard by her question. The Mr. Expose blog is how I actually have steady income. The two thrillers I've written certain don't qualify, since I've spent all year sending them to agents.

I concentrate on twisting the screwdriver and move on to the last boards of the frame. "Well, I do have some freelance work I do. But you won't have read any of it."

"Try me," she says.

Only two people know I'm Mr. Expose. Josie is one and Dane is the other. Neither would tell a living soul, so my secret is safe. "Hey, we're almost done." I stand and place my hands on my hips. "Let's put the mattress on the frame."

I grab one side and she gets the other. We walk the mattress over to the platform. "Thanks for helping me. I'd be hammering away with the meat tenderizer if you hadn't come along."

"Not a problem. What else do you need?"

She looks around the room. "Nothing really. I wish I had a television or more books. I'll get those later."

Harper's belongings are sparse. How does someone who's been married have so little in the way of housekeeping? Josie is single and her apartment is packed with enough furnishings for three houses.

"I'm so glad you came over. I thought maybe you didn't like me."

"I don't know you." I give her a pleasant smile. If I had a collared shirt on, I'd be pulling at my neckline.

"When I knocked on your door and introduced myself..."

"I didn't expect a new neighbor. That's all." But now the thing that's been bugging me resurfaces. I can't help myself. "Plus, I thought I knew you from somewhere. Have we met before?"

"No," she answers, shaking her head. "But I thought you looked familiar, too. Actually, I thought you were Joe Delaware, the famous country singer when I saw you one day at a bar I found downtown. I was eating lunch there and you were with Josie. Of course, I didn't know Josie then. Small world, huh?"

"Joe Delaware is a lot older than I am." I laugh. "And a lot richer."

Harper shakes her head. "Well, close up I can see the difference. You're a better looking guy than he is."

I don't do well with compliments. I know I'm not dog-turd ugly. Or so I've been told by Josie when her friends asked her to play matchmaker.

Instead of responding to her, I glance around the bare living room. "If you need a book to read, I have quite a few. You're welcome to borrow one."

"That'd be really nice."

"I need to get back to work if you don't need any more help. Come grab a book if you like." There. I'm still being neighborly.

I grab my toolbox and Harper follows me across the hall. She hesitates a little in the doorway as if waiting for an invitation.

Man, have I ever behaved like a dick.

"Come on in." I wave at the shelves lining one wall from floor to ceiling. "There's a rolling ladder at the end. Help yourself."

Harper lingers at the end shelf, browsing through the books at eye level. She has a tiny waist that nips in and I imagine my hands spanning across the entire width. For such a small thing, she has a fine ass. It's my Achilles' heel and I force my gaze up.

Too late.

I imagine grabbing her ass and pulling her

flush to my body, feeling the heat of her skin through her clothes.

I sit on the bar stool, one leg dangling, fighting a hard-on that I'll have to adjust when I stand. Still, I'm a glutton for punishment and reluctant to stop watching her since she isn't paying attention to me.

"Can I take this John Grisham one?" she asks and turns to face me.

I nod. "Take anything you want. But no dog ears. I hate those. Please use a bookmark."

"You're serious? I won't. You can trust me."

"My sister would turn down page corners on every book I owned. We used to fight over that. It's the reason she named her bookstore Dog Ears."

Harper pulls the Grisham book from the shelf. "You and your sister are very close, huh."

"I guess." I roll my head back and look at the ceiling. "She can drive me insane, but she's also my best friend. We're twins."

I don't know why I've told her this. The story is really one of those inane details.

"You don't look a thing alike. So you're not identical." She throws both hands to cover her face. "I cannot believe I said that." She drops her hands and her face turns a bright shade of pink.

I cannot quit grinning at the way she's so embarrassed over her thoughtless remark. "I hope we're not."

She holds up the book. "On that totally stupid note, I think I'll be leaving. Thanks for the book. I'll bring it back when I'm finished."

"You're welcome to borrow all you want. If you need help with something heavy, or whatever, please let me know."

"Thanks, Leo."

She closes the door behind her and I stare at it. Harper is someone I could be interested in. Not that I'm looking. But if I wanted more than a hook-up, Harper would be exactly the kind of girl I'd choose. She's the opposite of my ex, Tori—a woman I now know was all flash and dishonesty.

Grandma Lulu's Litmus Test

Harper

DESPERATE TIMES CALL FOR DESPERATE measures. Take reading for instance. I've never been opposed to the task. My daddy asked me read to a Bible verse a day and that was okay. A verse is pretty darned short. Now, I've suddenly taken a shine to the written word. Specifically, I'm fond of books that belong to Leo and must be borrowed and then returned.

I thought I had everything under control with fake reading until the second book I borrowed. Yesterday, I'd returned the book, ready to guide the conversation to what he might be writing.

"How did you like *Gone Girl*?" he asked me.

"Loved it. That book was such a page turner."

"What about the plot twist in the middle?"

I'd given him a puzzled look.

One corner of his mouth quirked. "You know. When you discover Amy's an unreliable narrator."

What. The. Heck. There went my easy ruse.

Now, I guess I'll have to really read.

It is interesting how his eyes sparkle when he asks me about the stories. He turns his head ever so slightly, like he might miss something important I have to say.

I'm lying on my bed and fluff two pillows underneath my head so I can better position my current read, a zombie novel. Leo's tastes range from classic to trendy. It's been a week of borrowing books and so far, those few minutes are the only time I see him. I've tried a little of everything he has in his library, as if I'm at some buffet taking a bite of this or that and knowing I can always go back for a different dish.

On the next page turn, I find a piece of paper serving as a bookmark. It's a business card for a hair stylist. Interesting. Wesley always went to a barbershop, as far as I know.

But then again, he had lots of secrets I only uncovered bit by bit. I grip the card tighter. I close my eyes for a second and shake off thinking ill of the dead.

I flip the card over. There's a phone number on the back and the word 'cell' printed above the numbers. There's also two tiny hearts drawn next to the name. I turn back to the front and examine it. The card lists a business name and at the bottom, "Stylist Tori."

I wonder if Tori borrowed this book also. Maybe Leo has lots of friends who borrow reading material.

My cell phone chimes and I grab it from the end of the bed. "Hello."

"Hi Harper. It's Josie."

"Hey." I gently place the card inside the book and close the cover. I haven't heard from her in a couple of days. "How are you?"

"I'm good. I've been the only one running the store because my help decided to go to Disney World. As if people deserve a vacation."

I'm silent, since I can't tell if she's kidding or not.

"Harper? You there? You OK?"

"Yeah. Things have been good here."

"Did you find a job yet?"

"Oh. I did. I'm going to be a concierge at a dog hotel."

"That's a joke, right?"

"Um...no." I sit up and pull my knees forward. "Well, that's what they call it. It's really a dog walker and assistant type thing at this glorified dog boarding business. But they can call me whatever they want at Le Frou Frous. I start work on Monday."

Josie's deep laugh puts the happy in my day. It's nice to talk to someone.

"Want to come by?" I ask.

"Oh. That's why I called. Could you go next

82

door and tell my brother to check his voicemail or pick up the phone?"

"Sure. Is that all you need?"

"Tell him I need help. It's not like I've asked him to pick up tampons or anything."

"He'll know what you're talking about?"

"Oh yeah. Just tell him I can't go pick up Grandma Lulu and take her to the quilting thing. He'll have to do it this week."

"Got it. Take your grandma to quilting."

"She's not really my grandma. She's my dad's second cousin. But we call her—"

There's a crashing sound in the background. Josie makes an irritated noise deep in her throat that resembles a warning growl. "Listen, I need to go. Some kid knocked over a shelf. Thanks."

Silence.

I glance at my cell to see she's disconnected. At least she thought of me.

I really had no friends in Tacoma. As soon as I made any, Wesley found reasons to dislike them. He'd say the females were bad influences on me. Once I went to the movies with a girl who lived down the road. Wesley accused me of meeting men with her. All I wanted was watch a movie and meet a bucket of buttered popcorn. Laugh and talk to another girl. Be silly.

Having a male friend was out of the question.

So, I've gotten accustomed to being self-sufficient, detached, alone. But I want it to be different here.

Our building is noisy in the mornings. The bakery downstairs rumbles with the banging of sheet pans into ovens long before customers enter the doors at 6:00 am. I don't mind the sounds. It comforts me in a way. The sweet smells remind me of childhood and Mama.

I walk across the hall to Leo's door and listen for a moment. Monitoring his schedule like I have, I know he's awake. It's puzzling to me if he gets any sleep at all since he wakes early and stays up late into the night. My soft knock brings him to the door immediately.

He's showered already with wet hair slicked off his handsome face. A smell of shampoo and wood and man envelopes me. I have an insane desire to step closer and inhale more of that goodness into my lungs. He's more scrumptious than the bakery's cinnamon rolls.

Somebody should package him up for resale.

Leo frowns at me and I get the feeling he's not a morning person. He really should work on his happiness factor.

"Hi Harper," he says.

His gaze travels down the length of my body and my nipples tighten. I'm wearing cotton pajamas, since I thought I'd spend the morning reading *Glorious Dead* in bed. My clothing is perfectly acceptable for messenger type duty. Except for the lack of a bra and the obvious headlights I'm sporting, I'm more covered than most of the girls he'd pass on the street.

"Hey. Josie called."

"What's wrong?" Alarm spreads across his face so fast I barely have time to stop it.

"Nothing. Whoa. Sorry. It's just she couldn't get you to answer your phone."

He exhales, and if anything, his expression grows darker. "I've told her to leave a message. I don't pick up when I'm writing."

My gaze narrows to an assessing squint. I recognize this unfriendly man as the Mr. Expose who is too rude and stubborn to look for my postcard.

"Don't shoot the messenger. I'm supposed to tell you that she can't take your grandma to some club thing..." I trail off, trying to remember exactly what Josie's message was.

Leo raises both eyebrows. "My grandmother is dead."

"No. I meant to say..." I'm flustered that I appear to be so inept. "Grandma Lulu."

He opens the door wide. "Were you even awake when she called you?" He again glances at what I'm wearing.

"Yes, I was. For your information, I was reading your book and then she called. But

85

you're so grumpy it made me forget what she said exactly."

"What book?" He grabs his phone from the end table. "*Glorious Dead*?"

"Yeah."

He studies his cell phone. "She's blowing up my phone. Ten missed calls. I hope she doesn't call you like that."

"No. It's the first time she's called me. But I'm so glad I have her number now." I try to tamp down the wistful tone to my voice, but it's out there and too late.

He punches the screen and holds the phone to his ear, listening to a voice mail. When he's finished, he sits on his bar stool. "You could've asked me for her number."

"You seem busy. I don't want to interrupt your creativity flow or whatever you do in here."

He chuckles. "The thing I said about Josie calling and messages? Well, she calls me a lot. Every day. I can't spend all my time on the phone with her."

"Must be nice." I sit on the arm of the sofa. "I mean, to have real family that you can share your life with."

Leo stares at me and then out the window. "It's good. When our parents died a few years back, we realized we can't take family for granted."

I nod. "What happened to your folks?"

"Plane crash. My dad was a pilot. He ran charter flights. They were on a trip to pick up some organ transplants and the engine failed."

A hollow feeling bottoms out deep in my stomach. I picture an aircraft encased in flames and the mental image takes my mind to the car wreck. To Wesley. I grip the side of the edge of the sofa, digging my nails into the leather arm. "That's terrible."

Leo's gaze flicks down to my hands and his eyebrows dip in concern. I inhale and relax my body.

"We don't have to talk about this," he says.

"I'm OK. But if it bothers you..."

"It was years ago." He stares at me silently for several seconds before turning his back to me to glance out the window. "Man, it's nice out there today. Not too muggy."

"Uh huh."

"Josie's message says I have to take Grandma Lulu to quilting. I guess I need some fresh air. I've been working on a deadline and haven't been out enough lately."

"Where does Grandma Lulu live?"

"Nursing home. It's about 25 miles from here and her quilting club meets at a senior citizens' center down the road. I have to wait a couple of hours in the area while she's there."

"I wish I could get out of here today. Could I tag along?"

He turns around slowly. "To take Grandma Lulu? Are you serious?"

"Oh. That was kind of pushy. Sorry." I get to my feet.

"It's not very exciting." One corner of his mouth quirks.

"I'll be in my pajamas all day if you don't take me. How's that for a party?"

He grins. "The quilters are gonna love you."

I hop from my perch on his sofa. "When do I have to be ready?"

"How about 9:30? She needs to be there at 10:00."

I nod and smile. "Got it. See you in a while."

***

Grandma Lulu isn't what I'd pictured. A complete opposite to my grandmothers back in Texas, Lulu is loud and rowdy. After the introductions in her tidy room at the nursing home, she shoves a twenty-pound canvas bag into my hands.

"Make sure you don't drop that. There are two jars of boysenberry jam inside," she says.

I nod and clutch the bag by both handles. "Yes, ma'am."

"Darlin, just call me Grandma Lulu. You need to eat more. What are your intentions with Leo?"

Leo walks ahead to open the retirement home door. "She's only a friend."

Grandma Lulu shakes her head. "Boy, I should tan your hide for stringing this girl along. Of course she's your friend. But that's not all. You've never brought a girl to meet me before." She scoots her walker along at a remarkable pace. The yellow tennis balls at the bottom of each leg thump against the linoleum.

"I'm only his neighbor." I follow her out the door.

"You a natural blonde?" she asks without turning to look at me.

Leo opens the door of his car he's pulled to the curb. "Grandma Lulu. Can you behave yourself?"

I glance over at Leo to see he's grinning. She's not bothering him at all.

"Yes, this is my natural color," I say. "But when I was a teenager I did let my friend put highlights on my hair once."

"I like the color it is. You shouldn't mess with what Mother Nature gave you." Her gaze moves from me to Leo. "You look good beside Leo. You'll make pretty babies."

My cheeks warm. "Thank you. About the color, I mean." Grandma Lulu is either ornery or set on matchmaking. Or both.

I look to Leo for some help. He ignores me and takes her walker to put into the trunk of his car.

At my extended hand, Grandma Lulu scoffs. "I don't need help sitting down, honey. It's the getting up that's the problem. That's the way of life and love. Falling is easy. Getting up is the hard part."

She maneuvers into the front passenger seat, and I get into the back. While I'm buckling my seatbelt, she whips around in the seat. "How old are you? You look too young for Leo."

I should be accustomed to elderly ladies like Grandma Lulu. Our church was full of the ones who'd passed the age of conversational filtering. I'm out of practice.

"Twenty-two." I fold my hands in my lap, waiting for the next question.

"Leo's twenty-four," she says. "Time for people to be settling down. I'd like to have some great-grandbabies before I'm dead. My grandchildren are scattered from New York to Alaska. Do they ever visit me? No. Leo and Josie are my only hope for holding some babies."

I've given up on denying dating Leo.

Leo starts the car and glances at Grandma Lulu. "Harper lived in Texas. Didn't you live there for a while?"

"When I was married to my second husband," she says. "You don't remember him. You were but a spark in your daddy's eye back then. Those were the days."

"Mm hm," Leo says. He glances up at the rearview mirror and grins.

"I miss home," I say and turn to the window. "I miss the heat and the wildflowers. There's nothing more beautiful than bluebonnets in the spring." My throat tightens at the fullness of the statement. For a brief, silly moment, I'm afraid I might cry so I dig my nails into my palms and inhale.

We're at a red traffic light. Our gazes meet in the rearview mirror. His eyes are so blue and knowing. It's as if he felt a shift in my emotions from the front seat. He'll never let me tag along again if I act all crazy.

Grandma Lulu sighs. "We should take a trip there. You and Harper and I could pack up and go. We're all single. Or at least I am."

I'm glad when he looks back to the road. After another ten minutes, we reach our destination.

The Talbot Seniors' Center is a large building with limestone walls and beautiful flowers in planters. Grandma Lulu allows Leo to help her out of the car and we walk her inside. Once we enter the building, we take an immediate left to a room full of elderly ladies and a couple of men. Some have chosen their seats already and a few stand near a table with desserts and coffee. A couple of the women immediately walk over to hug Leo.

Grandma Lulu makes her way over to a chair next to one of the few men.

I follow her and quietly place the canvas bag on the floor beside her chair. She turns to me and grabs my arm to pull me closer to her side. "William, this is Leo's girlfriend, Harper."

The man leans in to offer his hand. "Leo's girl. How nice."

This Leo's girlfriend thing won't die. Sometimes you just have to go with it. "Hi." I place my hand in his and he squeezes.

He winks at me. "Sure picked a pretty one." He looks past me.

Across the room, Leo politely listens as an older woman talks to him. He points at me and then strolls my way.

"Grandma Lulu, we'll be back in an hour. Harper and I have errands to run."

She's waves a hand at us, signaling that we should go on. I walk with Leo to the door and outside. "Errands?"

"I'm sorry. That was a lie. If it would make you feel better, I could definitely make up some errands. Want to take a walk?"

I laugh at him. "Sure. The lady you were talking to looked very disappointed when we left."

He smirks. "I swear. Some of those ladies flirt worse than a sixteen-year-old looking for a prom date. They'll do a little quilting in the next room, but they mostly talk."

"It seems like fun. I'm sure they're lonely. It's very sweet of you and Josie to bring Ms. Lulu here."

We duck our heads as we walk under a low hanging tree branch. Baskets of begonias hang along the wooden fence and litter flower petals across sidewalk.

"I don't mind. It's not like I have to set work hours, so it's no trouble." He slows his pace.

"What are you writing now?" I peer up at him. Maybe he's never mentioned the Mr. Expose blog because he's embarrassed or thinks I won't know about it. He published a new post today. I check it constantly to ensure my postcard isn't the image at the top of the page.

He stops in front of a gift shop and folds his arms while looking at the window decor. "I have to tell you something. As a writer, I'm constantly trying to analyze why people do the things they do. I watch them and look for clues. I listen to what they say. And then I listen more carefully to what they don't say."

"Uh huh." I'm not a people watcher, but even I can read the discomfort rolling off him in tense waves.

He changes subjects like a racecar changing lanes. "Why didn't you move back to Texas instead of coming here?"

"No reason. I like Nashville."

He is not deterred by my short answer. "I visited Hawaii, once. Really liked it, but I'm not moving there."

Maybe if I give him something—a real answer—he'll open up about his writing and his blog.

We turn to follow the sidewalk past another block of shops. "My parents love me. But they'd try to run my life if I went home, because they didn't want me to marry Wesley. I eloped and didn't give them a chance to talk me out of it. At eighteen, I thought I knew everything. I just left a note and it really hurt both of them. I'm an only child and it took a while before we made amends over the phone. I don't want them to think I can't make it on my own."

I've been wrong about so much; I can't stand another person judging me. Wrong about love, about my ability to give, about being a kind person. But for some reason, his opinion is important to me. I want him to think I'm a good person.

The answer satisfies Leo and he glances at his watch. "We can head back and wait in the air-conditioning until she's ready to leave."

"Oh, yeah," I say, disappointed that the time has passed so quickly.

"Thanks for coming along today. And for what it's worth, I see you as strong and capable.

You're hardly a failure."

I don't say anything. I can't tell if he's trying to make me feel better by giving me a compliment, or if he really believes what he's saying.

Leo puts a hand on the back of my bare neck and squeezes lightly. "We all need time to find ourselves."

His words do something weird to my chest. He doesn't know how terrible I am. How much I wanted Wesley to pay for what he'd done to me.

How careless I was with my thoughts and prayers and words.

***

From: isabellawarren@iconic.net
To: angelgirl@me.com

Dear Harper,

Thank you for taking my call last night. It's funny—the bond we've discovered through tragedy. I lie awake at night with no one to talk to about what's happened. I'd been married twelve years when Warren died—sorry, does it feel odd for me to use the name Warren? I wonder what he called himself and if he ever got confused.

That's not funny in the least, yet I cannot stop laughing at the thought. I may need to visit with a counselor, but somehow, right now talking with you does the trick.

The other night, I watched a show about sister wives. I wonder if they feel like we do. But that's all wrong. At least, they know about each other. It's easy to be bitter, but it's never directed at you. You've been hurt by his double life as much as I.

When I'm really angry, I remind myself that at least Warren was a good father to Charley. He was a good provider for her and she never suspected.
If you ever need anything, please tell me.

Yours truly,
Isabella

Passing Strange

Leo

HARD AND FAST RULES ARE meant to be broken. Or at least that's what I tell myself to justify having Harper in my apartment watching television.

"Is the volume too high?" she asks.

I shake my head and glance over my shoulder at her. "No. It's fine.

Even though I say this, Harper points the remote control at the TV and lowers the volume. "I can turn the closed caption on."

She turns the sound even lower and places the remote beside her on the sofa.

"Harper. Please quit worrying. You can't even hear it now."

"I can read lips."

I give up arguing with her. She's as stubborn as Josie. My fingers rest on my keyboard and I urge them to move, make magic in the form of a story.

Nothing.

I've always guarded my writing time. By habit, I rise early and work on Mr. Expose blog entries. Then I contact blog advertisers, conduct billing, create ads. In the late evenings, I work hard on my real passion—my novels.

I ask Josie not to interrupt. The guys don't drop by. I've never even allowed a girlfriend to cut into this ritual.

But now, Harper's on my sofa watching television while I work on my current manuscript. This is the third night in a row for her to sit in my living room and watch a movie. She rarely says a word while I bang away on the keyboard. I only offered because she won't buy a television for some reason, and I feel sorry for her.

It's how neighbors behave. Cordial, friendly, comfortable.

And everybody likes Harper—Josie, Dane, and my landlords. Grandma Lulu likes her so much that she's asked me to bring her again. I reminded Lulu that Harper is only a friend. Nothing more. Because I'm not interested in her for more than a platonic relationship.

All utter bullshit and dressed up excuses.

Each day when I see her, I want to know a little more about what's inside her head.

Yesterday, Harper borrowed Cormac McCarthy's book, *All the Pretty Horses*. When she returned the hardback today, we discussed it—the story, characters, the language. Even Josie, who is a serious reader, doesn't discuss novels with me...unless she's going on and on about who should star in the movie adaptations. Dane probably hasn't read a book since middle school.

I admit it. I love talking to her. She's a mix of smart and kooky. Sexy and sheltered. She amuses me. It doesn't hurt that she's hot, with a frail but fierce Emma Stone look.

I swivel around in my desk chair to face her. "Want a soda or water? Coffee?"

Her gaze flicks over to meet mine. "I'm fine."

"I'm getting something for myself. What'll you have?"

Her phone buzzes and she examines the display. She answers cheerfully. "Hi Josie."

While she listens to whatever Josie says, Harper traces an invisible pattern on her bare thigh and pulls the hem of her shorts down. "Oh," she says in a low voice as if I can't hear every word. "I'm at Leo's watching TV."

She stares and her lap while she listens and tugs again at the hem of her shorts. A nice pink bubblegum blush tinges her cheeks.

I stop watching her because it's driving me crazy that I can't hear what Josie's said to make her embarrassed. Time to grab my drink.

I'm standing with my back to Harper when she touches my back. She moves like a sneaky cat.

Harper holds out the phone. "She wants to

talk."

I take out a soda and hand her one. "Thanks," I say, taking the phone. "Hey, Josie."

"Watching TV? How come you don't watch TV with me?" Josie asks in a teasing tone.

"I'm working. She's watching a movie." I pop the tab on my can.

Harper makes her way back to the sofa. I'm distracted by the way her khaki shorts cling to her perfectly round ass. She's thin, but her ass is this masterpiece that would fit in my hands—

"Did you even hear what I said?" Josie's impatient voice interrupts my fantasy. "Your mind is somewhere else, isn't it."

It's like my sister has ESP. Which is creepier than hell when it comes to some things you don't want your sister to know. "What do you need? I've got to get back to work," I answer in a rough, no-nonsense voice.

"I said, since you're obviously *not* working, can Dane and I come over?"

"You're with Dane? You guys went on a date?"

"No. I helped him close tonight." Her tone challenges me to ask anything else.

"Oh," I say, not in the mood to antagonize her.

"I had a drink at Dastardly's and then helped him close. Let us come over. It'll be fun. When's the last time you had fun?"

Harper is watching me and when I catch her, she looks back to the television.

I sigh. "All right. You guys can drop by."

"Good. See you guys in a few," Josie says with barely contained glee.

"Bye." I walk over to hand Harper the phone. "Josie's coming over. And Dane. I should've asked if you can stay a while. I'm sure she's coming to see you."

Harper takes the phone from me and our fingers brush. A frisson of electricity passes between us that jolts me into needing more contact. I'm suddenly like a junkie, wondering if it'll feel that good a second time and with more skin. Lots of skin.

I back away and return to my desk. What's wrong with me? It's true I've been without a girlfriend for almost a year. That doesn't mean I've been celibate. It doesn't mean I've been satisfied either.

Hooking up is what it is…a brief meeting of two lonely bodies in the night. The problem is that one-night stands always leave me thinking about my ex-girlfriend later. I'm not ready to be relationship screwed again, so I end up avoiding a second time around with anyone.

Tori. She couldn't tell the truth if the fate of all mankind depended on it. Each time I see her name on my cell phone display, I cringe. She won't accept that it's over between us, and I'm not opening that door a crack in case I'm weak enough to walk through it again.

I sit at my desk, staring at my computer and wondering if there's a possibility of something between me and Harper. She's visited daily to borrow books, and now watch TV. But I'm not sure if she's into me or not.

I decide to give up on getting any work done and wait until Josie and Dane arrive. The television shares a wall with my desk. My desk is at the wrong angle to see the movie well, something I did on purpose when I arranged the furniture in this room.

Harper's so into the scene that it's like her body's been dragged inside the movie. Her hands ball into tight fists in her lap and send distress waves across the room. My desire to comfort her drives me to my feet.

"Which movie is this?" I stand and move to the center of the room, my arms folded.

"*What Dreams May Come*. It's an old one."

"I don't remember it. Robin Williams, huh. So, what's this about?"

"He died and then his wife commits suicide. He's searching for her in hell," Harper says in a tight voice without ever looking away from the screen. The movie is doing a number on her emotions.

I'm thinking about her phenomenal ass and conversation skills, and she's thinking about her dead husband.

Perfect.

"Harper?"

She glances over at me, then gives a slow blink as if to ground herself in this time and space. "Yeah?"

It bugs me that she's watching this movie and it's putting her head in a place from her past. I want her emotionally here in my apartment, not back in Washington. It's selfish, I know. But I am always honest with myself. Lying to yourself is the ultimate betrayal, a foolish indulgence which only gets you into more trouble. I smile so she'll focus on my face and remember she's sitting in my living room. "I think Josie and Dane will be here in ten minutes or less. Want to help me see if I have something to eat?"

"Oh," she says and straightens. She looks once more at the television and then hops to her feet in a single move, blonde hair swinging around her shoulder. "Sure. Sorry."

I take several steps and turn the television off. There's no way I want to compete with the movie.

"I have guacamole dip in the fridge if you'll get it out for us." I take one step to the right and bump into Harper. "Sorry, babe."

The endearment slips out. I'm not even sure where it came from, but she's been around so much lately that I've grown comfortable with her. Also, there's the fact I've been thinking of her in a different way. Maybe I should ask her out. Maybe she would cleanse the bad taste that Tori left. Then I back away from the idea because I get the feeling Harper's not ready.

"I, um...Guacamole." She walks quickly to the fridge and sticks her entire head in as she pokes around looking for it. Her head pops up above the door. "You sure have a lot of food in here."

"Just went grocery shopping last night. The guys are coming over here to play poker this week, so I needed supplies."

"You have a lot of liquor."

I laugh. "My friends drink a lot."

She doesn't say anything and pulls out a plastic container of store made guacamole. "Do you have chips?"

"Cabinet to your right."

She turns and opens the door. The cabinets hang high on the wall and she tiptoes to reach the bag of chips on a shelf.

"Here. Let me." I move behind her and reach above her head to grab the chips. With one hand resting on her shoulder, I lean in and retrieve it.

Her entire body tenses with the touch and she turns her head the slightest amount to stare into my eyes. Flecks of green glimmer in her hazel eyes, reminding me again of cool water.

A man could lie down in that gaze and drown.

"I'm in the way," she says and looks away.

"You're fine. Don't move." There's other things in the cabinet that I hadn't intended to get but suddenly seem like a good idea. Dane and Josie will be more interested in what I have to drink than eat. "What about pita chips? You like those?" I reach up to the shelf again.

She takes a step to the side and twists, so her body angles toward mine. We're two magnets, naturally pulling together until our bodies touch. Harper's face tilts up and her cheeks turn pink.

She wants me to kiss her. I don't doubt it. I lean closer and bring my mouth within inches of hers.

My apartment door opens. "Honey, we're home." Josie sings the phrase, doing her best to imitate something she's heard from an old TV show.

Harper pulls in a quick breath and shoves at my chest to put distance between us. I stumble back until the island bar hits my ass.

Is she embarrassed by Josie seeing us so close? If anything, Josie would throw a party to celebrate my interest in just about anyone, after Tori.

"Heard of knocking?" I ask Josie. Dane trails in behind her and gives Harper a curious look.

Josie raises one eyebrow but otherwise ignores me. "Hey, Harper. Cute outfit." She walks to the bar and places a brown paper takeout bag from Dastardly's on the counter. "We come bearing gifts."

Harper peers into the bag and her eyes widen. "More liquor?"

I slide the bag to me and remove a bottle of whiskey, a bottle of daiquiri mix, and a bottle of rum. "She travels equipped."

"Not my fault," Josie says. "Dane's trying to get me wasted so he can take advantage of me. As if..."

Dane smirks. "My plan has been discovered. Since Josie won't have me, maybe Harper will succumb to my charms."

His comment is said lightly enough that I know he's kidding. Dane walks over to the other side of the bar near Harper and slings an arm over her shoulders.

"She's smarter than that, man." I chuckle, but there's an uncomfortable panic that pelts me like a sudden hailstorm.

Dane is a flirt. He's always been ballsy and confident. But I don't want him making Harper think he's really interested.

And then there's Josie. In the second Dane has so carelessly paid attention to Harper, my sister's expression has fallen into a gloomy pit of doom.

Fuck Dane for being such an asshole.

"Let's mix some drinks then, people." I glance at Josie. "Can you grab something for me? Shot glasses are in my desk drawer."

"What the hell?" Dane laughs. "You doing the Hemingway thing and doing shots while you write?"

"You know who Hemingway is? I'm so impressed," I say dryly. Maybe the dude does read.

Thank God, he moves away from Harper. I exhale and hand the chips and dip to Harper. "Can you put these on the table?"

I spend several minutes helping Dane make daiquiris and wondering how to defuse the tension he's caused with Josie. I love my sister and could kick his ass.

Josie stands at the far end of the room and hooks her phone to my stereo speaker. Dane watches her as she absently dances to the music she starts. The noise muffles what she and Harper are saying to each other.

I pour daiquiris into two glasses for the girls and tilt my head toward Dane. "When in God's name are you two going to stop pretending?"

"Pretending what?" He examines a bottle opener he's taken from my drawer. Dane grins. "There's a breast for the handle."

"Put it back. Groomsman gift. I didn't buy it. Back to my question. You and Josie need to go out and start acting like grownups." I give him a cold stare but know he's not going to answer. Chickenshit.

I grab the two drinks and carry them to the table.

Josie turns the music down and meets me before I can set hers down. "Thanks!" She sips the icy drink.

Dane takes a chair on the opposite side of the table and sets down a couple of cans of soda tucked into the curve of his arm like a football. In his other hand, he holds the bottle of whiskey and promptly breaks the seal. "What do you guys want to do?" he asks.

I sit in the chair closest to where Harper's been waiting. Josie takes the remaining seat.

"Let's play 'Have you ever.'" Josie pushes Harper's drink in front of her.

"What are we? Twelve?" I ask and take the shot that Dane slides toward me.

"I hope not," Josie answers. "Twelve-year-olds should not be drinking."

Dane downs his shot. "I'm down with it. How does this game work? I haven't played."

"Liar," Josie says. "I ask the first question, 'Have you ever?' and then everyone who has must drink."

"I don't know about this. This game doesn't

seem like a good idea." Harper's voice hesitates like we've asked her to participate in a bank robbery.

Any other girl and I might think she's playing innocent, but not Harper. Man, she's cute.

Josie shrugs. "If you don't want to play, we won't."

"I've never played any party games." Harper takes a sip of drink and sits forward. "I want to."

I lay my hand flat on the table and tap with the beat of the music. I'm dying to play this stupid game. I can think of all kinds of things I'll discover about Harper.

But my motives are childish and selfish. Temptation beats a drum while chanting that I give in. I inhale. "Let's just play cards," I say.

Dane uses two fingers to nudge the shot glass. "Drink up, buddy."

"You don't want to play?" Harper's eyes glitter.

I raise one eyebrow. Then I make sure to look at Harper when I say my next words in case she needs an out. "I'll play if everyone wants to."

Josie looks to her left at Harper. "Here we go. Have you ever gotten arrested?" She raises her daiquiri to her lips. "Cheers," she says and takes a huge drink.

Harper's mouth drops into a cute little 'O' and she exhales. "Not me."

Dane takes the shot glass and upends it.

I grin at him. "Man, this doesn't bode well for you."

Josie turns to Harper again. "This is going to be fun. Your turn to ask a question."

"Have you ever cheated on a test?" Harper asks.

Dane rolls his eyes. "I cheat on every test."

Harper drinks from her daiquiri. "This tastes pretty good."

I don't take a drink and grin while Dane and Josie take their penalty.

I'm up for a question. What do I want to know about Harper? Maybe a sure bet so she'll have to drink. "Have you ever gossiped?"

We all take a drink. Harper's grin warms my chest. Or maybe it's the whiskey. Either way, I'm starting to feel mellow.

"My turn," Dane says. He pours liquor in both our shot glasses.

At this rate, I'm going to be wasted long before the girls finish their little icy drinks. Shit.

"Have you ever wished you were with someone else while on a date?" Dane asks.

I grin. Dane is an asshole. I lift my shot glass and so do Dane and Josie. "So much for romance," I say and drink the shot in one long pull.

We continue with a few inane questions that have us laughing because everything now qualifies as funny. Josie gets up from the table several times to make more daiquiris and brings one for Harper every time she refills her own.

It's Harper's turn and she stares at the table in concentration. No one rushes her. Finally, she raises her head. "Have you ever loved someone? I mean really, truly loved?"

The music still plays in the background, but there's a sonic boom sound in my head and my entire body clenches in response to the question. I didn't see that coming.

I take the shot in one gulp. The heat of the liquor burns my throat. The sensation is a welcome assault after that question.

I cannot take my eyes off Harper. It's such a serious question to ask. And then, she surprises me by not taking a drink.

Silver Lining

Harper

"HAVE YOU EVER LOVED SOMEONE? I mean really, truly loved?" I ask.

A languid blanket of euphoria folds around my body, and I sit back in my chair. Leo and Dane and Josie are all looking at me with room-sized expectation on their faces. I stare at the table so they won't influence my answer.

This drinking game should really be called the truth game. *The truth shall set you free.* Where have I heard that? The author who penned it must be the smartest person in the universe.

Because with only a few truths during this game, I am liberated.

Truth. I've done things in spite of my parents' rigid rules when I lived in their house.

Truth. Some of those things were fun and some were downright stupid.

Truth. I'm not sure I was ever really in love with Wesley. I was in love with love. Can you love someone and then hate him so much you can't stand the sight of him? Was I justified because he was a lying, cheating coward?

That seems like a fickle attitude. I married someone before God and witnesses at the chapel in Las Vegas. How can I ever trust that I will recognize love if I married a guy I only thought I loved?

I know I wouldn't go searching into hell for Wesley like the guy in the movie did.

What was my question? I look to Leo for help.

"My turn," Leo says.

Oh yeah. We are still playing the game.

I study the glass in front of me. Several rounds earlier, Josie brought me a different mixed drink. It's soda with liquor and doesn't taste as good as the daiquiris, but I drink the concoction anyway.

Leo, Leo, Leo. I lift my gaze to meet his. A sigh escapes my lips, and I stare at him and his very nice lips. It doesn't matter that he can see me staring. Because the truth is, it makes me happy to look at him, especially his mouth. I love his mouth.

Leo takes a drink from his shot glass even though I don't think he's asked a question. This makes me laugh. Well, he's certainly not playing by the rules of the game. Question, first. Drink, second.

He closes his eyes for a second and when he

opens them, he looks straight at me. "Have you ever had sex outside?"

Dane tips up the shot glass without hesitating or watching to see if anyone else will drink. Josie shakes her head and smirks.

I think hard. "Does inside a car count?" I ask.

Leo leans both elbows on the table, seeming to think about my question. "No. It has to be you and your lover in the great outdoors. Maybe you're on a blanket in the meadow with only the stars as a moonlight ceiling. Or he's pushed you up against a tree—"

Josie groans. "No details," she slurs loudly. "Ugh. Sister, here. Remember I'm here." She points at herself so we won't doubt her location.

Dane raises a hand like he's getting a teacher's attention in class. "I have. In an alley. That's not a meadow, but it counts."

Leo grins and turns his head toward Dane. "You are so predictable."

"It was hot." Dane raises an eyebrow. "Believe me."

"No drink for me," I answer. And then I take a drink from my glass anyway.

Leo takes his shot, but his gaze never leaves mine. His image must be in the dictionary beside the word 'sexy' and I vow to tell him this someday, when I feel bolder.

The way he stares at me makes my body

tingle and my nipples tighten, in direct contrast to the way my brain slows. I want to tell him how he makes me feel. No. That would be disastrous for some reason.

I search my mind for the reason I shouldn't grab him and push him into the bedroom. Perhaps, this drink is three drinks too many.

"I need to go home," I say.

"I'll walk you." Leo gets to his feet.

"No, I know the address." I giggle at my own joke.

Leo grabs my elbow. "I'll make sure."

"OK. But we are not having sex in a meadow." I smirk.

Leo doesn't respond. He could've argued at the very least. Even pretending he wanted to have sex with me would've made me exponentially happy.

He guides me from the table and out the door. I glance over my shoulder and wave at Dane and Josie. "Thanks for the game. This was fun. So. Much. Fun."

Leo's hand glides across my back to my opposite hip. "Steady."

"I am steady." I wobble to the door and he opens it. "Maybe not."

"Yeah," he says, his lips so close to my hair. A pleasant chill travels down my spine and I shiver.

"I live there," I say, pointing across the hall.

He laughs instead of answering.

I dig in my short's pocket. "No key. I had a key earlier. It's gone. Someone's stolen it."

The heat of Leo standing so close to me makes it difficult for me to concentrate on the key search. I throw up my hands in defeat.

"Let me." He moves flush to my back and his chest pushes against me as he leans in. His fingers edge to the top of my right pocket and push down inside.

My head falls back into the crook of his neck. "You can search all my clothes for a key. You just do whatever it takes. Leave no stone unturned."

His hand inside my pocket pulls my body closer against him behind me. He kisses the side of my head. "I'm tempted."

Leo pushes his hand deeper into my pocket and the thin fabric is really no barrier to the luscious feel of his fingers against my skin. He traces his fingers across the edge of my panties.

I moan. "Maybe you'll have to do this forever. I probably don't even have a key."

He pulls his hand out. "You do. Got it." Suddenly, there are beautiful masculine fingers and a stupid gold key in front of my face.

"Shoot." I grab for the key, but he dismisses my efforts.

He opens the door, and we both walk inside. His arm is still around me and he turns me toward him. "You going to be OK? I think I should put you to bed."

Every cell in my body hums a happy tune. The pleasant buzz of alcohol plays a sexy song, and I allow it to loosen my inhibitions. "I'll let you under one condition."

He inhales. "Anything the lady wants."

"I'd like a kiss."

Leo studies me, his blue eyes darkening. "You're drunk." Then he bends his heads and touches his lips to my cheek in a chaste kiss.

When he pulls back, I frown. "You don't want to kiss me."

"I did kiss you," he says, brow furrowed.

"I meant a real kiss. Like you want me. A passionate, I-might-fall-in-love-with-you kiss." I shouldn't have said it, but it's exactly what I mean.

"Babe," he says and laughs. "You have no idea."

"Kiss me again."

He puts his hands on the back of my neck and pulls me to him. When his head lowers this time, I close my eyes instantly.

Leo's lips part the seam of mine and I gasp as his tongue teases its way inside. The kiss accelerates like a bike coasting from the top of a hill. The thrill of the ride amps my heart rate and makes me want to hold on tighter.

His fingers tunnel into my hair and I grab

the front of his T-shirt.

Leo's mouth turns up at one corner in a smile I can feel and his lips move away from mine to trace kisses down my cheek and neck.

He gently kisses the base of my neck. "Is this what you had in mind?"

"Mmm..." I answer. My head swims a lazy circle, and I'm so drowsy that I can't seem to open my eyes.

I drop my hands from the tight hold on his shirt to rake a trail down his chest, his stomach, and hips. Sliding my fingers to the back of his waist, I drag him closer to me. His mouth finds mine again.

He wins the Oscar, or Emmy, or gold freaking medal for kissing. Hands down.

The tips of my fingers slide into the back of his shirt and run along his waist where his jeans hang on his slim hips. He shudders.

"Babe," he whispers against my lips.

His full erection presses against me, and I stop moving my hands. "You like this kiss," I tease against his lips. "Me, too."

Leo stops moving and puts a hateful inch of space between us. I groan a complaint.

"Bed," he says, his lips against the top of my head.

"I want more kisses. I want you to know you are so beautiful." I say to him with my eyes closed. "You are a beautiful enigma. The woods have secrets dark and deep..."

"You need to sleep this one off."

"I'm not sleepy. More kissing."

He leads me to my bedroom.

***

My brain slogs into gear. I open both eyes in unison and end up closing the right one to limit the sunlight burning a hole in my retinas. I have no idea of the time or the day, but I do know something.

There's a body on the other side of my bed.

A wave of nausea rolls around my stomach. I turn my head to see the lump beside me and the dark hair. If someone were in my bed...I'd expect blond. I'd expect Leo. I'd expect...a larger body.

"Hey," I say in a croak reminiscent of pond frogs on a summer night.

"What? I'm still asleep." Josie rolls onto her back.

"Oh, it's you."

"Who'd you expect?" she says, her eyes slitting open and pinning me with a knowing look.

"I don't know...oh, I'm going to be sick." I take a shallow breath and push down the feeling.

Josie gently pushes me to the edge of the bed. "Go. If you puke on me, I'll start puking."

I drop my legs off the side of the bed and go

119

to the floor. I'm on my hands and knees when Josie appears with a trash can.

"Here," she says. "Take it, but I can't stay. I cannot be around someone getting sick. It's a vomit phobia. Sorry!" She puts the back of her hand to her mouth and makes a gagging sound.

"I'm not puking! Stop."

"Just imagining. I'll go get Leo. I'm so sorry. Just watching you..." She places the trash bin near my head and then her footsteps recede.

I lift my body and move toward the trash can. I'm not going to vomit. I can do this.

Then I put my head inside the canister and retch. So much for not vomiting. Tears stream down my cheeks, and I quit trying to fight it.

A faint rustling sound alarms me that either Josie is braving the vomit or she's brought help. Please let it be the first.

"Here's a washcloth," Leo says in a low, soothing voice.

"Josie is a traitor." I take the washcloth from him and wipe my sweaty face and then my mouth.

"She has a low threshold for medical emergencies. I, on the other hand, am an excellent nurse."

"Gah," I say in a self-disgusted groan. "Better than a low threshold for alcohol."

He places a hand on my bare shoulder and squeezes. "I'm going to get you some water and aspirin."

I sit up with my back to the bed, laying my forehead on my bent knees. When he returns, I lift my head. "Thanks."

He hands me the glass and pills. "Try to drink all the water."

I can't do anything but obey. My head throbs in unison with my heartbeat. My mouth tastes like I've eaten something served in hell.

Leo takes the trash bin away and leaves the room, returning with a package of saltines. "Here. A couple of these on your stomach will help."

"I need to die. Now." I place a bite of cracker on my tongue and suck the salt before swallowing.

"Nah. You're going to make it." He sits beside me on the floor. "It's my fault. I should've said no to the game. You can blame me."

"You had more to drink than I did," I say in an accusing tone.

He nods. "I never get sick. Josie doesn't really either."

"Oh."

"Dane slept on my sofa, and he's going to be as sick as you are."

"I'm never drinking again."

Leo grins as he stares at the wall. "You were pretty funny."

"Did I do or say anything horrible?"

He looks up at the ceiling and then over at me. "You said you thought I was beautiful." Leo's mouth splits into a huge grin. "You can't take it back. Liquor loosened your tongue last night, for sure."

I cover my face with both hands. "Oh."

"Yes. You did. But it was nice. And we kissed. Do you remember that?"

I'd shoved this memory to the back of my brain, and it rushes forward. That kiss. Angels must've laid down their harps and sighed.

Mortifying heat singes my cheeks. I'd asked for it. I think I may've begged for it. "Well, I am going to crawl back under the covers and hide for the rest of the day."

"Good idea." Leo stands and offers his hands to me. "Come on. Back to bed. I'll drive Josie home and check on you later."

"Leo?"

"Hmm?"

"Thanks." I get into bed, still wearing my clothes from yesterday.

"Anytime. You were fun last night. Sorry you're paying for it today." He walks to my doorway and lingers, bracing both hands on each side of the threshold.

"Tell Josie bye."

He smiles. "Will do. If you feel better later, I'll take you out for something more than saltines. Don't fix lunch."

My heart skips rope, performing double-unders that keep my lungs from functioning. How long can a person live without oxygen? Must. Breathe. "I could eat here. You don't have to take care of me."

"Yeah, well, it's for my own good. Dane will be on my sofa, and it'll be great to leave him be for a while. So, rest up and I'll be back later."

Leo takes a few steps out of the room and then returns.

"You forget something?" I ask.

"Just wanted you to know I think you're beautiful, too."

I inhale. There are my lungs again. I didn't know I'd been holding my breath, but I obviously could forget to take in air again if he doesn't leave soon.

Before I can think of a witty reply, something casual and sitcom funny, he turns and leaves my apartment.

I asked Leo to kiss me. I do remember most of it—the pressure of his mouth on mine and the absolute feeling of rightness. It's as if his kiss fit perfectly into the hole in my heart, filling it up like putty to stopgap the blood pouring out.

How can I remember that kiss so well and be so fuzzy on the other parts of the night?

I snuggle my head into my pillow, thinking of Leo's kiss. The apartment is quiet except for the noises from the downstairs bakery. It's a Saturday and customers will come in throughout the day. I can never hear their conversations, but the door opens and closes. The metal pans clink against the oven racks.

I don't fall into sleep as I'd hoped, but I lie still and quell the nausea for a while. When it's safe to move, I crawl out of bed and into the shower.

Hours later, I'm sitting on the edge of my bed painting my nails when there's a soft knock at the door. I'm on my feet and running past the half wall that separates my bedroom from the living area. Then I stand with my hands flat on the door, check the peephole, and try to get my heart rate under control for the next ten seconds.

What am I doing? He didn't ask me to go on a date. Or did he? No. Lunch is not a date.

Besides, he's still Leo the neighbor-writer-postcard-hoarder. I pull the door open. "Hi."

Leo, who was attractive when I first saw him, gets more irresistible every day.

"Hey," he drawls and leans with his right hand high on my threshold. The movement puts him far too close to me.

I tense as I imagine throwing myself into his arms. He'd catch me with those very capable hands. And then I'd profess undying love after one kiss last night.

The thought triggers something at the edge of my memory, like an important box placed on a high shelf.

Last night, did I tell him about my postcard? No. I don't think so.

He's never admitted he writes Mr. Expose, as if it's some huge secret.

I shuffle uncomfortably. "Thanks for everything from, you know, earlier. Is Josie OK?"

"Yeah. She'll be fine. I told you. She doesn't get sick." He chuckles and walks past me into my apartment and sits on the arm of the sofa. It's my newest addition to the apartment, delivered just yesterday. It's comforting to see Leo making himself at home in my space.

I could get used to sharing everything with him.

"Ready for a bite to eat?" He unfolds his arms and stands.

Lunch and Leo, a combination too tempting to resist. "I could do that. But we have to go Dutch. I'll pay for mine."

Leo gets up and walks to the door. He gives me a slow grin, his wide mouth revealing even, white teeth. The gleam in his eyes shoots a thrill straight through my heart. "We can wrestle for the ticket."

Canary in the Coalmine

Leo

DRINKING ALWAYS MAKES ME RAVENOUS the next day. It's the way my metabolism works. Harper, on the other hand, still appears a little green around the edges and avoids looking at my plate.

She nibbles on a poached egg and toasted bagel. We're at Pistol's on Music Row since Harper says she hasn't been to many places besides Dastardly's. I'm having a steak scramble and relishing every bite, my appetite on full blast since waking up this morning.

Harper's not meeting my gaze, for some odd reason.

"Is your egg good? You're not eating much."

She presses her lips together and shakes her head quickly.

"Too soon after?" I motion with my fork at the food on her plate.

"Not if you have a stomach of steel—which you obviously do." One corner of her mouth tips up. "You had as much to drink as I did. I think."

I fork a bite of flank steak into my mouth and grin while I chew. "Um hm."

She rubs a hand over her eyes. "I never drink. Did I tell you my daddy is a Baptist preacher? I grew up thinking alcohol will send you straight to hell."

My mouth twitches a little in amusement. "A lot of folks will be toasting marshmallows there if that's true."

She gives a half-hearted laugh. "Bonfire party."

"Be careful if you're not used to drinking. I don't want anything bad to happen to you. Last year, Dane had his wait staff watching out for some guy who was going around dropping roofies in girls' drinks. I wouldn't want some guy to take advantage of you while you're wasted." I cringe at the thought of anything happening to her.

"I would never do anything stupid," she says.

"No." I grin and tear off a piece of toast. "But you were very friendly when you were drinking last night, and there are some really bad people in the world."

"Yeah. Don't I know it." She makes a face and grabs her water glass to concentrate on taking a sip.

Her expression is fierce. Has someone done something bad to her?

Harper places her glass on the table. "I knew I was safe with you. You wouldn't take advantage of me." She picks her water back up and takes a drink.

"Oh, but I wanted to."

Harper chokes. It takes her a few seconds to compose herself. Her gaze flicks up to meet mine. "It's not nice to tease. Are you trying to kill me? I almost died there."

She's playing it off like it's all a big joke, but my comment really got to her. I don't want her to be nervous, but she might be if she knew I had an ice-cold shower after leaving her apartment. "I had fun last night." I have an urge to reach across and haul her up to kiss me across the table.

"Me, too. Josie and Dane are crazy."

"Yeah. They are."

"I didn't know they were dating," she says.

Harper glances up at a couple of guys who sit at the table beside ours. One, a guy in a red plaid shirt, is giving her too much attention for my liking. I stare at him until he sees me and looks away.

I take a bite from the orange slice on my plate and shake my head. "They're not."

"But they really like each other."

"Yup," I agree.

"Are you positive?"

"Oh, yeah. But they are both hard-headed

and have this thing about remaining friends."

Harper pushes her plate to the side and rests her chin on her hand. "Oh," she says, understanding dawning in her eyes. "They think it will ruin their friendship."

"Um hm." I fork another bite of steak into my mouth. "We've known each other since we were kids."

"That's nice. So, is Dane your best friend?"

I shrug. "He's like a brother to me. Sometimes an irritating brother, but that's how it goes. I'm lucky that I stay in touch with a few of the guys I grew up with."

"I wish I had that. Wesley never liked anyone I made friends with."

I frown at her. Her husband must've been a jerk. "You'll make friends here. It takes time when you move somewhere new."

"I guess." She gives me a sad smile and looks away.

"Well, my sister thinks you're awesome. Dane, too. Tell me more about your life in Washington."

She fidgets uncomfortably. "So you, Dane, and Josie grew up here?"

Her change of subject is too quick. I want to know more about Washington, her dead husband, her life. But it's also good that she wants to know about me. "Yes. I moved away for college and then came right back here."

Something—a sound or a voice—catches my attention and my glance wanders to the restaurant door. Tori, my ex-girlfriend, stands beside a dark-haired girl I don't recognize. They both scope the tables, looking for an empty spot or to see if someone is almost finished with their food. She spots me before I have a chance to look away.

Our eyes lock. My heart rate quickens at the promise of a scene, because Tori is all about making every encounter a battle. Sweat breaks on my forehead and my appetite bails.

I command myself to break the laser tractor beam of Tori's stare.

I was stupid to bring Harper to Pistol's. I take a slow, deep breath and return my attention to Harper. "Did you say something?"

She gives me a wide-eyed look. "No. Are you OK?"

"Oh yeah. Fine. You finished?"

"Um hm..." She places the napkin from her lap on the table. "Ready when you are. Thanks. And remember, we're splitting the ticket."

The waitress stops by our table at this moment to drop the ticket on it. Harper makes a grab for the white slip of paper, but I scoop it up first. "On me."

Tori and her friend are walking toward us. Hell, no. She is not going to ruin what has been a great weekend for me.

I hold out my hand to Harper and she hesitates. If she doesn't take it, she leaves me standing here like a moron with Tori bearing down on me like a missile. The minute Harper places her small hand in mine, I want to fling her into my arms and kiss her.

My fingers fold around hers and I pull her to her feet.

Pistol's restaurant is laid back and I head to the register in the lobby, where patrons can also buy souvenir items like shot glasses and t-shirts. I'm hoping to escape a conversation with Tori. My day is obviously on a quick downhill slide when Tori weaves her way through the tables to ensure our paths will cross.

"Hi Leo." Tori's body moves forward and for a second, I'm afraid she's actually going to hug me. I've still got Harper's hand linked to mine, but Tori's never been very observant.

At the last second, her eyes flick to Harper and then down at our hands. Thank God.

"Hello Tori." I grit my teeth rather than say more. I want to ask her why the hell she would come here. She hates this place and knows it's my favorite.

Tori and her friend block our way past and I'm wondering if she's going to force a conversation.

Finally, she sighs. "I can see you're leaving. I'll call you later and we'll catch up. We have lots

131

to talk about." Tori steps to the side and looks at her friend. "We can grab Leo and his *friend's* table, since they're leaving."

Her emphasis on the word 'friend' is threatening and leaves me dreading our next conversation. I squeeze Harper's hand, whether to reassure me or her, I don't know.

Like a natural disaster, Tori moves away, leaving chaos in her wake. I didn't think she still had the ability to affect me. Being pissed means I still care, and I fight the anger that bubbles up inside me.

Harper and I walk to the storefront where I pay for our meal. Even though Tori is an entire room length away, I feel her presence inside my head. She's done exactly what she wanted. Put herself back into my thoughts.

I open the door and Harper walks out onto the sidewalk. "What happened to you back there?"

I glance over at her. "What do you mean?"

"Did you grab my hand because of that woman? Who is she?"

Who is she. Who is she? Answering that question could be a thesis paper. I walk ahead enough to give me some space for a few seconds. Time to get my head in the right place, with Harper. Then I stop walking since I'm being an asshole.

"I'm sorry," I say and put both hands behind

my head, still not able to meet her eyes. "It's a long story."

"So tell me."

"Harper," I say and take her hand in mine. It's warm and right. "I grabbed your hand because I wanted to hold it. But I can't talk about Tori here. Not now. Give me a little time, OK?"

If she were Tori, she'd argue. She'd pout. She'd insist.

"OK. Tell me later, then." Harper gives my hand a squeeze and meets my stride. My legs are much longer than hers, so I slow to keep our pace reasonable. There are no words between us as we return to the parking lot and get into my car.

By the time I pull into the lot behind our apartment building, Harper's asleep. I gently wake her and again insist on holding her hand while we walk inside. I pull her into my apartment and she doesn't resist.

I want to see her sitting among my things, immersing herself in my life like she has been for the past couple of weeks, so subtly that I didn't even realize she'd become part of it. The development wasn't anything forced or artificial and that's what I like so much about her.

"Here," I say, and lead her to one end of my sofa. I grab a blanket and drape it over her. Her eyes shine with something as she watches me arranging the folds of the soft material around her shoulders. My apartment is chilly and I only want her to be comfortable. But I also like touching the skin of her neck and jaw line.

I reach across and trace her lips with two fingers. Her breath hitches and her eyes flutter closed.

"What are you doing to me?" she asks.

"Nothing you don't want. What do you want?"

She doesn't speak. Instead, she pulls me to sit beside her. "I want to know about the girl at Pistol's."

"She's my past."

"Not really. It seems like she's your present. She said she was going to call you." Harper leans her head back and looks at the ceiling.

I sprawl my legs out and sling my arm along the back of the sofa. "I'd rather talk about us." Our proximity is a cozy, more-than-friends position. I twist a piece of her ponytail between my fingers, wishing I could take the holder out and let her hair fall loose around her shoulders.

"You might say that girl is none of my business. But I don't know anything about you."

"Her name is Tori." I rub my hand over the back of my neck. "We dated for a year. We broke up ten months ago. That's the story."

"Short story." Harper gives me a lazy smile.

"Come on. There's more than that."

"Tori and I had a bad break-up. Do you like that synopsis better?"

"She was happy to see you today." Harper eyes me knowingly. She swats my hand so I'll quit twirling her hair. "You're distracting me. Tori wants to get back together."

I imagine the cold, steel vault around my heart. Tori will never have the combination to unlock it ever again. "That isn't going to happen."

"Have you told her that?"

"Like a broken record." I smile at Harper, but she continues to frown as if I'm doing something wrong. "Tori has problems."

"We all have problems."

"True. But hers are no longer my concern. I'm only worried about mine and yours. My current problem is I want to kiss you so damn bad that I can't think of another thing. I want to kiss you when you're not drunk and you know it's my lips on yours."

She shakes her head. "I knew exactly who I was kissing last night. I wasn't that far gone."

I raise an eyebrow. "Good. So, let's try it again."

"What?" she asks, her eyes wide and dark. "Now? As in this minute?"

I chuckle and lean in so close our breaths mingle. "This first." I reach around remove the ponytail holder from her hair.

She pulls in air. "Oh."

There's a smell of something like raspberries and vanilla that makes me want to bury my face in her neck, but I restrain myself since she looks like a scared rabbit.

You'd think I'd just ripped off her panties or something. A corner of my mouth lifts involuntarily. "It's only a kiss."

I thread my fingers through her soft hair and grab the back of her neck to pull her forward. There's the smallest amount of resistance from her, and then like a dam breaking, she's meeting my lips.

I've never been this hungry for a kiss, for a way to feel how a woman thinks about me. My tongue pushes into her mouth and sweeps forward to tangle with hers. Her mouth is sweet and hot and intoxicating.

If a heartbeat can match rhythm with another, mine is searching for hers. Searching for a reason to find skin upon skin, heartbeat upon heartbeat. I push her gently back on the sofa and cover her body with mine. Her hands skate up, up, up my back and fist my shirt.

I moan into her mouth. Holy kiss of kisses. I silently pray: Please let me have a box of condoms in the bathroom. Don't let my lack of shopping lists be the downfall of me now.

Her nails rake gently when she loosens her

hold and drags down my back to grip my hips. I press against her, my erection evidence of the way she turns me on with a simple kiss.

She frees her lips from mine with a gasp. "Wait."

I rest my forehead on hers and catch my breath. "OK."

"I don't do this."

"Babe. We aren't doing anything, yet." 'Yet' is the operative word, since my brain has already stepped into the bedroom, her naked body under mine.

"I...um...Can we stop?"

It's enough to make a grown man cry. I lift my head and gaze into her warm, amber eyes. "Of course we can."

She covers her face with both hands. "This is so embarrassing."

"It's fine." I sit up and pull her into a sitting position with me. I keep my arm around her and kiss the top of her head.

"I don't know if I'm ready for this." She's deflecting. Maybe she regrets kissing me. Maybe she's feeling awkward. Maybe I should quit guessing.

"Harper, do you mind if I ask you something personal?"

"No. What is it?"

"Have you dated anyone since...well, since your husband died?"

Harper stares at me for what seems like eternity. Inside that stare, I feel the air go still and a million emotions flicker across her face—sorrow, confusion, distrust—but I'm left knowing one thing with certainty.

This girl has been through something bad. I've been there, or at least in a similar situation. So I know how she needs to talk about what's happened. I'm the last person to want to confide in people, but I did share my feelings with Josie.

I'm not going to avoid this topic. If she and I have a chance of getting to know each other better, I can't let it go. "It's OK to feel weird about this subject. Can we talk about it?"

She nods and laces her fingers together as if she's about to pray. "Yeah."

"How long has it been?"

"November. Last November."

"You doing OK?"

"Sure," she says, "I'm terrific. It takes time. That's all." She's not terrific and I don't expect her to be. But I'm not asking her to tell me everything. Just a little. Thing is, we're at this crossroad where she needs to open up to me.

A left turn and I accept her answer of 'terrific' and drop the topic.

A right turn and she gives me more. The truth.

I ball my fist and rub my knuckles across my mouth, wondering how hard to push. I shouldn't have pushed for the kiss. She seems more vulnerable than I've seen her. But last night was spectacular as far as kisses go. There's no misinterpreting that she wanted it.

I'm selfish and don't want to see a possibility of us fizzle away because she's afraid. "You're bullshitting me. I thought we were friends."

"I don't know what you want me to say."

"The truth. Tell me you hate waking up every day or that you miss him or that you don't understand why people leave us. Anything."

"I said I was fine." Harper looks across the sofa and at my bookshelves.

"Say you don't want to talk about it. Don't lie."

Color rises in her cheeks. "Oh, as if you're such an open book."

"What do you want to know? More about Tori? That topic's not my favorite."

She narrows her eyes. "What are you writing all day?"

Not a question I expected. It sounds like a desperate plea to change the subject away from our kiss, her husband, my ex-girlfriend. "You know the answer." My answer comes out in a patient sigh.

"I don't know anything. Be specific."

"Thriller. Political thriller. The story takes place following a presidential candidate who discovers a plot to take over the American government."

"And that's all you're writing."

"I write a few freelance things."

"So much for specifics."

"Babe, I'd bore you to tears with the details."

"I need to tell you something," she says, sitting straighter and looking nervous.

"You can tell me anything."

"It's about your writing." She takes a deep breath and pauses. "I..."

"Yeah?"

Harper opens her mouth to continue, only to be interrupted by an insistent knocking on my door.

"Hold that thought," I say. "It's probably Josie."

I get to my feet and glance at the clock. It's half-past one. Josie must be taking a late lunch. She has a knack for interrupting me when least convenient, so this figures.

The instant I open the door, the artillery of everything that is Tori rains down on me. She stands there with her tear-stained face and her expression that screams *victim*.

All so calculated and cunning.

She steps into the apartment without invitation and glances from Harper to me. "We need to talk. I wouldn't have come, but it's a matter of life and death."

Resting Bitch Face

Harper

THE POP CULTURE PHRASE "resting bitch face" hasn't meant much to me until today. Leo's ex-girlfriend has the expression down pat. As soon as she realizes he's not alone, her face takes on this mannequin quality, molded from rigid material and meant for display purposes only.

"I was just leaving," I say and rise from the sofa. I stoop to pick up the blanket that falls from my lap and fold it into a square. My hair is mussed and my lips swollen. I know what it must look like to the outsider.

A small and shallow part of me is glad of it. He's been kissing me, me, me!

"You can stay." Leo all but blocks me from moving to the door.

But Tori doesn't change her expression. She glances at Leo. "Do you want to discuss our relationship in front of *her*?"

She says the pronoun 'her' with a curl to her lip. It's the only change of expression she gives. For someone who has clearly been crying, she doesn't show much emotion.

"Want me to stay?" I ask, placing a hand on Leo's arm. His features give away everything. He doesn't want me to leave. Is he stressed over being alone with her? What has she done to him? I have the urge to pummel her, MMA style, even though I haven't actually been in a fight before. I never really had violent thoughts until everything came crashing down with Wesley.

His lips tighten and he exhales through his nose. "No, it's all right. I'll only be a minute."

"I'm Tori," Leo's ex interrupts.

I turn to acknowledge her. "Harper," I reply.

"He won't be long. I'll be finished with him in a while," she says to me with a queer jab in her voice. Oh yeah. I would really like to wait for her outside and trip her down the stairs. Perhaps I should look into anger management.

"It's not a problem," I say, the lie falling from my lips. I step around her and make for the door.

"Harper," Leo says to my back. I turn with my hand on the doorknob.

"Hmm?"

"I'll see you later," he says.

Not two minutes later, I'm inside my apartment and sitting at the island bar when I hear yelling. It's them. I'm shocked and curious at the way sound travels. I shouldn't be. I'm able to hear the bakery customers, so it makes sense that I can also hear across the hall.

Still, Leo is always so quiet as a neighbor that I never hear a thing from his apartment.

I make out his voice. "Get. Out." His yell is harsh and final. "You can't be honest now. It's too late." Pain weaves through the fabric of each word.

Her voice is quieter and I can't hear her words even though I've wandered to stand beside my door. I imagine them though.

There's a shriek and something hits a hard surface and shatters. Even though I cannot see through walls, I know she's thrown something. Her mannequin mask has slipped.

Leo is always sweet to me, yet there's some disagreement between them that has splintered their relationship. What drove them apart?

Maybe it's the way he keeps his secrets guarded so close to the chest.

His words to Tori echo in my head. *You can't be honest now. It's too late.*

I was five seconds away from confessing everything to Leo—about sending the postcard and following him. Lying to him this entire time.

What have I done? A disturbing darkness colors my emotions as I imagine how he'll react if I tell him about the postcard. I won't have to say anymore. He'll connect the dots and know the rest.

Maybe, he'll hate me so much he won't

speak to me again. And he'll tell Josie. Josie won't forgive me either. Why should she? I lay my head on the cool tile of the bar and attempt to stay calm.

What was I thinking? Do I simply throw away the best things in my life? For the first time, I'm with a guy who makes me happy. A guy who cares about what I think. Who wants to spend time with me. And Josie's a bonus. I need her.

True affection from real, honest people. Wesley took all that away from me.

I deserve a little happiness, don't I?

I go to my refrigerator and search for a cool drink. My body temperature has risen to boiling in the past minutes, listening to their voices, and then imagining how that fight could've been me and Leo.

You broke into my apartment? You went through my things?

Maybe if he gets to know me a little better, if we allow this attraction to evolve, he'll understand when I tell him everything. I'm such a coward, and I've lost so much this year. My entire identity dissolved with the disclosure of one police report when Wesley died. I can't risk it. I take a gulp of cool water.

The yelling next door stops abruptly and there's a final door slam.

My lungs burn with an effort to stay calm. I

take another gulp of water and wait in silence. I wait for hours with the expectation that he'll knock at my door and tell me what happened. That he'll pour his heart out to me and share whatever has turned him inside out.

I want him to be okay.

It's late afternoon before I give up on Leo. The afternoon sun is filtering in my windows, and I'm silly stupid for still waiting on him. We are not even a couple.

I decide that I can't sit in my apartment any longer. It's time for me to break free of the chains I've put upon myself and act like a grownup. A sane grownup.

The hallway is hot since the air-conditioning doesn't cool this space. I fan myself and knock softly on Leo's door. "It's Harper." The last thing I want is for Leo to suspect Tori is back for more.

He doesn't answer and I press my ear to the door. Then I quickly pull back in case he's looking at me through the peephole discovering that I am a psycho after all. A strand of my loose hair catches on something from the door and I struggle to loosen it.

So much appearing sane.

After he doesn't answer his door, I return to my apartment. One glance out my window tells me his vehicle is in the lot and he's at home.

I grab my purse and keys. I'll go and talk to Josie. I have to get out.

There's a doorway leading to metal stairs on the outside of the building. It tends to stick, so I'm surprised when I shove and hit something solid.

"Hey. Careful." Leo's husky voice reaches me as I get halfway through the door.

I'm so surprised to find him out on the landing that I don't know what to say at first. It seems silly to say I've been wondering where he is. He owes me no explanation. We've edged into that no-man's land between friendship and more. Still, I hurt because he hurts. Even more, I want to make her pay for whatever she's done to him.

Leo sits on the landing, before the first metal step that leads down to the parking lot. He's leaned back against the brick of the building with one knee cocked up. "Going somewhere?"

"Oh," I answer and look down at my purse. "I thought I'd get out for a while."

He narrows his eyes at me and takes a swig from his beer. "I wish you wouldn't. Can I convince you to stay?"

I give him a small smile. "Of course."

"Good," he says. He holds up the beer. "Can I get you a drink?"

I groan. "Really? I think I've had enough for one weekend."

He pats the space beside him. "You have a few minutes?"

"Sure," I say as nonchalantly as possible. I want to yell that I've been waiting inside for hours on the chance that he'll let me in on what happened earlier. The space on the landing is small and I have no choice but to sit near him. It's all I can do not to lean in and allow our bodies to touch, but I'm too unsure of where he's coming from in his current mood.

Leo switches his beer to his other hand and takes my hand in his. "Sorry about today."

His warm hand reassures me that we have a real bond. We're linked.

"There's nothing to be sorry about." I act as though it's not a big deal that I realized today how much I've relied on his company and voice and *him*. My throat tightens.

"I let her barge in and that was wrong. She has no place in my life whatsoever. It doesn't matter what she had to say, I shouldn't have let her—""

"She said it was a matter of life or death!" Of course, I've been wondering all day long if this was an exaggeration on her part, but it seemed petty to doubt.

He cocks an eyebrow. "Everything about Tori is urgent in her mind. No, it wasn't life or death. You and I need to talk. I have things to tell you."

"That's what we're doing." I glance away from the intensity in his eyes.

147

"You should've stayed earlier. She was the intruder. You belonged."

"I didn't want to get in the way," I say, my throat cinching like tiny strings being pulled. An inexplicable surge of gratitude overcomes me that for once, I'm not the outsider. I turn my face away toward the building opposite our parking lot and pretend to study it.

He touches my shoulder. "Have I told you all the things about you that I like so very much?"

I shake my head and turn back to meet his eyes. This is my mistake. He's so open with everything. The strings wrapped around my throat pull tighter and I have to look away quickly so he won't see my eyes water. So he won't sense how much he means to me. Does he even know what his words do to me? His affection has trickled in like water touching the edge of paper, saturating my life. It feels as though I've known him only a few days and an eternity at the same time.

"Hey, no tears," he says, leaning his forehead against mine. He threads fingers through hair that he pushes back from my cheeks.

I enjoy the feel of his hands framing my face as he forces me to continue eye contact.

"It's all right." Leo smiles. "It's OK to feel things, you know."

"I know." I give a self-derisive laugh. The

sound is hollow and unnatural—like a ball bouncing against the walls of an empty room.

Maybe the room is my heart, waiting to be filled with something and Leo is the ball bouncing into me, bringing me joy I haven't known in a long, long time.

He pulls back and caresses the base of my neck with one hand. "We were interrupted earlier." He licks his lips.

My heart is pounding like a kettledrum. I study my freckled knees so I can stay calm. I'm not good with conversations like this.

Leo's fingers grasp my chin and turn my head to look at him. "You feel the same way about me, don't you?"

The kettle drumbeat quickens in my chest. I nod since my mouth is so dry I couldn't speak if I wanted to.

"Tori and I are over. I promise you that. But it took a while to get past everything. And I guess that's okay because what we had mattered. People shouldn't get over something quickly if it does, right? You know what though? I knew beyond a shadow of a doubt today that Tori and I are over. Sometimes you say the words to convince yourself. That if you say them enough you'll feel them. Months ago, that would've been the case. But today...I said them because they are the truth."

"I need to tell you about Wesley."

"Your husband mattered to you. I get that it takes time. But you need to know that I'm a very patient guy when it comes to the things I want."

"You don't understand. There are things I have to tell you." My voice is small and unsure. Where do I begin? What do I say? How much do I tell before he wonders if I'm a freak? What kind of idiot doesn't realize her own husband had another wife? An entire family hidden away in a different city.

Crapola. I detest liars since my life with Wesley was one huge lie. I have to tell him about the postcard and breaking into his apartment to find it. I have to ask that he give that postcard to me. I have to stop him from printing the blog post.

He moves in and kisses me hard on the mouth. It's sudden and purposeful. His lips devour me whole as they demand a response I'm only too willing to give. When he pulls back from the kiss, he grins at me like a kid who's found money on the street.

"I love the way you say 'Crapola,' instead of real cursing." He touches the end of my nose with his index finger.

"Huh?"

"You're so funny. The way you don't actually curse is one of the cutest things about you."

I must've said the word aloud. "There are bad things about me." Should I tell him? Say,

I'm sorry I've deceived you, but I only did so in the beginning.

"I find that very hard to believe." He leans toward me and kisses the corner of my mouth. "I'm crazy about the way you lick your lips when you're nervous. It just makes me want to kiss them."

Leo leans in and I wait for him to kiss me again. Instead, he swoops over to my left ear and places his lips against it. The tip of his tongue flicks my ear lobe and he laughs, the sound all husky and male. "I like the way you look at me when you think I'm not watching. I hope you're imagining all the naughty things you want to do with me."

I gulp and heat rushes, a divining rod straight to the core of me. My body trembles in response.

He's right. I have fantasized about him. Last night, I begged for a kiss. In my dreams, I've kissed him over and over again.

I rest my cheek against his and relish the feel of his afternoon scruff on my skin. "Want to go inside? Watch a movie or something?"

"Something," he mutters. He rises and holds out a hand. I take it, my limbs unsteady. My heart pounding so hard I'm sure he can hear it.

The hallway between the outer door and Leo's apartment extends on thirty feet or so in reality. Still, it seems an eternity until he leads

151

me inside his apartment and pushes me against the door.

I gasp as his mouth drags kisses along my jaw and neck. "You have no idea how good that feels."

He hesitates and smiles against my neck. "I think I do." His words are warm as summer sunshine.

My hands glide over his shoulders and along his biceps. "I love your arms."

"Really..." he says and laughs into my throat. "That's too bad. I love your mouth."

He kisses me softly. "And your neck." He nibbles down to my collarbone. "And this spot." He moves my shirt aside and places his lips in the hollow of my throat.

"Ah. Yeah." I close my eyes. "I think I like those spots on you, too."

Leo steps back and takes my hand. He guides me through his living area and to his bedroom. He sits on the edge of the bed. I don't protest, but my eyes widen. I've only ever been with Wesley and have no real experience as a lover. Wesley was a lights out, missionary style, five-minute man. It was a disappointment I previously blamed on myself and my tortured self-esteem.

But I knew there could be more from the movies I'd seen on the pay cable channels. I probably learned more from HBO than I ever did in sex ed class. There appeared to be a lot more passion going on than I'd experienced.

And honestly, I want Leo to know how much I feel for him. No room for half-truths or lies in this physical space between us.

He scoots back on the pillows and opens one arm to indicate that I'm to join him. "We can lie in here and watch television. Or we can nap or we can talk about all the other places I want to kiss you. It's your choice."

There's beauty in the way Leo's eyes go hooded when I crawl my way toward him and pause near his hips.

I rise to my knees. "There are places I want to kiss."

His eyes close briefly and his nostrils flare as if he's trying to maintain self-control. He opens his eyes. "Show me."

"Take off your shirt." I lick my lips.

There's the beautiful look again. The one where his eyes tell me he could devour me. He sits up and tugs his T-shirt over his head and hands it to me. I take it, wishing I could commandeer the shirt for my own to sleep in. It's such a juvenile thought, but I still may do it. I carefully place the shirt on the end of the bed.

"Now what?" he asks. His voice is deep and low.

Good question. I allow myself to soak up the

visual. Shirtless Leo, leaning up on his elbows, eager for me to do whatever I please. I move my left leg over the top of him and straddle his hips. I'm still on my knees, but I slowly lower myself to sit squarely on him. The ridge of his hard erection pushes against me. It takes all my willpower not to rub myself against him.

He drops back on the pillows, but never takes his eyes from mine.

"I'd like to kiss here." I bend my head to kiss his shoulder. The muscles tense beneath my lips. "And here," I say, moving to tease my lips across one pec.

I sit up and grin at him. "I love your muscles."

He tilts his hips up, pressing his hard-on into me. "You should take your shirt off."

I sigh playfully. "If you insist."

"I insist."

I pull my shirt off and toss it on the floor. His hips move against the apex of my thighs in almost an involuntary movement. Leo makes a low, guttural sound deep in his throat. One small mix of low notes and tones representing surprise, pleasure, and desire.

I'll do anything to hear it again.

Playing By Heart

Leo

"BABE. YOU ARE EVERYTHING RIGHT in the world."
It's all I can come up with and it's downright
embarrassing. I'm not sure I can call myself a
writer after that cheeseball line. I want to say
something beautiful and timeless. Something
worthy of being printed on a page.

I revel in the perfect lines of her body. My
greedy hands want to take and take, but I keep
them still.

Harper leans down and kisses the center of
my chest. The feel of her mouth on my skin
ignites an urgency in me. She sits back and dips
her head, looking down at herself. Her hair falls
forward and hides her face.

What is she thinking about?

My mouth goes dry when she unfastens her
bra with one flick of the wrist. The lacy cups fall
away and she shrugs out of it.

"I'm trying to be bold," she whispers.

There's something about the way she then
lifts her chin, high and challenging, as if daring

me to stop her. She gives a shaky laugh. And then she looks away and I can tell she's nervous.

"You don't have to be anything but yourself with me. We don't have to do this. You can put your shirt back on. Baby, do whatever feels comfortable. We can go into the living room and watch television. This doesn't have to go further." I sit up slowly and put my hands on the sides of her face. I'm pushing her. She's not some one-night stand I've brought home for a hook-up. I am a moron in the first degree.

Her eyebrows draw together and her eyes search mine.

"What? Tell me what's wrong." I rest my forehead against hers and breathe her in. The essence of her skin must be filled with brown sugar and oranges because she smells like Christmas to me. A beautiful package of what my heart desires.

"Don't you want me?"

Her words are brutal because they tell me too much about her. She's vulnerable and fragile.

"You don't know, do you"?" I take a deep breath. Not only am I ready for us to open up physically, I want to bare my soul to her. "I have wanted you from the minute I first laid eyes on you."

"Yeah?"

I stroke the side of her cheek with one hand. "Yeah. And then it kept getting worse. You'd come over in those tiny shorts and borrow a cup of sugar—""

She laughs. "I never borrowed any sugar."

I kiss the side of her neck, dragging the tip of my tongue along her skin and leaving goose bumps in my wake. "Ok. Books, then. Same thing. But the shorts. Killing. Me." I nibble on her earlobe and press my cock into the soft spot between her legs. "Every. Single. Day. So if you think I don't want you, you'd better think again. Do you want me?"

"I want you." She states it as simply as someone walking up and saying they want an ice cream.

I move her from my lap, get to my knees, and slowly unzip her shorts. She reaches up and unzips my jeans. I lean in and kiss the corner of her mouth, starting out slow. Her hands grip the back of my neck and the simple touch sends one hundred degrees of heat straight to my cock. I try to slow down, but it's too late. Try to pull back, but my mouth has an agenda and shifts to her breasts.

She's perfection to me. Her slender frame thrums with electricity, muscles tense with each pass of my lips. I suck and bite and tease along her perky breasts down to the dip of her navel. My tongue flicks into the valley of her belly and she squirms.

I glance up through my lashes at her. I peel the shorts slowly down her hips and her panties with them. She helps me by sitting back so I can take them. The thin material of her panties is soaked and a thrill runs through me, zinging every cell as I discard them on the floor. I grin at the way she's watching me, her cheeks so flushed and her nipples tight little peaks begging for my mouth.

I'm at the edge of the bed, so I stand and push my briefs and jeans to the floor. My body is so ready for hers. I swear I could come hands-free purely from the lusty look she's giving me.

I take a couple of steps to my nightstand and retrieve a condom to place near us. She surprises me by grabbing my hand and pulling me onto the bed. If my body had its way, I'd push inside her in one stroke and then another and another until I found my release. My urgency for her would take over. Instead, I want her to set the pace.

It's a tangle of sheets as I roll her on top of me. "Ride me," I whisper, my voice scraping every vowel and consonant.

She has this expression of shock—only for an instant—and then it's replaced with excitement. "Tell me if I'm doing it right."

"You can't do anything wrong." I grab the condom and roll it on while she watches. My heart slams hard against my chest.

Harper moves her body over my hips and places her entrance over the head of my cock. My pulse—all the blood in my body—is focused on one thing. Filling her. Making her understand how much my body yearns to be inside hers.

I grab her hips and lift myself to slide inside. I shake with the effort to go slowly. Each centimeter inside her incites me to push harder, go faster. She's so fucking tight.

"It's been a while," she says, squeezing her eyes tight.

I pull out and thrust in, one long stroke, unable to stop. "Does it feel good, baby?"

"Ahh..." She hangs her head and squeezes her eyelids shut. "Yes."

"Move however it feels good. Up and down. Fast. Slow." My last words sound guttural, restraint forcing me to resort to one-word, monosyllabic speech.

Harper sets a rhythm, her body sliding faster and faster until I'm gritting my teeth in an ecstatic pain. I forget about her fragility.

I dig my fingers into her hips, urging her to continue. We're a streamlined instrument that demonstrates how two bodies become one.

In the quiet of my apartment, there's only the labored sound of our breathing and the glorious music of skin hitting skin, rising to an ultimate crescendo. Although her eyes are closed and her eyebrows drawn, I can't stop watching her. I reach down where our bodies meet and rub my thumb against her. Her lips smash together as if the pleasure is too much to bear. The moment I sense her orgasm coming, a tensing and pulsing of her body around my cock, I wish I could slow it down so I could memorize her face.

She groans, the sounds hitching as each wave of pleasure rolls through her.

My own release chases hers. My fingers dig into her hips as I quit fighting it and thrust long and hard. Giving everything of my body in the final seconds of claiming her.

Mine.

I thrust a second time, although we're both spent and it's a half-hearted stroke to tell her I'd do it again if I had any strength left. She languorously bends to place her head on my shoulder and licks away the salt of my sweat.

"I've never..." she whispers and her lips tickle my collarbone.

"Never what," I prompt. My eyes are closed, but I open them to peek down at the top of her head.

She's breathing as hard as I am. "That. I've never. It's the first. Orgasm."

Harper lifts her hips and pulls away. It's as if I've lost a part of me, a sanctuary I've never visited before.

She relaxes her body and rolls to lie beside me on her belly.

I'd be a liar if I said I didn't like hearing it. I want to be better than her former husband. But then, I don't want to compete with a dead man. There's no honor in being jealous of a man six feet under.

"Hey," I say into her mass of hair. It's strewn across my chest and sticking to the warm skin of her back. I lift it and blow across her neck.

"Hmm?" She places her hand on my chest and one finger traces over my nipple.

"Don't go anywhere." I get out of bed, and walk to the bathroom so I can dispose of the condom. My apartment is small and it's not a stone's throw from one end to the other.

I make a quick trip into the kitchen and grab a couple of bottled waters. When I walk back in, she hasn't moved. "You need to stay hydrated after last night."

She lifts her head. "Thanks."

I make a nest of pillows against the headboard and drag her to sit with me. Twisting the cap off, I offer a drink of mine. She lifts the bottle to her lips and it's sinful that I get half-hard just watching her throat work as she drinks. "You've ruined me for other women," I say. "I guess that was your plan."

She chokes on her water. I pat her gently on

the back.

"Stop doing that." Harper laughs at my expression of mock confusion. She pokes me in the ribs. "Stop waiting until I take a drink to say something funny."

"You think I'm kidding?" I take the bottle from her and guzzle it.

"Yeah. I do."

I place the water on the nightstand and pull her to lie back in my arms. "No joke. I'll never find another like you. You don't take yourself seriously. You like to read as much as I do. You're absolutely gorgeous. And most of all, you're real. Real and honest."

"Mmm..." she says.

"And I forgot about your ass. Oh my God, your ass."

She giggles and I smile into her hair.

I like the sound too much, so I continue. "Your ass is the stuff men dream of."

"So poetic," she says.

"Yeah. Did I tell you I'm a writer?"

She gives an unladylike snort. "I think so." She looks at the ceiling and then tilts her head back to make eye contact with me. Her expression is suddenly as somber as a storm cloud. "Do you want to know about my past?"

"If you want to tell me." Tori kept too much from me, but Harper would never do that. It's not in her nature. "Do you mind if I bring up something from last night?"

"Oh no. What else did I do?" She covers her face with both hands.

I laugh, trying to keep the conversation light. "No. It's something from the game. You asked if anyone had ever been in love."

"Oh." Her hands drop. "Did I?"

"Um hm..." I wait a beat and wait to see if she remembers.

"I'm really fuzzy about that part of the night. I think I do remember it."

"You didn't drink which means 'no'. So. I don't know if that was the drunk part of your brain not keeping up with the game or the honest part of your brain knowing the right answer."

"This is embarrassing. I got married when I was eighteen. I ran off with Wesley without my parents' blessing. Didn't tell my friends. Just left because I thought I knew him."

I stroke her arm. "I doubt you're the first or last teenager to do that."

"I should've known better. I was raised better. And I was grown."

"How'd you meet him?"

"I worked at a grocery store the summer after I graduated. Wesley came in one night and he was in line behind this lady and her two kids. She looked dirt poor and the kids were crying. She's trying to pay and she's short of the amount. Wesley reaches over and plunks a one hundred dollar bill on the counter and says for her to buy her groceries and keep the change."

I nod. "That was a nice thing to do."

Her mouth tightens and she smoothes the comforter over her legs. "He was. He was a nice guy. I remember thinking, 'Wow. He's one of the good ones.'"

All my muscles tense. I stare hard at the wall and take a deep breath. Do I really want to go here? Hear the dead man immortalized?

Something wet drops onto my arm. "Babe. Hey. Oh, please don't cry."

"I'm not," she lies.

I turn her toward me and wipe underneath her eyes with my thumbs. "You're a terrible liar."

"I'm a good liar. Just have a little something in my eye." Her laugh is husky.

Then her resolve crumbles and fat tears stream down her cheeks. "He was nice when I met him. He was all the things a guy is supposed to be."

"People look for what they want to see. It's the way we're made. Always searching for that ideal."

"There was a baby. I was pregnant. That's why I ran off with him. I couldn't face my daddy. I miscarried a week after I married Wesley."

"Shh..." I say, rocking her against my chest.

I search for the right words to make her understand that it's all right, but there are none.

"We moved out to Tacoma. The house was a rental in the middle of nowhere, and I didn't have a car. He left for weeks at a time to work. He'd return and bring flowers and nice words. I was so confused. I didn't know if I loved him or hated him. I really didn't feel anything for a while. I've never told anyone that." Her words are muffled against my chest.

She's given me the gift of her trust with something she's carried around all alone. I've had the luxury of Josie when times were rough. As much as she can be a pain in the ass, she's my rock. Never judgmental. Always a phone call away. Hell, I even have friends who silently carry my secrets from the past.

Harper's had no one and that knowledge of her isolation twists inside me like a furious cyclone. Her husband is dead and that should be enough to quiet my anger. I need him out of our bed.

"He wasn't who I thought he was," she says. Harper's mouth turns up at the corners in a derisive smile. "I was so blind."

"Shh…" I don't want to talk about him in the place where I make love to her. It needs to wait until another time because this bed is a place for her to feel cherished, not relive bad memories. I turn her face toward me. I kiss the end of her nose and her curves melt into me. Our naked bodies are flush to each other and my desire for her stirs, despite the fact that I need to console and comfort.

I kiss her tenderly. My tongue strokes hers, saying she's beautiful, desirable, mine.

She fits against me, her soft places molding to my hard.

"Do you have anywhere you need to be?" she asks.

I grin and push my erection against her. "Is that an invitation? I know one specific place." I suck her bottom lip into my mouth and gently grab it between my teeth.

When I release her mouth, she sighs. "It's scary how good this feels."

"Yeah. I know." She's right. I should be scared. I should be terrified. I'd told myself that I wouldn't jump into another relationship so soon after Tori.

But when feelings this intense slap you in the face, you don't ignore them.

Nosy Harper

Harper

From: angelgirl@me.com
To: isabellawarren@iconic.net

Dear Isabella,

I start a new job this week. Thanks for offering money, but I'm really OK. I'm glad that Wesley/Warren's money will take care of you and Charley.

Your friend,
Harper

***

LEO STANDS IN MY DOORWAY with a smile so bright it could light a small city. "I brought you breakfast. First day on a new job and I can't have you leaving hungry."

"How did you have time?" I step aside so he can enter. He smells like soap and happiness.

"I'm resourceful." He places the tray of food on the bar. "I ran downstairs. I'm a hunter/gatherer like that."

"I left your bed an hour ago. That line had to be out the door at this time of the morning." I glance at the clock. Eight a.m. is rush hour for the guys in the bakery.

"A friend of mine was in line. I begged to cut in."

If a guy like Leo asks you to dance naked in the streets with him, you consider it. I'm convinced he could charm the last stitch of clothing off a homeless woman. She'd probably pay him for the honor.

I didn't mind being naked with him—especially last night in his apartment.

I am afraid of the charm and I don't trust my judgment. Wesley had that same way about him in the beginning. The too-easy ability he possessed to make me feel special.

That charm fell away like a tree shedding its leaves in the fall, until one day, I knew he was different. By that point, it was the full-fledged winter of our relationship.

Wesley never allowed me to work. He made sure I couldn't. The house in Tacoma was too far on the outskirts. I didn't own a car.

I was stuck.

Leo's charm is different. It's the charm of his honesty. It's the intensity that glows from his eyes when he listens to you speak. It's the way he encourages me to do what's right for me.

Deep down in that back-of-the-closet spot of my soul, I know that Wesley and Leo are as different as Satan and Gabriel.

I'm more scared after the weekend with Leo than I've ever been in my life. He's a glittering thing in a world full of rubble. That silver tinsel that attracts a bird foraging for nest materials. He could make a home beautiful.

And this is what I did with Wesley. Saw the possibilities of us before we'd had a chance to really know each other. My stomach clenches.

Leo happily offers me the bagel and I take a bite. "Umm…"

He wipes a corner of my mouth with one finger and sticks it into his own. "Don't make all those sexy sounds. You won't get to work on time."

"I'm a little excited," I say.

"I keep telling you not to say such things to me, you wicked girl." He winks and takes another bite of the bagel and then offers it to me. Although there are more pastries on the tray, I love sharing with him.

I grab the orange juice and peel away the cap. "What are you up to today?"

"Online meeting this morning with an advertiser."

"Sounds fun."

"It's not. It's like listening to Charlie Brown's teacher talk for an hour. Mwa, mwa-mwa. Mwa-mwa." He drags me forward and into his arms. "I can't wait for this day to be over."

"Why do you do it then? This thing that you fund with ads..."

When I say 'this thing', I wait for him to give me that tiny nugget of disclosure.

"Bills. Ambition. Freedom. It's OK until I get my novels published." He shrugs. "But you," he says, changing the subject, "need to go work for the man. I'll be here when you get back." He swats me on the behind and heads out the door.

I know it's unfair to expect total disclosure about everything in his life, but I need his dirty laundry exposed before I can lay out mine. Then I'll know how much I need to tone mine down.

I can make myself sound more misled than plain stupid. Right?

At Le Frou Frous Pooch Hotel, I meet the manager, Tom, who instructs me on my duties. He's a young guy, probably younger than I am. He drags his fingers across his too long bangs as he talks to all the dogs like they're people.

"Want to go for a walk with Ms. Harper?" he says to a sheepdog name Louis. "All right then. Be easy on her. Don't pull on the lead."

All the tasks are more fun than work and I smile all morning as I walk dogs and generally play harder than I have in years.

When he gives me an hour for lunch, I leave and head to Dastardly's, where I'm supposed to meet Josie.

She's seated at the bar, so I join her. The place is packed and Dane is serving tables along with his waitstaff.

"Hi," I say, positioning myself on the wood stool. She's already ordered her food and the pasta smells heavenly. I'm starved after all the energy I've used with the dogs.

"Hey yourself." Josie cocks an eyebrow and grins. She continues to chew a bite of pasta while keeping eye contact.

"What?"

"Oh, don't play coy with me. I've talked to my brother." She bumps her elbow against mine.

"I'm not," I say and take the one-sheet paper menu that Dane flicks in my direction.

"Tell me everything. Well, not *everything*. Some details would be too weird. But you and Leo? I knew this was going to happen."

"Why is that?"

"You're his type. I'm so glad for him to be rid of Tori the witch."

"You liked her that much, huh?"

Josie suddenly frowns. "I'm not sure of how much I should say about their thing. I wouldn't want to share stuff Leo hasn't told you. But I hate that woman."

"I met her."

Josie stabs a bite of her pasta and swings her dark hair to one side. She raises her eyebrows. "Oh? How'd that happen? I was hoping she'd moved, since I haven't run into her in a while."

"We went to breakfast on Saturday morning and bumped into her. Then she came by his apartment later."

She drops her fork. It clangs onto the concrete floor of Dastardly's, but she doesn't bother to retrieve it. "Shit. No way."

I nod. "She...um...seemed upset, but Leo said it wasn't important." Her reaction unsettles me. "Take my fork," I say, unwrapping the rolled napkin that someone placed in front of me at some point.

"Forget about the fork." Josie looks like she's about to explode.

"It's OK. He was a little upset afterward, but I think he's fine now."

"Do not let that woman near him. Do you hear?" Josie's mouth tightens. "You have no idea, no idea at all, what a lying, conniving piece of work she is. She almost broke him. I swear I told her I'd run her over in my car if she dared to step foot near his place." She pushes her plate away.

And I thought I might need anger management. "What did she do?" I can't help but ask.

Josie's lost in her own world and it's not a happy place. She's staring at the bottles of booze lining the wall of the bar as if she'd like target practice on them.

"Josie?"

"Oh. Leo needs to tell you. Not me. I know it's not fair since we're friends, but he's my brother. He would kill me if I went around blabbing his history with her."

"I understand."

"Maybe we can pool our money together and pay a cheap hitman." She cuts her eyes toward me with a calculated look.

"You aren't serious."

"No. If I take out a hit, I won't tell you. It'll be on the down low with no accomplices. You can rest easy."

"Thanks. I'll remember to never make you mad."

Josie looks at the menu I'm holding and points to the waitress behind the bar. The girl moves to stand in front of me.

"You guys need to hire some help," Josie says to her.

"What can I get you?" The girl ignores Josie and asks me.

"Club sandwich and Diet Coke. Thanks." I smile at the girl and turn to Josie.

Josie leans in. "I was sort of kidding about

the hitman. But don't put up with Tori hanging around. She's trouble."

Dane comes up behind me and squeezes my shoulder. "Hey sugar."

"Hi." I look back at him.

"Josie," he says. "You teaching Harper all your bad habits?"

"Every single one." She grins at him.

"Dane! A little help?" The girl tending bar calls to him.

He shakes his head. "Always a crisis. Catch you girls later." Dane hurries away to the kitchen.

The rest of lunch goes by quickly, with Josie telling me stories of her bookstore customers and talking about a band she wants to see in concert. Even though I attempt to concentrate on the conversation, I can't help but worry about her reaction to the subject of Tori.

I can't understand Leo if I don't know what he's been through. The fact that he's not telling me things is so familiar. Wesley never told me anything—what he liked, didn't like, where he went. His past.

***

Leo has a fascinating way of working on his novel. He types frantically for at least five minutes. Then he pauses and sits back for

174

thirty seconds with his hands touching the keys of his laptop. His fingertips move in a caress over the keyboard as he stares straight ahead. Then frantic typing again. It's like his brain cycles in five-minute runs until he deposits all the words into the computer.

He rolls his head from side to side and sits back in the chair, then twirls it around to face me. "Is anything wrong?"

"No. Why?"

"You've been very quiet."

"Watching the movie." I point at the television with a lazy finger and tuck my feet underneath me on the sofa.

He stands and strolls across the room, eyeing me tiger-like and grinning. "I need a break."

"Pretend I'm not here. Would you still be stopping your work?"

"But you are here." He sits beside me on the sofa and takes my hand, kissing each knuckle with his soft lips and a smile.

Using my free hand, I reach across and move the piece of hair that's fallen over his eyes. He catches my wrist and smells it. Literally puts his nose to the skin and inhales. "I have no clue what you are made of, but whatever it is, the smell makes me ravenous."

"Scented lotion," I mutter, hypnotized. Sitting this close, I can't do more than concentrate on the perfect parts of his face and the imperfect parts I love even more. His crooked smile, something I thought he affected, but is all charming him. The wide mouth with lips that draw the eye.

His beautiful blue eyes. Some girls would call them ocean-colored or sapphire. To me, they're heaven-blue.

"Nah. It's pure you. I'm positive," he says.

"What is?" I've lost the thread of our conversation. Concentrate.

My stomach makes a low rumbling protest. Getting home at the end of the day after working with dogs, I needed an immediate shower and then headed straight to Leo's. I'd forgotten about dinner.

He chuckles and releases my wrist. "I'm hungry, too. I think I'll run to the corner and get something for us. What do you want?"

"Lasagna." I look down at my tank and sleep shorts. "Want me to change and come with?"

He shakes his head and gets to his feet. "Nah. You should stay. You've been on your feet all day. I'll be back before you know it."

Our building lies in the middle of every ethnic eatery a person can imagine—Thai, Mexican, Chinese—all served till late in the night. I know he'll only be a half-hour if he orders ahead. Still, I'll miss the separation of that short time. I reconsider running across and changing clothes.

I grab his free hand, the one not already dialing some number on his cell. "Hey."

"What babe?" He holds the phone to his ear and waits for me to tell him.

"I want you to know that I've had the..." I search for a way to finish without sounding like I'm ready to throw on a wedding dress.

"Yes," he releases my hand and holds up a finger to indicate I should wait. "Two orders of lasagna and a large salad. No. Does that come with garlic bread? Ok. Yeah. Thanks."

I'd been close to saying it was the best three days of my life. "Nothing."

He arches one eyebrow. "Methinks the lady tells an untruth."

I lift one shoulder. "I've had a craving for lasagna for days."

He smirks. "We'll take care of this craving. I've had a certain craving all day."

I feel pleasurable warmth creep into my face. "Is everything a sexual innuendo now? Go."

Leo laughs. "I won't be long."

After he leaves, I stretch out on the sofa as if I've belonged in his apartment forever. The television is still on, the tiny fan on his desk still whirs, his laptop monitor still glows.

He's left his life running and waiting with me in it. I'm not an outsider to him, but a part of his day. I hop up, walk to his desk, and let my fingers run along the worn wood. The things that he keeps nearby while he works fascinate me. There's a shiny, very expensive pen on a pad where he's jotted down words that mean nothing to me in their randomness.

And it's not like he's writing my name on the page, but I want to connect the words to me—beauty, lust, love, ache. A random phrase floating above a sun and stars and galaxy drawn at the top of his page. *'One world struck by an asteroid and now its path has been rewritten.'*

He must be brainstorming for his novel and those words help him. I feel guilty looking at the pad now in my accidental snooping, but it's also intriguing to see the way he thinks. Across the desk, there's a couple of envelopes he hasn't opened.

At the edge, there's a funny looking box. It's fabricated to look like a thick hardback book, dark burgundy cover with gold embossed lettering. I reach and pull it to me. It looks like the type of storage box where you'd keep photos.

I can't help myself. The lure of seeing pictures of Leo has me giddy. I lift the lid and it's packed, but not with photos.

Postcards. Every shape and size. The top one has a colorful photo of the Brooklyn Bridge.

I turn it over and read, despite the warning screams in my head telling me I should stop.

The next postcard has a mustache on it. And the next is a photo of a diner. There's at least a couple of hundred in the box. My hands shake as I lift the stack up. I feel the weight of all the people who have written Mr. Expose— Leo. Their pain and fear and fury. Their pleas for help.

My plea and then my request to rescind. And the way he so coldly addressed my emails.

No wonder I didn't find these the time I broke into his apartment. The box camouflages them so well. Leo's written a range of dates on the paper stuck to the inside lid. Each white square has three lines for noting something about the contents. Although this one doesn't list the time period of my postcard, I realize he could've found my postcard. Easily. If he'd wanted to.

I set the cards inside and turn slowly, as if I have a Tyrannosaurus rex breathing at my ear. Because that's what it feels like—a realization so big, it fills the room and I can't do anything but cut my eyes to the thing that's been in front of me the entire time. This is where he hides the Mr. Expose postcards.

My pulse booms in my ears, sounding like the gong of a hammer hitting the inside of an empty barrel.

At the top of Leo's bookshelf that spans one wall, there's a row of book spines identical to the faux one on the box. Anyone looking would assume it's a row of classics—books that he considers precious. They are on a shelf too high for me to reach without using the stepladder.

I've never bothered. All the books I've wanted to read are within my reach.

A knock at the door causes me to jump. I hastily make sure the box is back in place, that I haven't screwed up his organized desk.

I walk to the door with my entire body shaking so badly that I might as well have 'guilty' stamped on my forehead. The right thing to do would be to stay silent and not attempt to answer the door. It's late and I doubt if it's Josie.

My instincts scream a bad feeling as I squint into the peephole. Tori. I should've known better. There's too much between them that I don't know about. Besides, she's everything I'm not—confident, beautiful, and sexy. With my heart in my throat, I examine her. She's wearing a tight, white, silky tank and an extremely short mini-skirt. A sit-the-wrong-way-and-flash-your-panties skirt.

My hand is on the knob. Why is she here? I heard him tell her that she's not to come back. My fingers curl into my palms. Open it or ignore her?

I open the door because I want her to see me and to understand once and for all that she needs to back off. Leo wants me in his life.

She eyes me and looks over my shoulder. When her gaze returns to mine, it's dismissive, as though I don't matter. "I'm here to see Leo."

"He's not home." I cross my arms over my chest.

"Oh." She cocks her head to one side and her judgmental gaze travels from my face down the length of my body. My pajamas aren't meant to be sexy. It's a comfortable, cotton set that I've worn for a while.

I hope my clothing says I don't have to try hard to have Leo. That he likes me just the way I am. "Do you want to leave a message?"

Her mouth forms a straight line in a half-smile, half-grimace. "I don't think I do. I'm sure I'll see him later."

"OK, then. Bye." I move to close the door and she puts a hand out to stop it from shutting.

"Listen. I'm not your enemy. I'm sure you are very nice. And that we could be friends under different circumstances. But Leo is not over me. I hurt him really badly and I'll never forgive myself for it. I don't want you to fool yourself. You're only a rebound for him."

I'm shocked at her gall. "I heard him tell you to stay away."

She studies her shoes that make her legs

look incredible. I imagine one well-placed kick to her shins making her topple. Hopefully, I'd leave a nasty bruise.

Tori looks up at me. "He's afraid I'll hurt him again. And I can't blame him for being scared. But Leo and I are getting back together. I plan to leave my husband so I can be with him. Leo begged me to get a divorce."

I suck in air. Tori is married? She and Leo were having an affair?

My head feels light and my body numb. This can't be true. She's a liar. Josie would've told me something like this. Then I remember that Josie didn't really tell me anything.

"Sorry," Tori says from somewhere miles outside my head. "I can tell you really like Leo. But he's not over me and I'm not over him. Take my advice. Step back before you get your heart broken."

Without responding to her—because my response still might be to kick her in the shins—I back away and quietly close the door.

Tori's statement about being married has to be true. I could ask Leo and easily confirm what she's said. He would date a married woman?

Can a man not be faithful to one woman? Are all men liars and cheats?

A fissure cracks open the wounds in my barely healed heart.

Why am I so afraid to know the truth from

Leo and to tell him the truth?

I feel my doubt hacking away at my heart—a wooden moll splitting my very core—tearing me in two.

I glance at the wall clock and then at the box of postcards and back to the clock. Leo will be back soon.

I should get the card now, in case Tori is right. In case I've been a fool, a rebound, a temporary replacement. I was wrong about Wesley and I could be wrong about Leo.

He cannot post my card in Mr. Expose.

He's not told me everything and I can't trust him.

I scoot a wood ladder over from one end of the bookcases. The books with the faux spines matching the box are at the top and I pull the one on the end out and balance it. Lifting the lid, I examine the dates inscribed on the inside label.

Not the right one.

Matching Leo's meticulous personality, the boxes are in chronological order on the shelf and it takes only minutes to locate the one that should have my card. My heart slams against my ribs.

I finger through the cards. Several slip out of my grasp and litter the floor.

With one foot in the bookshelf and the other on the ladder, I lean on the books and try to breathe. All I have to do is stay calm and get my postcard. I'll hear him walking up. I can always hear him.

As I use my thumb to fan the cards, the pink postcard suddenly appears. Score! I exhale and move down the ladder so I can pick up the mess I've made.

Click. My skin tingles in alarm.

"Hey babe." Leo stands in the doorway with two takeout bags and a look of utter confusion.

One Fell Swoop

Leo

HARPER'S FOOT SLIPS FROM THE LADDER rung, and she reaches out to grab something to hold. It's no use. She tumbles to the side away from the bookshelf and hits the floor with a sickening pop. The floor is painted concrete with no rugs in front of the bookshelf. The sound of her body crashing against the surface causes me to flinch. It's like watching one of those car crash commercials on television in slow motion.

My muscles have trouble taking directions from my brain. I drop the bags of takeout and run to her. "God, Harper. Don't move."

She's flat on her back but sits up, obviously determined not to do as I say. "I'm OK."

Postcards are strewn for at least ten feet surrounding us. I kneel into the space beside her. "Careful. Is anything bruised? Broken?"

Her eyes water and she looks away, sucking in air.

"I knew you were hurt. I'm going to take you to the emergency room."

"No! I'm fine." She begins picking up postcards in her immediate reach.

"Leave them." I put my arms around her body. "You scared the fuck out of me."

"I'm sorry." She begins picking up cards again.

I run my fingers along the back of her head to feel for any bumps. Nothing. No blood. I allow myself to calm down. "I didn't mean to startle you when I came in."

She must've been looking for a book and grabbed one of my storage boxes by mistake. "Baby, you're shaking. Are you positive you're OK?" I draw back.

"Yes, yes." Her voice has a strained edge. "I shouldn't have been in your things."

I frown at her expression. Something is off and I can't put for my finger on her mood. Maybe the fall frightened her as much as it did me. "Come on." I hold out a hand to help her up.

"Aren't you mad?"

"No. I mean, I'm just glad you didn't kill yourself when you hit this floor."

Harper continues picking up the postcards. She wasn't looking for a book; does she know what the cards are? I still her hands and take the cards from her. "I've got this," I say. "Let's get you to the sofa."

"I'm fine." Her voice is now soft and

regretful. She has to be embarrassed, being caught snooping.

Why do I feel bad for her? Normally, I'd be pissed. Only Josie and Dane know I'm Mr. Expose. And now Harper has glimpsed a part of my life that I've vowed to keep a secret.

I put my arm around Harper and kiss her head. "Come on. Let's see if the lasagna survived. I dropped our dinner when you did the sky dive from my ladder."

Harper shrugs me off and goes to the bag. "I'm OK. I'll get the food out."

I can't figure out what's wrong with her. "OK. I'll pick up this."

All my storage boxes contain three months of postcards. I carefully log all the cards by scanning them as an image into the computer, but I can't let myself throw the physical ones away. I save them like some nostalgic hoarder.

It takes me a few minutes to pick up the cards. Although I tag them and put them in a special order when I store the cards, I don't have time for that now. I have a moody woman on my hands and I'm confused. Harper is not that type.

She stares at me, her body as tense as I've never seen it.

"What's wrong, babe?"

"Can we talk about the postcards? About Mr. Expose?"

My eyes widen. She's called out the name of my blog and had time to read one of the cards. How long had she been on the ladder, reading?

"It's for a website I run."

"Is everything you do a big secret?"

I'm taken off-guard by her tone. Why do I suddenly need to defend myself? It reminds me of the way Tori always quizzed me about how I paid my bills and how much I made. "That's all you need to know. I'd appreciate not talking about it anymore," I say coolly. "And you should forget you saw the postcards."

"It's not like you're running a porn site." She's breathing hard. "I want to talk about it."

Why the hell is she so angry? "But it is confidential and my business. People trust me. If I were a psychiatrist, you wouldn't expect me to divulge client records."

She squeezes her eyes closed. "I knew you were Mr. Expose before today."

Her sudden admission feels all wrong, twisting in my gut like a soured meal. I search my brain for some time I've slipped and said something. "Why haven't you said anything? I need to know what's going on."

"I sent you a card. I asked that you return it and you wouldn't. I knew who you were when I moved into my apartment." She opens her eyes. "I've lied to you. I want you to know that I'm sorry. I'm really sorry."

"Fuck, Harper. I don't get it." But I do get it. I thought she'd been following me and that things were too convenient. Why would a postcard spur all that? And how can I look at her without wondering what else is a lie?

She's pale and I have to stop myself from going to her. I want to comfort her. Comfort myself. But I've been with a woman who lied to me too many times and this shift in my world with Harper cuts me.

She is a liar.

I inhale slowly and make my way to the sofa. "I don't know you at all, do I? You sent me emails. You were the one who kept writing me, over and over. Right?"

She nods and twists her hands. "I should've told you in the beginning. But this thing with us isn't a lie. I...um... I didn't know I was going to feel like I do about you."

I rub my hands over my face. I feel hot, and cold. "I've been honest with you. I have this thing about people lying to me."

"Honest? You aren't honest about what you do with that blog. I've hinted around, tried to bring it up and you won't talk about it. Is that honest?"

My temper paws at the gate of my self-control. "Don't try to turn this on me. That's work. It's confidential. My pen name's a secret because I don't tell people about it. It's not a personal thing between you and me."

"What about Tori?"

"What about her?"

"Were you with her while she was married?"

It's a simple question. Yet the answer is very complicated. I pause and attempt to give her an answer, but I'm angry now. How has this conversation turned to my ex? How did she know this about Tori?

Harper raises an eyebrow. "No answer? I only need a yes or no. I don't want any explanation."

"That's convenient."

"Yes or no." She stands with her arms folded over her chest.

She doesn't want an explanation. My pulse thrums in my ears. Tori was a liar. Harper is a liar. I want to reverse the past hour and go back to before. I don't want to know she's exactly like Tori. "Yes."

Harper doesn't meet my gaze. Her eyes are filled with tears and I'm pissed that I want to stop her pain. At the same time, I want her to hurt like she's hurting me.

She walks out my door and quietly closes it.

***

I don't leave my apartment for two days. Josie drops in and attempts to quiz me about what happened between Harper and me, but I won't engage. I guess that Josie is the one who told Harper the details of my relationship with Tori.

Josie can be my ally, but she also interferes. When she discovers Harper's lies, she'll get all up in arms like she did over Tori. It's more than I can stand right now. My sister threatened to do Tori physical harm more than once and they weren't even friends. Josie's like a gangster that way.

Sometimes the twin thing is just too much. Too stifling. Too invasive.

A knock at my door sends prickles of dread through me. I peer through the peephole, then open the door wide. Dane strolls in with Gunner, a friend from my school days and one I haven't seen lately. It'd be hard to turn them away.

Dane takes a seat on my sofa and Gunner grabs a barstool.

"What's going on?" I turn the television volume down.

"Thinking about going fishing. You up for it?"

I shake my head. "I don't think so. I have too much to do."

Gunner looks around my apartment. "Nice place."

"Thanks. You like your new one?" I ask him.

"I haven't seen you much since you moved back."

"Yeah. It's taken me a while to get everything set up with the business. I haven't had time to do anything since I started it. I've got a day off." Gunner's a guy who works harder than anyone I know with his own landscaping business. When he moved to Arkansas as a teen, I thought I'd seen the last of him.

I'm glad to see him back. A guy can never have too many good friends. My mind wanders to Harper and how I miss her. Is she sitting across the hall alone and thinking about me? But no. I glance at the clock and realize she's at work.

Dane puts his feet up on the trunk in front of him. "How are you and Harper doing? Have you seen her lately?"

Silence.

This isn't the type of conversations we usually have. He's treading on serious ground. "You talked to Josie?"

He doesn't even pretend. "She mentioned it."

"She send you over here?" I give him a look. He and my sister should not be joining forces against me.

"Nah. I came on my own. For the fishing." He glances at Gunner. "Right, Gun?"

"Bullshit." I smile. It's fake and hard-as-hell

to execute since I haven't felt anything close to a smile since Harper walked out my door.

Gunner leans back against the bar and stretches his legs to the floor. He's a tall guy— still built like the star football player he was when I went to school with him. The landscaping business agrees with him. "Women. They make life a helluva lot tougher than it should be."

Dane nods, as if he has women problems. The only problem he has is running from his feelings for my sister. All other women throw themselves at him. Owning a bar has its advantages and disadvantages. Drunk, lonely women could fall into both categories.

He puts his feet down and leans up with elbows on his knees. "Tori came in last night."

There's a reason he's telling me this. Tori still visits Dastardly's on a regular basis, so her appearance isn't news. "Oh yeah?" I ask.

"She said you two might get back together and that Harper is causing both of you problems." Dane examines his cuticles and picks at one.

"Man. You know that's a lie." I take a deep breath.

"Uh huh. Sure. But she's loud. She said some pretty bad things about what she'd like to do to Harper." Dane glances up.

"She is insane." I usually don't exaggerate

193

or moan and bitch about Tori, but she's a burr in my side that I'm ready to be rid of. I should've tried harder to cut her out. She's like a festering wound. The thought that she'd hurt Harper makes me want to do her physical harm.

Not that I'd hit a woman. But Tori needs her mouth taped shut.

"She knows Harper is your neighbor." Dane nods as if he's telling me something new.

"Yeah. She came by once when Harper was here."

Gunner picks up a flyer on my bar and studies it. Poor guy is ready to be on with his fishing day.

Dane shakes his head. "I wonder if she's bothered Harper. Tori asked me fifty questions about her. I didn't know most of the answers and even if I did, I wouldn't tell Tori."

"I don't think so." I flash back to Harper telling Tori that she's my neighbor. "She was asking last night?"

"Um hm." Dane looks at the door as if he can see through it and across the hall. "Just thought you'd want to know in case she's harassing Harper."

"Thanks man." I'll make sure Tori stays away from her.

"So. What do you say we go hit the river? The water's not too low and you need this. Come on. Gun's here and I need to work on my tan.

You're looking pretty pasty yourself."

I stare at the windows and think about Harper. If I sit here any longer, I'll be tempted to go next door and demand we talk through whatever has happened between us and what she wrote on that postcard.

Two nights ago, I picked up the postcard mess and organized them as I always do. Each postcard tagged with an inventory number I created. It's a way to match it to the image file on my computer. A way to match a postcard from 'Betrayed Woman' to the image file.

Harper took more than my heart across the hall. She stole that fucking postcard.

Perfect Storm

Harper

From: angelgirl@me.com
To: isabellawarren@iconic.net

Isabella,

I wonder if my compass in life has been destroyed and I'll never understand true north. What I mean is, will I know when love is real? I can't understand what's happened to me in the last four years. How could I be so wrong about someone? So blind to the false things he portrayed?

I hope you find true north someday. I hope we both do.

I hope Charley is doing well. Of course I don't mind if she emails me. It's sweet that she wants to be my friend since you are. Also, I know I don't have to say this, but I'd never reveal our true connection to her. I'm glad I don't have to make the decision about telling her about her father. I don't envy you in that.

Hugs,

Harper

***

MY BAD LUCK HASN'T RUN ITS COURSE. I'm not certain how Tori discovered where I worked, but she has. Seeing her leave Le Frou Frou's surprises me. She isn't carrying a dog out. Maybe she's dropping one off.

I don't say a word to her as we pass each other on the sidewalk outside. She's wearing shorts and platform heels that probably cause traffic to stop when she walks by. It's all I can do not to purposely bump her into oncoming cars.

People get put away for stuff like that. Orange is not my color.

I open the front door, prepared to put my purse away in cabinet when Tom signals me from the office door. I head there first. Maybe he's giving me different duties today.

"Hi, Tom." I try desperately to drum up enthusiasm.

He runs his fingers through his dark hair. "Have a seat."

"OK." I sit in the plastic chair in front of his desk.

Tom takes his place behind the desk. "Do you remember walking Hitler, the German shepherd yesterday?"

"Sure I do." An uneasy feeling crawls up my spine.

"Someone saw you kicking Hitler because he wouldn't cross the road with you."

I gasp. Literally draw in air with a horrific sound and begin to hyperventilate. "No. That's not true."

"A bystander reported seeing everything."

I whip around and look toward the exit. "I hope you're not talking about the girl who just left. She used to date my boyfriend—I mean ex-boyfriend. She made the story up."

Tom's lips tighten and he straightens in his chair. How can I prove he's wrong? He knows me. He's seen me with the dogs.

He links his hands on the desk. "It doesn't matter who reported the incident. I can't have someone working here who treats animals with cruelty."

"You're missing the part where I said I didn't do anything like that. I love the dogs. I love this job."

"She said she can bring someone else in who also witnessed what happened. They followed you here and that's how she knew it wasn't your dog. Not that it matters. Animals deserve better treatment." Tom stands and puts his hands on his hips. "I really thought you'd work out. We get along and—"

Hung without a true jury. I have to give it to Tori for being cunning. If she wanted to punish me today, she found a perfect way.

"Thanks, Tom. Thanks for believing a stranger."

"Your last check—"

"Mail it." I leave the office and hope I can make it to the truck without crying.

Inside the truck, I break down. It's the hottest day of the summer on record and I sit inside the hot cab of my vehicle crying for everything I've lost. I know I'm not at fault for losing my job. That was a sucky twist, compliments of Tori. But everything else is something I could've prevented.

If only I'd never sent the postcard. If only I'd asked Leo in person for it instead of deciding I'd take what I wanted. If only I'd never deceived him.

My life is a long list of regrets.

But I do have the postcard now and it won't be printed. I wipe the hot tears from my cheeks with the backs of my hands.

I check myself in the mirror. I resemble a zombie with dark circles framing my eyes.

I'll be okay. I can do this.

I could go home to my folks. Pretend the last four years never happened.

And never see Leo again. My chest constricts into a tight ball of misery and I slump into the seat.

The ding of my cell phone alerts me of a text. Josie's tried to contact me over the past few days and I've avoided her. My stomach cramps at the thought of losing her as well. I've waited for the text that calls me a liar for the things I've done to Leo, but that hasn't come. Yet.

I'm not sure what Leo is waiting for by not telling her.

I drag the phone out of my purse.

Josie: *I'm tired of this. What is going on?*

My heart thumps hard against my ribcage. I can't tell her because I'm a coward. I can't lose her. Not today. It'll have to wait until tomorrow.

Me: *I'll tell you later. Have to go.*

When I was a little girl, Daddy always said that prayer fixes everything. He's probably right. But I don't think God wants me to sit around waiting for him to do everything.

I sat around for four years knowing that Wesley hid things, lied, and generally applied for asshole husband of the year. It was a bad plan. Really no plan, except for the money I socked away from the household allowance Wesley gave me.

I promise myself this time I'm only waiting a

day to tell Josie about the lies. I turn on the engine and the AC blows warm air on my face. My head swims from the heat, the stress, and the lack of sleep.

Why hadn't I sat in the air-conditioning while having my meltdown?

I shift into reverse and back out of the spot.

A horn blares and metal crunches somewhere in my awareness. My car slams sideways, my airbag deploys, my head snaps back and forward and back. The smell of burning rubber assaults me.

My car alarms blares into my ears. Something wet slides down my nose.

Then, blackness descends.

***

I dream of June bugs on my body, skittering around in quick circles, their tiny legs digging into the pores of my skin. Surprisingly, I don't feel like screaming. I don't feel like anything really.

"She's awake," a woman says in a voice too chipper for my liking. "Can you open your eyes? You have visitors."

I attempt to see through half-mast lidded eyes. "No."

There's a low laugh. "I think she's OK," a familiar voice says.

I roll my head to the side and see my hand being held. "Hi. Where are we?"

Josie rubs our linked hands. "Hey crazy. You had an accident. It's a miracle that you aren't dead. I was the last number in your phone and they called me. We have to watch you for a concussion."

"Oh yeah?"

"Yeah. And when you do something, you go all out. No half-assed accident for you. No, ma'am."

"What...do...you mean?" A movement from the corner catches my eye. It's Leo, sitting in a chair as far from me as possible. He stares at me, his face expressionless.

"You were backing out of a parking spot. A semi pulled in going way too fast and barreled into you. He dragged you across the lot and into a dumpster. Well, you in your truck. You hit your head on the window. You're going to be really sore for a while." Josie squeezes my fingers.

That explains the bandage over my left eye and the feeling that my limbs aren't attached. That I'm floating above the entire room.

I can't take my gaze from Leo's. He doesn't look away and I'm like a fly caught in the spider's web. I'm unable to move or escape. Perhaps I wish to die this way—locked in his heaven-blue gaze.

"Don't remember," I say. I smack my lips together. "Thirsty."

To my surprise, Leo rises from his seat and leaves the room. My pulse quickens and I can't breathe. "Don't," I say, but it's too late. He's gone.

"He'll be back, sweetie. Don't worry."

I turn my head from her and bite the inside of my mouth hard. There's a metallic taste and then I close my eyes. As well meaning as Josie is, she is not a substitute for the loss of him.

"Do you want to sit up?" Leo asks.

When I open my eyes, he's there and holds a straw to my lips. A small sound escapes my lips, like a hurt animal, but I don't care. I nod.

I take a careful sip through the straw. He pulls it away too quickly and water dribbles down my chin.

"Sip it. You're stuck with me as a nurse and lucky I'm not letting Josie help you."

"Maybe I should be doing that." She points at the Styrofoam cup. "At least I wouldn't drown her." Josie laughs deep in her throat, a diabolical sound.

"Kiss my ass." Leo grins for the first time since I noticed him in the corner. "Harper, help me out a little. Small sip. Look up at me when you're finished."

I do as he says and he takes the drink away. He looks tired. Dark circles under his eyes make his eyes look like a midnight sky.

"You need more to drink? Was that enough?" He holds the Styrofoam cup against his chest.

"Missed you," I whisper. The words slip out before I can think about them.

He looks away. "Josie, can you give us a minute?"

"Yes. Definitely." She hops to her feet and leaves the room.

"I'm so sorry." I keep my voice steady.

"I know. Me, too." He sits in Josie's chair.

Then, he reaches over to hold my hand and I can finally breathe again. I give him a bright smile even though my face feels numb and my lips are cracked.

I lick my lips. "Do you forgive me?"

"Yeah," he says. "I can. We can be friends."

"Friends?" My throat works convulsively trying to find a way to work past the giant lump.

"Yes. I've missed you. I have. But I can't trust you."

"That's—" My throat refuses to let the words out. There's a moment when my eyebrows squeeze together in a plea. "Not forgiving."

"It is. You and I have a different understanding of what we want. I want to date someone I can trust. Someone I might someday spend a lifetime with. I can't waste your time or mine if it's not you."

He releases my hand and places his face in both palms. "It won't be easy at first. I know." He shrugs. "But we were friends before this. We can be friends again."

"Fuck you."

He looks shocked for a second and color drains from his face. Did he think I'd so easily take his suggestion?

"OK then." He gets to his feet. "You need some time to get used to the idea. Wow. I've never heard you this angry. Must be the drugs. I'll go get Josie."

He turns and walks toward the door.

I choke I'm so furious. "Friends. OK. Guess my feelings for you were a lot stronger than that."

Leo's steps slow. He faces the door, but I can still hear him. "You're wrong. And that's exactly the problem."

***

Josie and Leo take me home the next day. Home. I'm not sure I know the meaning. It's supposed to be a place that feels safe and happy.

It's neither.

I realize I've entered a dark place in my life and have to salvage myself. If it means letting Leo go, then so be it. Still, it hurts like no other hurt. As Josie says, it hurts like a mother-effer.

I'd obviously given Leo all the round edges and corners of my heart, the open places and hidden ones. The only thing I hadn't given him was what he needed most—my fears. Because that's where all the truth lives—in the ugly, honest parts we try not to reveal about ourselves.

Maybe if I'd given him my ugly truths, he'd have given me his.

On day two after my accident, I call Mama and Daddy for an hour-long conversation. It's the most real heart-to-heart we've had since I eloped with Wesley. Sure, they both catch themselves trying to tell me what to do, but for once, they talk to me as an adult.

Josie attempts to be neutral Switzerland. She asks me to do things, brings me books, and never mentions Leo. It's my third day home from the hospital and I smile at her happy face in my doorway.

"Don't you have better things to do during lunch?" I ask.

"Nope. This is me, earning my angel wings." She sweeps in with a white bag. "Brought you a burger. Dane sent it and said you can kiss him later."

"I'm not hungry. I'll eat it for dinner."

She walks to the bar and pulls out the contents. "You've lost weight. Which normally,

I'd be envious of and wanting to go on the old car crash diet too, but hey. You need to gain a little. Eat."

I roll my eyes. "Whatever."

"When do you go back to work?"

"I don't."

She slows in opening the to-go container with my burger. "You quit?"

"Mentally? I quit. Officially? I think I was fired." I slide the burger my way so I can stop talking and eat. The damage that Tori's done can't be reversed and I'm really over it. When she finds out Leo and I aren't together, she'll be thrilled and leave me alone forever.

"No one would fire you. Forgive me for saying this, but you are such a goodie two-shoes. What did you do? Turn down your manager? Tell him to go suck his own—"

"Someone complained about me."

"What about?"

"Can we drop it?"

"No." Josie grabs her burger container from the bag. "I'm your friend and I deserve to know what's going on. There's a story that goes with this and the fact that you aren't telling it bothers me."

"OK. It was Tori. Are you happy? Tori lied about seeing me doing something really bad to one of the dogs and Tom fired me."

Josie slaps both hands onto the bar. "I am

going to hunt her down like the vermin she is and kill her. Honest-to-God—"

"Don't swear. And you aren't killing anyone. She's done. She won't bother me again."

"I'm telling Leo. You can't stop me."

I shrug, but the mention of his name drives a blade through my sternum. "You know what? I don't care. I can't keep any more secrets."

She raises an eyebrow. "You have some more I need to know about?"

Dread hovers in my stomach, making my pulse speed up. I'm like a skydiver about to make that jump from the plane. No going back.

"Leo won't tell you because he's too honorable or something. I don't know why. But I'm going to tell you because you've been a true friend to me. You don't deserve anything but the truth."

"What is it?" Josie tilts her head.

"When I met you in Dog Ears, I had seen you eating with Leo."

"Yeah, so? You told me that the first time. I'd forgotten about that."

"I'd been watching Leo. I wanted to meet him. I had ulterior motives." Should I add the part about Leo being Mr. Expose? It doesn't seem right that I should tell his secrets.

"You think you're the first girl to get chummy with me to meet Leo?" Josie laughs. "Crazy. Is this all you're worried about me knowing? Answer me. Are we really friends or are you faking it?"

"Real. You're the best friend I've had since high school. And I don't even know those girls anymore."

"Good. Now that we've decided to be all BFF and everything, we can eat." She winks at me.

For the first time in days, I smile.

The $64,000 Question

Leo

IF A WOMAN CAN RUIN YOU, what does that say about you as a person? Tori came close to killing any self-respect I possessed. I wanted her so badly, I considered sharing her with another man. Not that I knew about the other man until I was already in dick deep. I was a man drowning in desire and desperation. Ready to believe everything she told me.

So, I'm irritated when Josie drops in for the sole purpose of bringing up the subject of Tori. I've told her that it's taboo. I've buried that past and don't speak her name. Now, Josie wants to bring her up like resurrecting some horrible voodoo talisman that keeps popping back up.

Josie sits at my bar, peeling the label from a beer bottle and leaving curls of paper in a mess. "Tori did something to Harper."

I rub two fingers over the knot forming at the base of my neck. "What did she do?"

I prepare myself for whatever trash talk Tori has thrown Harper's way. Tori and Josie have gotten into several yelling matches outside of Dastardly's. I'm lucky Josie hasn't decked her yet.

"She got Harper fired."

The words echo in my brain because I need time to process. I stare at Josie. She'd never make this up. I know it's the truth, but I cannot comprehend how this has happened. "Details, Josie. Details."

Josie repeats her conversation with Harper. Each word drops a stone into my stomach, sitting heavy and insoluble. I'm going to need a vat of Tums to combat the indigestion. I massage my forehead, wishing I could erase this awful feeling that I've let Harper down. "Why am I finding this out now? Why didn't Harper tell me?"

She glances at me with her patented you're-a-dumbass look. "Have you set foot across the hall since the accident?"

I hate that Josie's even mentioned the wreck. Every time I picture that semi hitting Harper in her truck, I want to vomit.

"No," I say. "We both need some space."

"You mean *you* did."

"Josie..."

"Don't Josie me." She lowers her voice and shakes her head. "Can you not be such a guy for a minute?"

"I am a guy."

"Whatever. Are you trying to lose her? Because you're doing a fine job. She's lost her husband in the past year. Lost her job. Maybe you decided that you guys couldn't get along or whatever, but at least you could act like a man and not hide over here."

"These doors open both ways. If she wanted to be friends, she'd come over. I told her I wanted us to be friends. She hasn't been knocking."

"What a cop out." Josie gets off the barstool and throws her bottle in the trash. I figure she's about to leave since I'm not agreeing with everything she says.

She turns to me and grabs her phone. "If you really want to be her friend, you'll help me with something."

I hesitate. "Maybe."

"It's Harper's birthday on Friday. She won't leave her apartment and I want to get her to Dastardly's. Food and cake. That sort of thing."

"What do you want me to do? Take her there?"

"No. I'll bring her. She won't come with you." Josie's tone is light and she's not trying to be shitty.

Still, I'm hurt that my sister is right. I don't know that Harper would go anywhere with me. The trip home from the hospital had been painfully cold and impersonal. "OK, give me an assignment."

"I'll email you. There's a list of stuff I need done. I can't leave the store to run all my errands and you have time."

"What? You have as much time as I do. I'm not your honey-do. You need to find one of those."

"You don't want to make Harper's birthday nice?"

"Hold on. I said I would. Text or email the list to me."

"Dane said we can have the back room at Dastardly's. You'll be able to store decorations in the closet there. OK?" She sticks her bottom lip out at my expression. "Pleeeeasse."

"Why couldn't I have a brother? Remind me why I let you come in and boss me around?"

"'Cause you love me." Josie smirks and heads for the door.

"Yeah. Guess so."

She ignores my grumbling and pauses with her hand on the knob. "I think you should tell Tori I'm going to find myself a nice Mafia boyfriend to take her out if she even thinks about pulling any shit again. Capiche?"

"I'll tell her today."

"You do that. I'll send her a copy of The Godfather if that'll make it clear."

"Out. Go."

Josie beams at me over her shoulder as she

leaves.

I grab my phone and open the messaging app. My phone is filled with missed calls, voicemails, and unanswered texts from Tori. I'd come close to blocking her number.

Me: *I'd like to talk to you*
Tori: *WHEN? <3*
Me: *Now if you can get away*
Tori: *2:00?*
Me: *Yes*
Tori: *YOUR PLACE?*
Me: *No*
Tori: *:(*
Me: *Tonton Park*
Tori: *K <3 <3 <3*

***

Tori pulls her car in beside mine in the lot. I've had time to let my anger simmer to a low boil. She waits for me to get out before she exits.

"What a nice surprise." Tori leans in and hugs me.

I don't have time to react before the contact is over. Once, I'd have given both nuts and a pinkie finger for this woman. The hug is meaningless now. No thrill, no need, nothing.

"Let's walk." I don't trust my anger unless I can rid myself of the pent-up frustration about what she's done. I probably won't resort to yelling if we are around other people.

She looks down at her high heels. Tori always dresses, even for work at the salon, as if she's going clubbing. When we dated, it was a fact that amused me and made me hard for her at the same time. But I see now that she works hard to advertise herself.

I'm tempted to choose a walking trail as punishment.

"I guess I can. If I trip, you'll have to catch me," she says.

I respond by pointing to some kids' playground equipment. "OK, then. We'll sit."

Tori's frowning. I'm not exactly falling into her plan for a nice, afternoon rendezvous. I sit on a bench and she takes the spot next to me.

"You and I need to talk about some things that have happened."

"I agree. I want you to know I've made a decision." Tori smiles at me. It's a little scary because she looks away and seems shy. It's not her usual confident fall-under-my-spell smile she usually flashes.

"What about?"

"Us." Her gaze flicks to mine. "I'm leaving him."

She says 'him' as if he doesn't have a name. Or maybe she is foolish enough to think I've forgotten about her husband.

"Tori—"

She grabs my hand with both hers. "I know you didn't get the open marriage agreement. It worked for me and James until I met you. That's why I couldn't tell you in the first place. I knew you wanted all of me. But I'm leaving James. We can get married. Or live together for a while if that's what you—"

I pull back in surprise. Her long nails press into my skin. She reminds me of some eagle trying to hold onto its prey. I snatch my hand away. "It's not going to happen. Ever. If you need to leave him, then do. But don't do it for me because I keep telling you we're over."

"I know I hurt you. I know and I promise I'll never do it again. But you can't give up on us. I know you loved me."

I shake my head. "It's all in the past. I don't know how many ways I can tell you. You have to put the notion out of your head that we'll get back together. We can't go back. You told too many lies. And that hurt, Tori. It did. But I don't want us anymore."

"I know you don't believe me this time. But I swear I can prove myself to you."

"Tori. Stop it. I'm not in love with you." I hold my knuckles against my forehead to stop myself from slamming them into the park bench. Anything to make her shut up. "I didn't come here for this. I came to tell you to leave

Harper alone."

"What?"

"Don't talk to her. Don't ask about her. Don't breathe the same air she does."

"Or what? You'll do what? I know you turned to that little whore because you were lonely. But you can't just replace me. We have something together."

I stand and point at Tori. "Be careful. You don't have the right to breathe her name. Don't make me do something drastic."

"What does that mean? Drastic?" Tori grabs her keys and gets to her feet. "You can't threaten me."

A man jogs by and slows down as if he needs to protect Tori. He stops in front of us and I glare at him.

"Is there a problem here?" he asks, putting his hands on his sides and catching his breath.

Tori gives him her sweetest smile. "No. Just a lovers' quarrel." Then she turns and walks away.

After returning to my apartment, I consider drinking my way through the afternoon. It's not really my style, but I'm so pissed that working isn't in the cards for me. I spend an hour tossing a handball against the wall of my bedroom.

My hand is sore and I don't feel any better

for engaging in the mindless activity. That's when I remember I'm supposed to be doing some errands for Josie. I check my email to find a very short list: *1. Order a birthday cake, 2. Pick up a birthday card, 3. Buy an eReader.* Hell. Harper doesn't need an eReader. She can borrow books from me.

I pause and feel a little sick. Maybe she's mentioned getting one and that's the reason Josie has it on the list.

It's late in the day, but Erik is manning the phone at the bakery and takes my last minute order for Harper's birthday cake. Even though Josie wasn't specific, I order a chocolate cake because I know Harper will like it.

The card's easy but the eReader isn't. This late, I'd have to pay overnight shipping to get it in time. Or go to a mall.

I call Josie. "Hey. Why can't you just get her some books from the store?"

"Because I want to get her an ereader. Then she can download whatever she wants."

"You don't have those in stock?"

"No, doofus. I run a bookstore. Electronic devices are the competition. I mean, I have cases, but I don't carry the electronics. Never mind. I'll go buy one after I close the store."

"I'm getting it." I grab my keys and grimace. Shopping.

An hour later, I'm stuck in rush hour traffic,

trying to find a bookstore not as antiquated as Dog Ears or an electronics store. It gives me too much time to think—about how Harper still hasn't explained the whole husband drama on the postcard.

It actually has kick-ass potential as a blog post. Harper's postcard. Monogamy. The human dilemma. What makes some accept this tradition while others embrace multiple partners. It's what my advertisers pay for—sensationalism.

But I'd never post it. She put too many names in for it to be anonymous. I don't know what she was thinking or wasn't thinking.

The irony of our common experiences, our distrust of each other, isn't lost on me. She had husband who conned her. Married her. Or maybe didn't actually marry her. I don't even know if her marriage was legal.

I had a woman who told me she loved me with an intensity that left me a believer, but failed to tell me about her husband.

Finally, I arrive at the store and grab an iPad with wifi. It's more than Josie sent me to buy, but I pay the difference. It'll give Harper a way to watch movies if she doesn't feel like reading.

In the parking lot, my cell rings and it's Gunner. I answer with one hand and open my car door. "Hey man. What's up?"

"How are you?"

"Good. Out running errands. Can I give you a call back?"

"Dane thought I should call you. He can't get away. He's tending bar. Your ex, Tori, is here at his place."

"Yeah? I don't care." I start the engine.

"She says she's going to see Harper and teach her a lesson. I guess she doesn't realize that Dane will tell you everything she says."

"Is she still there?"

"I'm at the end of the bar and I can still hear her talking. Anyway, Dane thought you should know and maybe warn Harper not to open her door to any..."

"Any what?" I can't think straight I'm so angry.

"I quote here, lethal bitch like Tori."

"Will do. Thanks." I grimace and wonder if Dane's opinion of Tori is a brotherhood thing or if he felt this way the entire time I dated her. It doesn't matter.

I should've made it clear to Tori that Harper and I aren't dating. Then I wouldn't have to worry about Harper. Tori would back off.

It seems like an eternity before I pull into the lot behind our building. Harper's lights are dim. The wreck totaled her truck, leaving her without a vehicle, so I knew she'd be at home. There's the glow of a lamp that shows through her windows and I wonder what she's doing.

220

Reading? I wrack my brain trying to remember if she still has any of my books.

When I make it to my door, I pause and listen as if I can hear through walls. The silence is eerie. Be a man. We can be friends and I can take the first step. One step for all dudes everywhere who want to be friends after it's over.

I peck softly on her door. "Harper? It's me."

Silence weighs heavy as lead in the air between me and the door. She's on the other side of it, ignoring me or cursing me. I know it.

"Harper. I know you're in there. I thought you might want to...Hey, you want to borrow a book?"

Lame, lame, lame. What I really want is to see her face. See her curl up on my sofa with her feet tucked underneath her while she watches television. Talk with her about nothing in particular.

I lean against the wall of the hallway, checking my phone for email and browsing the internet so she can have the chance to change her mind and open the door.

Tori's pissed and could show up. She's not quite right in the head at the moment.

The outside door to the building doesn't have a lock. I haven't worried about this fact in the past, but it looks like an open invitation to every psycho who might want to harm Harper.

Inside my apartment, I find a bungee cord that will work to rig the door closed from the inside.

I use the cord to secure the door to a barbell from my place. It looks like a seventh grade booby trap, but I'll have the landlords do something about installing a real lock. I keep thinking she'll be curious with all the banging around and investigate and I'm disappointed when she doesn't.

If anything happened to Harper because of me, I wouldn't be able to live with myself. Tomorrow, I'll convince her that we can be friends.

Tonight, I'll try to convince myself that it's all I want from her.

Olive Branch

Harper

I FROWN AS I LOOK THROUGH the peephole. Leo knocks softly at my door. Nine o'clock in the morning is too early for me to put my emotional guard up. I'm not sure why he's outside my door.

I press my face to the peephole again so I can take in the full effect of him. He's really quite overwhelming with his gorgeous eyes framed by long, dark lashes. If eyes are truly the windows to the soul, I wonder what Leo's say about him.

Passionate. Beautiful. Intense.

Boom. Bababababoom. He bangs on the door, literally making me stumble back a foot and grab my chest. Is he trying to kill me? I return to the peephole and regular breathing.

"Harper. If you don't answer the door, I'm going down to the bakery and getting Eric's key. He'll give it to me." He glares at the door. Then his gaze moves exactly to the peephole and I slink to the side in one smooth step.

"OK. I'm getting the key," he says.

I place my hand on the deadbolt and turn the tiny knob. "Just a minute."

When I open the door, he stands with his arms folded across his chest. "May I come in?"

I shrug and take a step back.

"I knocked last night, but you must've been asleep," he says.

Our eyes meet. He doesn't believe that and I don't feel like defending myself. "Did you need something?" I ask. It's a grand effort to speak the words evenly and detached.

"Why, yes. I did." He strolls across the room and sits on a barstool. He's wearing a T-shirt, cargo shorts and is barefoot. I stare at his tan legs, finely sprinkled with hair. I remember the feel of them as they rubbed up and down the length of mine when we lay in bed together the morning after our first time together.

It was more soothing than sexual. An affectionate play with my toes stretching to touch his. His legs capturing mine between his.

"I need a favor." He tilts his head and gives me a soft smile that reaches his eyes. "Please."

I want to tell him I'm busy or that I have no desire to do him a favor. He shouldn't ask me to do anything for him because my poor heart is already pining away enough as it is. No, no, no. He knew that 'please' at the end would get to me. "Yes. What do you want me to do?"

He grins. It's a little boy gleeful grin that makes my chest squeeze like I'm being hugged by a bear. "Great. It may take a while. You don't have anything to do right now, do you?"

"No." I eye him suspiciously.

"Change into some old clothes. I'll be back over in ten minutes." He glances at my bare feet. I'm still in my sleep shorts and a tank. "You have tennis shoes?"

"Um...yeah. Sure." I need my head examined by a professional. There has to be a medical term for this.

Yes, it's insanity. That's it.

"Wear them." He hops up from his seat and leaves me staring after him.

True to his word, he returns for me in ten minutes wearing a ballcap and carrying a backpack over one shoulder. I lock up and follow him outside. "Are you going to tell me what you want me to do?"

"I will." He squints into the sun. "Get in."

Leo opens the door of his car and runs around to get in. Once inside, he finds a pair of sunglasses in the console. "Here. Wear them."

"Am I incognito?" I smirk. It's going to be tough to be grumpy when he's so cheerful.

He leans forward and slides them onto my face. His fingers casually touch my skin and the contact sears me as if he's touched some forbidden part of me.

My gasp must've been audible, or maybe I flinched. I'm not sure, but the air in the car changes and he looks away.

"We need to hit the road." He starts the engine and we head out.

I spend my time watching the metro area change to residential and then to country. We drive in silence. No radio. No conversation. Just the sounds of the outside world telling me that life goes on. I imagine it saying that I'll be okay. Hundreds of people we've passed have experienced far worse than I and they are all okay.

We drive underneath a canopy of trees. Horses run in a pasture, edging parallel to a white, board fence that reminds me of a movie scene.

Leo makes right turn onto a private road which only allows one car. From the corner of my eye, he glances over at me. I force myself to look straight ahead.

"Almost there," he says.

"What is this place?"

"You'll see."

"Is there a reason you won't tell me? Let me guess. This is a body farm."

"What?" His tone is curious laced with amused. "What are you talking about?"

"I saw it on television and then read a book about it. This is my punishment for not telling the truth. You're sentencing me to hard labor at The Body Farm. You know. That place where they study how corpses rot."

He laughs, the sound all deep and throaty, tickling along my ears. "There are no dead bodies here. That place isn't in Nashville. It's in Knoxville."

I smile to myself. The joy in making him laugh is enough to fuel my happiness for a week. I'm pathetic.

We turn down another one-car lane and a lake appears out of nowhere. The bright sun glints off the water. "Hey. What's this?" I bounce in my seat and the belt strains against my body. I haven't been to a lake since going out with my dad as a kid.

"This is a secret." Leo pulls off to the side of the road. "We'll have to walk the rest."

There's no path, but Leo seems to know where he's going. Someone has bush-hogged the grass so it's not high and I'm glad I wore tennis shoes. I haven't really done much outside since walking the dogs at Le Frou Frou's.

I inhale and put my face up to the heavens. "Okay. Even if this is a body farm, I'm in. It's great out here."

The sunlight warms my skin and soul.

"Keep up." Leo walks around a cluster of bushes and I follow obediently.

Like a desert mirage, a dock and boathouse appear. There are a couple of small fishing boats in a slip at one end. The boathouse is old and worn.

"Who owns this?" I step onto the wooden dock and follow Leo.

"Gunner's neighbor."

"We're trespassing?" The question comes out as more of a squeak than I intended.

"No. The guy doesn't stick around much and asked my friend Gunner to keep an eye on things. Gun takes care of the horses for him. The guy told Gunner he could fish anytime he wants. He said we could use the fishing supplies."

Leo leads the way into the unlocked boathouse. Inside, he grabs two fishing rods and a tackle box. There's a refrigerator in the corner and he opens it and grabs a white Styrofoam container. "Ready?"

I nod and go with him out onto the dock. He places his backpack in the shade of the building, sits at the end of the wooden planks, and takes off his shoes and socks. "Have a seat." He pats a spot next to him.

The wood dock is at least eight feet wide, plenty of room to sit on opposite ends. Still, it's silly to sit so far apart that I can't reach the tackle. I sit a foot from Leo.

"We're going to fish?" I take my shoes off and

let my feet dangle close to the water. I can almost touch it.

Leo opens the tackle box and begins threading a bobber onto the translucent line. "Um hm."

"Oh."

He flips the lid of the Styrofoam container up and pulls out a long worm. "Bait your own hook or do I need to do it?"

"I can." I take the rod and worm from him. "So, what's this favor?"

He shrugs and gives me a patient look. "I needed a fishing partner."

"And Gunner or Dane couldn't?"

"I didn't ask either of them. I wanted to fish with you."

I stop breathing for a second and concentrate on the worm's wiggly body. I cruelly spear him onto the hook. I feel your pain, Mr. Worm. I'm a worm on a hook. He's baited me.

"Plus," he says. "I heard it's your birthday and thought it would be fun."

"Ah." I lift my gaze to his, my pulse picking up speed. A lump forms in my throat as his thoughtfulness. "Did Josie tell you?"

He nods and finishes preparing his own rod. "She mentioned it."

"Well, you didn't have to do this. I know you have work to do at home. We don't have to stay."

"You wouldn't answer your door last night.

You only answered this morning under threats that I'd get a key. And believe me. I would have. Can we at least call a truce for today?"

I shrug and put my thumb on the release button of the reel. I flick the rod back and forward, releasing the button at the perfect time. The line casts out in a beautiful arc and plops into the water.

"Have you ever been horrified and terribly excited at the same time?"

I glance over at him, confused. "No. I don't know."

"I'm excited that you actually know how to fish and horrified because I wanted to be better at it than you."

I giggle. I hate gigglers, for the most part. Giggling isn't pretty unless it's done by a five-year-old girl or a ninety-year-old woman. Still, I can't help myself with Leo. "I'll teach you how."

He clucks his tongue. "Over-confident much? Let's see who catches more fish by lunchtime. We have to release them, but we should keep count."

"You're on." I grin lazily.

"Who taught you to fish?"

"My daddy. It's been a long time though."

Leo doesn't have a bobber on his line. He reels in slowly and finally the fishing lure appears, spinning hypnotically. "My dad taught me to fish, too."

"And Josie?"

"Oh yeah. She followed me and the guys around everywhere. She didn't know she was a girl until we graduated high school."

"Then what happened?"

"I don't know. We went to different colleges. She figured it out then, I think. Or at least she decided to have a boyfriend during that time."

"Oh." I watch my bobber sit on the top of the water. "I wanted to go to college once. I thought I'd make a good nurse."

"So why didn't you?" He stops reeling in his line and looks at me.

"I told you. I met Wesley and got married and that was that."

"Married people attend college."

I give him an exasperated look. "Some do, I'm sure. Wesley liked for me to stay at home."

"And you did what Wesley wanted."

My temper threatens to poke its prairie dog head above ground. "Yes. I lived too far from town and didn't have a car or a job."

Leo raises an eyebrow. "Easy there. Only asking."

"You want to know everything. I can tell. But it's all behind me and I'm sorry about deceiving you. I've said that."

"Why did you email me as Angel?"

"I don't know. Sometimes people do stupid things. No one's called me Angel in years except my parents. Wesley never did. It's my middle name. I guess I was so mad that I wanted to go back to the innocent time when people called me Angel. But you can never go back. Angel was a kid. Harper is an adult."

"That makes sense." One corner of his mouth lifts in encouragement.

I hesitate. "Your turn. Why didn't you tell me you dated a married woman? You had an affair."

"I didn't know she was married. I stopped seeing her when I found out." He pauses, examining my face.

I'm glad for the sunglasses that hide my eyes. I tear up immediately. I'd assumed he knew. That he'd been deceitful and the kind of guy I could never be with again after Wesley. "Good."

The one word is so insufficient. I cringe just thinking about the way I now expect the worst of people instead of the best.

"I'm sorry about what Tori did. Josie told me. Hey, I'll help you find another job. And Tori's not going to bother you again. I swear it."

So, has he been talking to Tori? Are they back together like Tori said and that's why she won't bother me? My throat has tightened like a fist encloses it. Squeezing and squeezing. But I won't let myself cry. I turn away from him, just in case a tear slips through.

"You're not speaking to me now?"

His cajoling, teasing tone triggers the tears and I stay turned away from him.

I feel a hand on my back and I jump, startled by the touch. Sensitive to everything. The movement is too sudden and I lose my balance on the edge of the dock.

The shock of cold water hits my body. I flail, sucking in water, my lungs and nose and throat burning with the invasion.

Then something pins me and I struggle against it. Kicking and pushing. Panic screaming like a banshee inside my brain.

My head clears the surface of the water and I sputter. Everything inside me is on fire. I cough and struggle for oxygen. I fight the restraint holding me. Still, the arms around me don't let go.

Leo carries me out of the water and places me on the grass. I turn my head and cough water until my lungs cry relief.

"Harper. Are you OK?" Leo's hair lies plastered to his head and water runs in rivulets down his cheeks and eyelashes.

I shake my head no, but I mean yes. But I'm not okay. I'll never be okay without him.

He rubs his hand over his face. "The water's not deep. Only twelve feet or so. You just went down so fast. Fuck. You sunk like a rock."

"I got scared. I can't swim." I give him the

tiniest of smiles. Not that the fact is relevant at this point as I lie half-drowned on the grass in my drenched clothes. Or maybe it is. Maybe I've always fallen in too deep because I don't think ahead.

He draws in a deep breath and sweeps pieces of hair from my eyes. His hand shakes and he laughs nervously. "I wasn't going to let you drown, babe."

Babe. I don't think he even realizes he's said it. "I'm OK," I say and attempt to sit.

I stare into his eyes, the color of skies and water and serenity. A place where I could find myself again. My instincts tell me that he loves hard and true. That he puts a lot of thought into giving his heart to someone. But I've lost my chance to be the person he wants.

After several minutes, Leo grabs my hand and pulls me up. "Come on." His gruff voice cuts into my melancholy.

Maybe he's read my thoughts and regrets that we can't start over.

I'm wobbly and shaken, but not hurt. We walk to the boathouse and Leo has me sit in a lawn chair that he finds inside. "Don't fall out of this."

"Ha ha. I'll try." But I'm far from the water and still trembling. My clothes stick to my skin like a wetsuit.

I'd worn a white T-shirt and thin, tan cotton

shorts. Now, both reveal my bra and panties as if I have nothing on over them.

Leo's heated gaze ignites shivers along my body. I press my knees together and look away.

"The boards of the dock are too hot to lie on. I'll find a blanket and we can get some sun. It'll dry your clothes."

He disappears inside the boathouse and returns with a large blanket that he spreads on the grass. "Take your clothes off."

"Excuse me?" I suck in air and hope he can't read my mind. A thousand hot images of us together flash through my head.

"Not everything. Strip down to your—" He motions toward me with his hand and seems hesitant. "Down to your panties and bra. I'll put those on the dock and we can sunbathe until they dry."

"No."

"Don't be silly. It's not as if you'll be naked. They'll dry faster off and we can enjoy the sun. I brought SPF 30 sunscreen and forgot about it. If that's what you're worried about..."

As if that is my main concern. A sunburn.

"What about your clothes?"

"What about them?" He pulls off his shirt. Warm, golden skin greets me and a happy trail of blond hair leads like an arrow to a place now off-limits to me.

My mouth goes dry.

"Shorts. Your shorts are wet, too." The devil made me say it.

He actually squirms. Leo places his hands on his hips and looks down, shaking his head. "No, I don't think it's a good idea if we both get naked."

"That's what I thought. You must not think we can just be friends."

His brow creases. "What's that mean?"

"Two things. You think it's OK for me to be exposed, but you're going to keep your goods all covered up. And you are afraid you won't be able to control yourself."

Leo grins. "You sure are sassy today." He pulls his cargo shorts down and stands in black briefs. Skimpy black briefs.

Not-enough-left-to-the-imagination briefs.

My heart does a catapult into my mouth, curving my lips into a spontaneous smile. No chickening out now. He thinks we can only be friends?

I shimmy out of my wet shorts and drape them over the chair. Then comes my shirt. The warmth of Leo's hot gaze is hotter than the sun. I catch him looking, and he looks embarrassed.

I wring water from my hair with one hand and walk to the blanket.

Leo stays on his side of the blanket and sprays sunscreen on his face and chest. I spray myself, even though I'm tempted to ask him to do it. We lie side by side on the blanket, our bodies not touching but painfully aware of each other.

Today hasn't been so bad, aside from nearly drowning. Happy birthday to me.

Catch-22

Leo

I LIE ON THE BLANKET BESIDE Harper and listen to her steady breathing. The sun should make me sleepy, but it doesn't. I keep seeing the moment her head disappeared underneath the water. My chest tightens painfully.

What if the water had been deeper? What if she'd been alone? What if by some freak of nature accident I'd lost a grip on her?

I allow my arm to brush against hers. The touch assures me. She's still here. Alive. First the semi hits her, now this. My stomach twists, and I remember feeling like this another time.

I'll never forget the death notification visit about Mom and Dad. At least the company sent a person instead of a phone call. Weeks later, I did research afterward, as would any writer worthy of his word processor. There's only one plane crash for every 1.2 million flights a year. One in a million chance that I'd lose the people I love.

It's a much higher chance that the person I

love will be unfaithful. I did research on that one as well. Estimated 30 to 60 percent of married people commit infidelity.

And if that person isn't honest from the beginning, what are my odds then?

There are too many variables that say my luck is precarious when it comes to Harper.

I turn my head to the side and study her. We've only been in the sunshine for half an hour, but she's dry and I am, too. Still, I can't bring myself to wake her.

A butterfly lands on the swell of her breast, opening and closing its wings in a colorful display. She wrinkles her nose and her eyelids flutter open.

I shut my eyes.

"Hey," she says, her voice croaky from sleep. "Are you awake?"

"Hm?" I pretend to wake and lean up on one elbow. "I am now."

"I think I'm getting too much sun." She pulls the fabric of her bra away to see the pink tan line.

I quickly look away. She's killing me. Slowly. "We should go. I need to get back to do some things anyway."

By the time we leave the lake to head back home, I'm exhausted from the effort of keeping my gaze and hands to myself. Harper's a mess with her tangled hair, wrinkled clothes, and sunburned nose. Absolutely gorgeous.

It's all I can do to stay focused on the road. I put the cruise control on and glance over at her again.

"I saw you staring at me when you thought I wasn't looking." Harper appears to be napping and you wouldn't even know she'd said anything. Her head rolls my direction her lips curve into a smile.

"You want to know the truth?" I click the car blinker once and change lanes.

"No. Lie to me." She cracks one eye open and peers at me.

"I was counting your freckles. Watching to make sure you didn't burn. Of course, I failed at that." I pause dramatically. "OK. I've been caught. I'm a guy. Of course I looked."

She laughs. "I don't have freckles in the places you were looking."

I click the button on my steering wheel to turn some music on. A pop song comes on and I sing along with the parts I know.

Harper's lips curve into a smile. She sits quietly with her eyes closed for several miles. I think she's fallen asleep until she mutters something.

"What was that?" I turn the music down.

She sighs. "Thanks for bringing me. Do you mind if I ask you a question?"

"Ask."

"About Tori."

My hand tightens on the steering wheel. I flex my fingers to relax. "OK."

"Is Tori the outdoors type? Did you go fishing and stuff with her?"

"You've got to be kidding." I throw her a sidelong glance.

"What was your favorite thing about her?"

On the list of possible questions she could ask, this doesn't even make the list. "I don't know."

"Sure, you do. You were attracted to her because she was smart or something."

I laugh at this. "Um, no. That wasn't it. Why do you want to know?"

"She doesn't seem like your type." Harper stretches her arms above her head, cat-like in her movement. "I'm surprised you went for her."

"Me, too." I drop my shoulders and try to relax. Harper's tone is conversational, and I can tell she's not picking a fight. Not like Josie does when we talk about Tori.

"She's hot, if you like that high-priced call-girl kind of thing." Harper's tone drips acid.

Maybe I was wrong about the fight. I laugh anyway. "She works hard for it."

Harper sits up and turns to me, drawing one leg underneath the other in the seat. She grins. "Oh, you're going to have to explain that."

It feels so good to be talking with Harper. I

shouldn't be talking badly about Tori. I hate it when people are malicious about their exes. Two people make a relationship work and two people ruin one. I understand I was to blame for some things.

But for once, it's like I'm lifting a thousand pound burden to say the things I've never voiced aloud.

"She works in a salon. I'd bet she clocks a hundred hours a month purely on her appearance. Hair, color, nails, tan, some other shit I can't even remember." I keep my tone flat, so I don't sound bitter. These things aren't really what would keep me from loving someone.

"And you didn't like that?" Harper asks.

"I ignored it. I mean—don't get me wrong—I appreciated the result at the time. But looking back, it's crazy. That is her focus in life. Looking the way she does."

"So, how'd you *not* know she was married?"

And now we get to the crux of the relationship problems. Harper doesn't mess around. I look at her and back to the road. "I should have. All the clues were there if I'd paid any attention at all." I pause. "It's like a mystery novel where you see all the details you missed because you were distracted by the wrong things."

"Tell me the clues." Her voice coaxes me

with its softness.

"She always came to my place. Never me to hers. She said she had a roommate that I never met. She said she lived in Germantown but wasn't familiar with a bookstore there I mentioned. One day, I kept trying to call her and it would go straight to voicemail. I was out in Green Hills picking up something. It was around lunchtime. And there she was, holding hands with some guy."

"I'm so sorry," Harper says in a commiserate tone.

I have no doubt she understands the feeling of being duped. "I'm not. She was a liar and a cheat—two things I won't tolerate."

She's not laughing. "Sorry."

I grin humorlessly. "Yeah, well, I'm glad I found out. She was never going to tell me."

"She wasn't worried her husband would find out?"

"He already knew. They have an understanding. She dates other people. He does, too. They have an open marriage."

"That's twisted."

"Like a snake."

She takes a deep gulp of air and sits straighter in her seat. "Wesley and I weren't really married. I found out he already had a wife. That doesn't work unless you live in Utah."

I nearly swerve off the road trying to look at

243

her. The tires make squealing sounds when I take a curve too quickly. I've known about her husband ever since I looked up the postcard I was missing. The image scan told me why she'd want it back.

"Hey, don't kill us!" She yanks on her seatbelt like she's checking it. Then, she's silent for several seconds.

I pull over to the side of the road and turn to her. "Why haven't you told me this before?"

Why couldn't she tell me this in the beginning? Why hide the truth until now? My desire to forgive her for everything wars deep inside me. I switch back and forth between wanting to start all over and needing to run.

"Because I felt stupid." She traces a pattern of freckles on her thigh, then looks up at me. Hurt and anger radiates from her gaze. "Can you imagine how it feels to know you've ignored all the clues—clues like you talk about. Things I should've seen. The police came to our house, because the wreck was in Tacoma. I was asked to identify the body. That's when everything got weird, because he had another wallet in the glove compartment of his truck. Another set of identification and another place of residence."

I shake my head. "You couldn't know. Who would guess something like that? It's insane."

"I didn't tell you because it's embarrassing. What kind of loser doesn't catch on to something that huge? Husband gone for weeks on end. No visit to meet his parents. No old friends calling him. So much was missing. I should've known."

"No. You couldn't. Don't ever call yourself a loser. You're the sweetest, kindest person I know." I'm so pissed about her admission, I can barely contain my anger. Anger at him. Anger at myself for not seeing she's as messed up as I am when it comes to relationships.

I grip the steering wheel until my fingers hurt. I relax my hold and flex my fingers of my right hand and then my left. "If I hadn't caught you rifling through my things in the bookshelf, would you've told me everything?"

She pauses, her gaze fixed on the dashboard. Then she pivots in her seat to look at me, her expression earnest. "I don't know." She shrugs. "I'd like to say I would have, but the truth is scary. I thought if you knew, I'd lose you. And I was right, wasn't I."

I turn back to focus on the road. I wanted her to say that she'd planned to tell me. Maybe I didn't want to hear the truth, after all.

***

I'm antsy since Josie turned me down when I offered to drive them both to Dastardly's. I'm supposed to show up at 8:30. It's 7:00 and the bar is crowded already with patrons ready to start their weekend early. I scan the room and spot Dane. He's behind the bar, so I make my way there.

It takes him several minutes to wait on a few customers. I stand, since all the bar stools have already been taken.

The girl to my right gives me a once over. "Hey there."

"Hi." I glance away from her so she won't take my greeting as some invitation to start a conversation.

"Want to buy me a drink?" she asks.

I turn back to her. "Sorry. I'm with friends."

Dane approaches and winks at the girl beside me. He turns my way. "What'll you have?"

"Nothing. Just came to say hi before I go to the back. Josie and Harper here yet?"

"Oh yeah. And a room full of women." He studies me. "You don't want to go back there. I think this is like an all-female thing. No men allowed."

His statement doesn't bother me. I figure Josie's asked all her buddies so they can meet Harper. I have to give it to my sister for being sweet and trying so hard to help Harper make friends.

"I'll go on back."

Dane gets a weird look on his face, all wide

eyes and arched eyebrows. "Hey," he says. "I don't think it's a good idea. Do you know what's going on in there?"

One corner of my mouth twitches. He must think I'm afraid of a little cake and singing. "Sure. All fun and games. I'm secure in my masculinity." I smirk at him.

He shakes his head, grinning. "You're the man. Seriously."

Someone calls his name across the bar, and he's gone to take care of the customer.

At the back of the room, I hear chants and squeals. I can't help but feel so proud of my sister for doing this for Harper. It's surprising that a bunch of girls sound louder than a bunch of guys rallying for their favorite football team.

I turn the knob and walk inside, closing the door behind me. It's a large banquet room, one that can host up to twenty-five people. The room is filled and there's loud music playing from an iPod and speaker setup. A couple of women stand in front of me, but I'm a head taller so I can see clearly.

I shake my head, unsure that I'm not seeing things. There, at the opposite end of the room, is my Harper, on a platform stage with a Happy Birthday Girl crown on her head. And beside her? A shirtless guy in tight, white, sailor pants giving her a lap dance.

He removes her crown and replaces it with

the fake naval cap he's wearing. His hips gyrate so close to her face, it's a miracle he's not knocking her teeth out.

No. Hell, no. We are not playing Navy.

I push the girl in front of me aside and walk briskly past the ones trying to get a better look at the show.

"Take it off!" a female voice yells at me. My mouth tightens, and I shake my head.

Harper glances up and sees me. We lock eyes. There are a dozen women in the room and a very confident, half-naked dude, but in that moment, it's just the two of us in the whole universe.

Navy realizes she's not paying attention and places his fingers on her chin. He turns Harper's head toward him. In a smooth move, Navy grabs her hand and rubs it down his oiled chest.

I make it to the stage and grab his hand in a strong hold to remove it from hers. "Off-limits." The bass of the music is loud and I'm in his face. Navy doesn't have to hear me. He reads my face. He nods amiably and dances his way back a foot, looking around for his next target.

Harper gives me a meek smile. "Leo."

"Could I have a word with you?" I grab her hand.

Josie comes stomping onto the stage. "No, you don't," she yells. "You weren't even supposed to be here yet."

"I'm early," I say, through gritted teeth. "You can take care of Navy here."

I drag Harper behind me through the crowd of women who totally ignore me in favor of the stage. As I open the door to exit, I glance over my shoulder to see Josie dancing with the male stripper. I make a mental note to have a word with her later. Many words that I can't repeat in public.

"Hey, I can't leave my own party." Harper drags her feet like a kid being hauled out of the grocery store after eating a handful of stolen candy.

I pay no attention to her protests and lead her straight to Dane's office. I close the door behind me, making sure to turn the lock.

My head is crazy-full of thoughts that burn me. The image of Navy touching her—his hands on her and her gaze on him—of her wanting him... But I know I'm acting like a jealous boyfriend, and I have no right. I've told her we are only going to be friends.

But after today and the thing between us at the lake, I admit I'm a liar. I can't be friends and nothing more.

It would be much easier if I could pretend it's all physical.

Harper looks up at me and she's still wearing that damned Navy cap. Her face is flushed and she's breathing hard.

I remove the cap and toss it to the floor. "Having fun?" I ask in a low voice.

"I...uh...was. It's the first birthday party anyone's ever thrown for me. And that guy was embarrassing but funny. Don't be mad at Josie. She was trying to make this night special. Fun."

My jealously dissipates, fizzling out like unknotted balloon. I am an ass. I step toward her. The birthday girl doesn't deserve to be yanked out of her party by a lunatic. I'll make it up to her. "What if I give you a private dance?"

"Sure. If you think you're up for it." Her words challenge me. She cocks one eyebrow and grins.

Dane's office is small with a desk and his chair behind it. I move to an imaginary beat, stepping toward her with each small movement of my hips. I grab her hips and move her body with mine. She closes her eyes and joins my rhythm.

Our bodies pull toward each other until we're touching. I dance her to the edge of Dane's desk and put my hands on her waist. She's easy to lift onto the desk. My hands linger on her waist.

I keep dancing to the beat and move between her legs. She's wearing a short, silky dress that rides higher as I push my body into the space. My hands skate down her bare thighs. Harper shivers. She closes her eyes and her head falls back.

Her reaction heats me like a human blowtorch. I'm heating her skin with each touch of my hands. She'd better not be thinking of Navy guy.

"Look at me." My voice grates husky and low. I'm not even sure she hears me.

Then, her eyes flutter open, the pupils dark and dilated. She runs the tips up her tongue across her lips.

I still move to a beat, but bend my head to lightly kiss those soft, wet lips. "Happy birthday."

One corner of her mouth tips. "Thanks," she whispers.

The sound of live music from the front of Dastardly's bleeds into the back room. The hard rock guitar riff fits my mood. Reckless.

I trail my finger down Harper's throat, down the opening of her shirt, down to hem of the dress that's riding up to frame her thighs indecently.

"What..." She trails off when my fingers brush against her inner thighs inside the hem of the dress.

"Shh..." I grin and never break eye contact with her.

There's a pulse throbbing in her throat that's probably in time to the throb in my pants.

I rub a finger to the edge of her panties.

Harper drops her forehead onto my chest. I can feel her breathing quicken. It hitches when I squeeze her bare thigh with one hand. My other continues to tease, my fingers stroking along the silky fabric.

"Want this?" I ask.

She nods against my chest.

"Say, 'Please, Leo. I want this for my birthday.'" I tease her with the press of one finger against the damp fabric.

"Yes, please, Leo." Her head's still down on my chest, and she places both hands on my shirt. Her fingers curl into the fabric.

I move the crotch of her panties aside and stroke the tender flesh. I rest my finger at her entrance and kiss the top of her hair. "Want more?"

She nods and attempts to pull me closer. There's no way to get closer unless I'm inside her. And even though that's what I want, I restrain myself. This is a present for her, not me.

I slowly push my finger inside her and she squirms on the edge of the desk. I add a second finger and she gasps.

"Too much?" I say while continuing to pump my fingers in a rhythm.

She lifts her chin and looks at me wild-eyed. Frantically shaking her head as if she's afraid

I'll abandon her.

I bend and slant my lips against hers. She's hungry for me. Her tongue thrusts into my mouth immediately. I suck on it and she moans. The sound is edgy, wounded, needy.

I love it.

My free hand moves to the top of her panties. I should've ripped these off her by now, but I risk insanity at the thought of her going back into the bar without them.

I continue to pulse inside her opening with one hand and my other dips down into her panties from the top, skims the sensitive flesh it seeks, finds her sweet spot. I rub once with my thumb, and she jolts against me.

Her lips break away from mine, and she stares into my eyes. "What are you doing to me?"

I give her a heated look, not slowing the pace of my busy fingers. "Making the birthday girl blow out the candles."

She's not even hearing me, or she'd smile at my cheesy line. My thumb plays back and forth in a quick motion over her clit. Her pleasure builds in sync with my movements. Her head is back enough for me to see the moment she breaks apart and it's breathtaking. The most beautiful thing I've ever seen, and I don't want anyone else to see it. Ever.

Her forehead creases at the end and she

shakes her head. Her face is unreadable. "What about you?" she asks.

I shrug and feel strangely vulnerable. Thrown off-balance by the intensity of the last few minutes when I only wanted her pleasure. I can't remember if it's always been like this when I was with someone else, because her face and scent and body are too close. I can only think about being with her.

She is filling my head. If I tell her how she's grabbing a hold of me—each day a little more even though I've pushed her away—will she disappoint me like Tori did?

Will I ever be able to trust her?

A knock sounds at the door and Harper jumps. I stumble back, embarrassed that I've taken what I wanted here in Dane's office. Even though I'm not the one who got off, the last few minutes were about me and what I want.

I need her to want me—in every way—and the thought scares me shitless.

I've behaved like a child. One minute demanding we downgrade to friendship and the next minute proving I'm more desirable than a guy in a stripper getup.

The thought sends an uneasy shaft of fear into my gut. I rub my hand over my face. Her scent mocks me.

There's another knock on the door. "Hey, somebody in there?" It's Dane's voice, and he's pissed.

"Come on, birthday girl. Time to get back to the party." I grab her by the waist and place her on her feet. Her confused eyes cause my stomach to bottom out, making me mad at myself. I pull her by the hand toward the door.

Tori's lies did a number on me. But I'm honestly okay about losing her. Jaded about dating, but really fucking okay.

Betrayal from Harper wouldn't leave me jaded. She could crush me.

Sleight of Hand

Harper

NO ONE USES POSTCARDS ANYMORE. No one except for Leo and the random traveler who can't get a freaking cell signal in Siberia.

This postcard that I've stolen back from Leo taunts me. The words on the card have an ugly voice that speaks of my impulsiveness. My hurt. My life that was nothing but a lie for four years.

I grip the pink postcard with two fingers, intending to rip it straight down the center and then into giblets. My fingers are poised at the top between two Rhododendron flowers and above the statement, 'Finest Beauty of the Evergreen State.' I allow a tiny tear in the paper. It should be the impetus I need to shred the evidence. Continue until there's nothing left of my life in Tacoma.

My hands shake and I drop it onto my bed. I need to return it to Leo. Am I crazy? Thinking it's OK to steal?

I fold the postcard and tuck it into my back pocket. Saturday mornings in our building are noisy. The downstairs bakery bustles with activity and the pan banging and voices are louder than normal. I walk across the hall to Leo's.

He answers after only one knock. He's wearing track pants, a T-shirt, and a wary expression. "Morning."

"Hi. Um...can we talk?"

"I have a few minutes." His answer is even, not cold or warm. His tone edges on impersonal.

This is not the response I expected. I'm not a door-to-door salesman or something. He stands back to let me enter. "Thank you for the gift. Josie said the ereader was from both of you. That was too generous. I love it."

"I'm glad."

"About last night," I say, wondering if I should sit or stand since he's made it sound as if he doesn't have time for a conversation. If only I'd said I'll come back or this will take more than a few minutes.

"About that," he says, rubbing the back of his neck. "I got carried away. This thing with being friends will be tricky since we've—"

My mouth opens. Not to actually form words because I have no clue what would come out. Last night meant nothing? Because I'd bet my last chocolate bar it was hot and emotional and special. It was certainly not something I practice with my friends.

I shut my gaping mouth. My gullibility is limitless. "We are back to this? The friend thing?"

"Don't read too much into it. We're both adults. Just because we had a little fun in Dane's office—"

I slap him and the pop of my hand against his cheek rings out in the room, seeming to echo. He flinches, but stays standing in the same spot with his impassive face. My heart beats faster, pushing air from my lungs as it tries to fill my chest with its fury. "You are unbelievable. I've never felt so used. So degraded." My throat catches. "So cheap."

"It got out of control." He looks away and then back to meet my gaze.

"What? Your pride? Didn't want some stripper touching me, so you needed to prove something?" My chest rises and falls like I've been running.

"It was my fault."

"Yeah. It was. But you can't do that to me. Friends don't behave this way and lovers don't either. I don't know what your game is, but I'm not playing. I'm done. You're vile and I pity the woman who is ever fooled by you."

Leo's rubs his fingers along the crease between his eyes. "Come on. You're upset. We can forget about last night. People make mistakes. I made a mistake."

I smash my lips together so I won't cry. At least when Wesley literally screwed me and left for weeks on end to go to his real family, I didn't know what was going on. It's my excuse for not doing something at the time. I back away from Leo. "I deserve better treatment than being some toy for when you feel like playing around."

"It wasn't like that."

"Oh wasn't it? I really am an idiot. I thought yesterday made you see how much you missed us together. That there was actually something real there. But no."

He looks up at the ceiling as if he can't meet my gaze. "You're overreacting. I didn't mean—"

"That I was a hook-up? That you were horny and I was a pushover?"

He gaze drops to mine immediately. "You know that's not what I meant. You deserve better than a purely physical relationship. I'm not ready to give you more."

His soft voice bleeds sincerity, and I hate him for it.

"Can you do one decent thing for me? Just one and I promise to never bother you again."

He stares at me. "Yeah." His voice is low and for a minute, I swear it's filled with regret.

"Don't print this." I pull the postcard from my pocket and fling it at him. "I took this the day I found all the blog cards."

The paper flips in the air and falls short on

the floor between us.

"You didn't trust me? You could've asked for it instead of taking what you wanted."

The hurt inside me coils. Strike at him. Make him feel like he's not that important. I shrug. "I did ask for it, but you treated me like an unreasonable ditz. The postcard was the reason I moved next door. Mission accomplished."

"Then why give it back now? You suddenly trust me?" He narrows his eyes and his cold voice makes me want to see some emotion from him. Anything.

"You're right. I don't trust you. Thanks for the reminder." I bend to pick up the card. Making eye contact again, I tear it in half once. Then again and again and again until only small pieces are left. I release them and they flutter to my feet. "Have a nice life, Leo."

A flicker of something I recognize passes across his face. Hurt.

I flee to the safety of my apartment with my chest tight. I can't let what happened last night happen again.

I'm lying on my bed with my cell rings. It's a relief when Josie's name pops up on the caller ID.

"Hello," I say, tentatively. She and Leo are close and I am well aware of what will happen if she's forced to choose sides. I'll lose her.

"Hey," Josie says, pausing for a long second. "I want to apologize for last night. I should've cleared the stripper with you but I thought it would be so much fun to see the surprise on your face."

"Yeah. I was surprised. Did I tell you thanks?"

"Um... about fifty times." She laughs. "Did you and Leo get into a fight last night over that?"

"No." It's the truth. What we did was the exact opposite of fighting.

She exhales into the phone. "Good. I've been worried. I mean, I did it knowing that Leo would be jealous no matter what he says. That's why I told him not to show up until later."

"It's fine. Can we not talk about Leo?"

Silence.

"I'm confused," she says. "Didn't you ride home with Leo after the cake?"

"Yeah, but there's nothing going on between us. It's over."

"You are bullshitting me. Did you see his face when he dragged you out of the chair last night?"

"Yes. But we can't make it work. I don't want to talk about your brother. I need help finding a job and a car."

Josie pauses, then sighs. "I'm coming over and we can take care of the car shopping today."

"How am I ever going to pay you back for all your good deeds?"

"I'll think of something." There's a pat-on-the-back tone in her voice that tells me everything will work out.

I smile at that. We disconnect. Even through the phone line, she's stable. Kooky and loud, but stable. For the first time in a long while, I know what I want. Roots. Family. Purpose.

Love. Real love that doesn't flash from hot to cold. A chill passes over me as I think about how awful my words were to Leo. I'm not that girl. A vindictive, ugly person.

He's wrong for thinking he can turn me on and off, but it's my fault for not staying away from him. We can't be friends. He's probably not going to try again anyway, after I was so hateful. But if he comes on to me again, I'll be stronger next time.

Josie arrives in half an hour. I get into her Mustang convertible. She's smiling but not her talkative self. It's okay with me if we stay silent. My round this morning with Leo still has me feeling as though I've been sucker-punched.

"Want to look anywhere in particular?" Josie checks traffic and pulls out.

"I'm on a budget. Nothing as nice as yours. Something to get me places."

"Gotcha." She accelerates and pulls her hair off her neck. "It's a little hot. We could've borrowed Leo's car."

I don't respond to her comment. The last thing I want is to be indebted to him for anything. The wind blows onto my face and the temperature warms me. Leo's chilly conversation with me has left me feeling frozen and empty.

Maybe my heart's actually stopped and I don't know it yet.

"Harper," Josie says. "I wasn't going to bring him up, but I have to."

"No, you don't."

"Yes. I do. He's my brother and I love him. I want him to be happy. I want you to be happy. But he's not going to tell you things he should. He's weird like that."

Cold is more like it.

"He's hurt me." I stare up and blink back the tears. "He really has. One minute he's incredibly sensitive and romantic and…perfect. But he keeps shutting down and I don't know who I'm going to get, Romeo or Voldemort. Today…" I cover my mouth with one hand and turn to the window so I can get myself under control.

"Tori still calls him. I found out he met with her the other day."

I can't stop the tears now. "Oh, geez. You are not helping me feel better."

"No," she says, frantically shaking her head.

"He's trying to make her stop calling and texting and dropping by his place. And it was after I told him that she got you fired. It wasn't a reconciliation thing. Lord, no. She's mental."

I search my purse for a tissue. "He may deserve her."

Josie puts her free hand on my arm. "You don't mean that."

"No," I say, my bottom lip trembling with the effort to stop my blubbering. "No, I don't. Sorry. That wasn't a nice thing to say."

Josie hits her blinker and pulls into the nearest parking lot. "Ice cream is required. Now."

We've parked in front of an ice cream shop and it suddenly seems like the perfect anecdote to a good cry.

I wipe my face with the tissue. "OK."

We stand in the line until our turn to order. I point at the ice cream buckets with the most decadent chocolate I can see and order three scoops. Then I request caramel on top.

Josie eyes my order. "There's a reason we are buddies." She licks her lips and orders the same for herself.

We sit knee to knee at the small parlor table and suddenly the world is brighter and definitely sweeter. I have a good friend. I dig into my ice cream.

"Let me talk and you listen. Eat your ice

cream," Josie says.

I nod and stuff a large spoonful into my mouth.

"Leo caught her with her husband. He broke it off. She said she'd left her husband. They got back together again. He discovered she'd lied. She said her husband abused her. That was a lie. I cannot tell you how many lies he believed. Over and over again."

My mouth full of ice cream is numb, but my heart isn't. He's as broken as I am.

Josie's lips purse. "For a smart guy, he can be really stupid. And that's the part that scares him. He was incredibly stupid when it came to Tori. He kept holding on because you want to believe in people you love."

"So, he loves her?" The words pass through my lips in a strained whisper. I'm not sure if it's the ice cream or my question that causes me to feel as though I've been stabbed through the chest with an icicle.

"Oh. Should've said loved. Past tense. And I'm sure she's killed any love there was. I mean, how can anyone stand that kind of abuse of trust? But she wove her spell on him and had this kind of sexual hold over Leo that I can't explain. She's like Calypso."

I frown. "You mean the one who held Odysseus captive?"

She rolls her eyes. "Oh come on. I do read. I

just mean Leo had trouble breaking it off and Tori's obsessive."

"And he doesn't still secretly want her? Do you think that's why he keeps pushing me away?"

"Shut up." Her eyes flash hotly. "Believe me when I say this. If he were to let her back in, I could not call him brother. Seriously. Some stupidity is beyond forgiving."

"I get it. My husband had someone else." I begin eating the ice cream fast, shoving in spoonfuls so I won't have to speak. *Husband.*

"You're going to get an ice cream headache." Josie suppresses a grin.

I stop inhaling the treat in front of me and look at her. Really look. She deserves the truth. "I was little more than a mistress, but I didn't know it. He had a family and a kid. He also had one heck of an ID forger."

Josie stops with her spoon midway to her mouth. "Stop. You're kidding, right?"

"No."

"I thought Leo was the only person with luck that hellacious."

I nod. "He's not the only one who's been stupid. I was four years of stupid."

"Makes me feel kind of good about my love life."

"You don't have a love life."

"Um...yes. Right." She spoons a large bite of

266

ice cream into her mouth and then squeezes her eyes shut. "Brain freeze!"

"I'm looking for happiness and there's so much weighing on both of us. It's too much."

"We're both young. I vote we just have fun. But I had to make you understand where Leo's coming from so you don't take it so hard. OK?"

"Here's to fun." I hold up my mostly empty container to toast hers.

She clinks her container against mine. "To fun. By the way, I have the stripper guy's phone number...if you're interested."

Pay the Piper

Leo

IT'S BEEN TWO WEEKS SINCE Harper's birthday party. I've stared at the same doodle of a giant fly with a man's head for the last twenty minutes. The words won't come. I don't believe in writer's block. Never have. I have a name for the current state I'm in. It's called Harper block. I grin to myself at the thought. Maybe I should add it to Wikipedia.

If she were on my sofa watching her sappy movie of the week, then maybe I'd be able to write. Be able add a page to my manuscript that seems to be at a standstill.

I grab my keys and stride to the door, so ready to get out that I am inside my car and driving before I have a plan. I make a quick call and discover that Gunner is at Dastardly's, along with my buddy, Aiden. This is what I need. A guys' night out.

I finally find a parking spot in a public lot several blocks away. It's a perpetual Saturday night in Nashville. People hang around on the sidewalks in front of the more popular bars. The music is loud and drifts out from open doors, beckoning with a lazy finger for people to come inside.

There's a cover charge tonight, but the bouncer nods at me to go inside.

I elbow my way through the crowd. It's standing room only, but Gunner motions at me from across the room. He and Aiden sit at a table with a couple of girls.

"Hey man. What do ya know? Miracles do happen. Somebody unglued your fingers from that computer." Gunner grins. He's already three sheets to the wind, by the look of him.

I smile back and Aiden scoots over to make room. "Good to see you."

The band is jamming with a mix of old rock and roll, songs they've remixed to fit their sound. There's an extra chair at the next table and I ask if I can have it. When I turn around to scoot in next to Gunner, the two girls have moved apart so I can sit between them.

"Hi. I'm Stacey," the girl to my left says in my ear so she can be heard above the music.

"Leo. Nice to meet you."

"Nice to meet you, too."

She places her hand on my forearm and puts her mouth close to my ear again. "I think my friend wants to go home with your friend." Her gaze flicks to Gunner and her friend.

"So," I say, moving back an inch so we aren't so close. "They just met?"

"Uh huh." She shakes her head. "I hate going out with Cherry. She's fun and everything, but she always ends up hooking up and she leaves me stranded."

I laugh. "The fun ones always do."

"What do you do, Leo, beside look handsome?"

I tell myself she's just being friendly. Still, unlike Gunner, I'm not looking for a hook-up. I back up another couple of inches. "Writer. You?"

"Dental hygienist." She sips from her frozen drink.

Aiden gets up and wanders off through the thick crowd and I lose sight of him. Another band takes the stage and begins preparing for their set.

Coming here was a bad idea. Stacey keeps talking to me and she's nice. Pretty. But I can barely pay attention to anything she's saying, because I can't quit thinking about Harper.

Stacey puts her hand on my arm again to get my attention. "Hey, the waitress is here to take orders. What do you want?"

I shake my head. "Nothing."

Stacey turns to the waitress who stands somewhere behind my chair. Her hand is still on my arm. "He'll have a beer. Whatever you have on tap. I'll have a Sex on the Beach."

"I'm not drinking," I say, leaning toward her since she's either deaf or determined. When I lean back, I pull my arm from her grasp and make certain my body isn't in easy reach again.

"Someone will drink it. Not to worry, handsome."

She doesn't touch me again but continues to attempt conversation. Some girls are just like that—touching you when they want. Perhaps I'm being paranoid that she's interested in me for more than a diversion while her friend gets friendlier by the minute with Gunner.

A beer appears in front of me and a frozen drink in front of Stacey. She reaches for her bag. "I'll get yours."

I shake my head and reach into my pocket for my wallet. She is not buying me a drink. I pivot in my chair slightly so I can hand the waitress money for my beer. My gaze travels up the length of the waitress in the revealing black shorts and tight t-shirts that all Dastardly's waitresses wear. A shock reverberates through me as if I've fallen twenty feet and hit the ground flat on my back. I need to blink to clear my vision.

Harper's hair is down, curling in ringlets down her back, and she's wearing makeup. Those shorts make her legs go on for miles of beautiful skin.

This cannot be. Harper stands behind me, waiting for payment.

"You work here?" This is the dumbest thing I've said in ages. I hand her a twenty dollar bill.

Harper gives a couple of bills back. "No," she yells. "I walk around scamming folks for money, but no one has caught on yet."

Funny girl. She walks away and I stare at her retreating backside until I can't see her through the crowd.

"Thanks for getting mine," Stacey says.

It's then that I realize that Harper gave me only a couple of bucks, assuming I was paying for both mine and Stacey's. She thought we were together. My gut is churning with a terrible need to jump from the chair and race after Harper. Why would she think I was paying for a girl's drink?

"Sure," I say.

I glance around the table. Gunner and the friend are sitting close and they look like a couple. As if they came here together. Stacey's not sitting quite as close to me, but we do appear to be on a fucking double date.

I feel hollow inside and hear a ringing in my ears. She thinks I'm on a date.

"It was nice to meet you," I say to Stacey. I get to my feet and walk through the crowd. I've left the beer on the table. Harper stands beside a table near the back and the restrooms where she's serving a table of four guys. Two of them are telling her something and she smiles at them.

Her smile. She always looks pretty, but there's a transformation that takes place when she gives you that genuine smile—a stamp of approval for whatever you've said or done. It gives me a buzz to think about that feeling.

Now, some strangers are the recipients of her smile and my chest burns. I tell myself to get over it and go home because tonight isn't working out.

Instead of leaving, I find a spot along the wall where I can watch the band and keep an eye on her. My phone vibrates in my pocket. I check the display.

Josie: *What r u doing dork?*

Me: *Dastardlys*

Josie: *Yes. I know that. What u doing holding up that wall?*

I scan the room. Josie waves at me from the bar where she sits on a stool.

Me: *When did Harper start working here?*

Josie: *Last week*

Me: *Why didn't you tell me?*

Josie: *Did you ask me about Harper and I forgot?*

I roll my head in a circle, stretching the tense muscles of my neck.

Me: *It's too dangerous for her to work here.*

Josie closes her eyes and shakes her head. She bends her head to continue texting.

Josie: *She's a big girl*

Me: *What about drunks hitting on her?*

Josie hops from her seat and pushes her way through the crowd until she reaches me. She flings one arm across my shoulders. "You can't have it both ways. You're either dating her or not." She yells above the music near my head.

I roll my eyes. "She doesn't have anyone to look out for her."

"Who was your friend over there?" Josie drinks from her beer bottle and uses it to point to the table I left.

"Her name is Stacey and I don't really know her. Tell Harper I don't know that chic."

Josie laughs. "Oh no you don't. Tell her yourself. We're not in fifth grade. Besides, why do you care what Harper thinks?"

I shrug as if it's no big deal even though I can't seem to quit searching the room for her. "I don't want her to think I hook-up with random girls in bars."

"She won't." Josie waves at someone entering and I follow her gaze.

"Do I know that guy?"

"Yeah. You saw him the other night when you dragged Harper away. See you later."

I squint at the guy, trying to place him.

There were no guys at that birthday party. There was a room full of women. Except for one guy.

I stare across the room at Josie as she talks to him. He's tall, thickly built like he spends an inordinate amount of time in the gym. He turns and then I'm certain of his identity. It's Navy, without the flashing lights and music and white pants.

Josie looks around for a moment and points at someone. I look where she might be pointing.

Harper. Harper who isn't paying attention as she takes a drink order from a guy. The customer is old enough to be her father, but he's looking at her in an un-fatherly way.

My sister is trying to kill me.

I force myself to watch the band for as long as I can to remove my focus from Harper. From the corner of my eye, I glimpse her at the table near me. She's good. I don't remember her saying if she's even waited tables before, but she's quick to buzz around the room delivering drinks. I silently scold myself when I realize I'm still watching her.

At some point, Gunner and the two girls leave their table. I've searched the room for Aiden, but assume he's left for some other entertainment for the night. It's after midnight and the place is still crammed with customers.

There's a small area in front of the band for

dancing. Several partiers are doing a version of line dancing.

My sister still sits at the bar with Navy. His back has been to me most of the time while he talks to Josie. Suddenly, Harper appears and she's changed clothes. Her shift must've ended and she's ready to leave.

I push off from the wall, prepared to offer a walk to her car. Before I can make it more than a couple of steps, Josie, Navy, and Harper walk to the small dance floor. The three of them begin to dance.

It's all harmless. No touching or grinding. A small favor for my already tortured emotions.

Returning to my spot on the wall, I can't help but seethe. My skin warms with anger directed only at myself. I want to be out there dancing with Harper and receiving her bubbly smile.

She laughs, her head thrown back in pure delight from something said. I don't know if my sister or Navy makes that happen, but I can't watch anymore. I weave my way through the crowd quickly.

Outside on the sidewalk, I can finally breathe.

Jesus. I'm a fool. I don't want her. I want her. I want her so much I can taste the salt of her skin from the last time we made love.

When I arrive home, I sit at my desk with a

goal in mind. I have one particular scene in my novel that I'm in the mood to write. It's several chapters ahead and although I write in a linear fashion, I open the file in my writing software.

The characters in *The Incident* meet for a rendezvous in a hotel room. It's a gritty scene. No flower petals strewn across the floor. No champagne chilling in a silver-plated bucket.

No murmured phrases that glide off the tongue to entice and persuade.

It's a scene of stolen moments and urgency. Their touching is quick and fraught with yearning. Afterward, they hardly speak because they have no need.

Their communication has been a wordless demand.

I type the final sentence of the scene and glance at the laptop clock. In half an hour, I've written more than I have for days. And it's good. I know it is, because I was transported into the hotel room with them—an invited voyeur into my characters' lives.

A noise sounds in the hallway and I glance at the clock. It's 3:30 am and I've lost track of time. Since having my landlord install a lock on the exterior door, there's only one person who has access.

I'm refreshed from the sheer joy of getting some words onto the screen. I could easily run a mile or lift weights. Adrenaline surges through my entire being. It's a rush only another writer can understand.

I swing the door open so I can talk to Harper.

Navy—sans white pants getup—stands with her at the end of the hallway. They aren't hand-in-hand, but she's knocks into him when she takes a step.

I'm frozen. Do I go back inside and wish I'd never seen them coming in together? She's not my sister or my tenant. I can't tell her not to have a guest.

Still, my mind races, trying to come up with some excuse to kick his ass.

They walk together toward me and she's looking at her feet. I have no doubt she's been drinking. When she lifts her head, she sees me for the first time and there's mascara under her red-rimmed eyes. Tear stains track down her cheeks.

"What the fuck?" I allow my door to slam shut behind me. "What's going on?"

"Nothing." Harper turns toward her apartment. "Leo, it's nothing. Go back inside."

"What did you do, man?" There's a sharpened edge to my voice.

"I didn't—" he says in a softly accented voice, Italian maybe.

Harper whips around and glares at me. "Antonio didn't do anything. He was only making sure I get inside my apartment."

"I'll bet he was."

"I don't know what your problem is." Antonio the Navy stripper has balls to look me straight in the face. "I suggest you leave this situation to me."

Right. "And I asked you what you did to her. She's been crying."

"That is none of your business. The lady told you I did nothing." He raises one eyebrow at me and nods as if we are finished with the conversation. He turns away and stands waiting while Harper puts her key in the lock.

"Harper," I say. "Answer me. What did he do? You've been crying."

She ignores me. There's no way he's going inside. She should know better than to let some stranger bring her home. What is she thinking? At the very least, he's aiming for a good time. She'll regret it tomorrow.

His hand is now on the center of her back, and I grab his shoulder with my fingers digging into his bulk.

Navy shrugs me off and looks at Harper. "Do you want me to take care of this nuisance?"

That's when my brain abandons logical thought.

I draw back and punch him. The smash of knuckles against cartilage makes a faintly crunching sound. Blood courses down his face.

Pain explodes through my hand and shoots straight up my arm.

Harper screams as if I've hit her. I drag him away a few feet to make sure we aren't too close.

It's been a long time since I've been in a fight. I wonder if I'll regret it later. Probably not. It feels too damn good.

Get Religion

Harper

MY SHIFT BEGINS IN TEN MINUTES. I pick at the Dastardly's shorts, pulling them down to cover more leg. The uniform is sized for a girl in middle school.

"Let Harper tell the story one more time." Dane shoots a foam basketball toward the hoop mounted on his office door. It falls short.

Josie retrieves the squishy orange ball and shoots. The ball glides in. "It's pretty unbelievable. My brother is a raging madman. Antonio is huge. What was Leo thinking? A writer can't type with broken fingers."

"He's lucky that Antonio let it go. And Leo's fingers aren't broken. They're probably only bruised." I stare at my own knuckles in my lap. I can still see how Leo's bloodied knuckles looked when I pulled his hands from their grip on Antonio's shirt.

I focus on Dane's desk and then look away. It makes me blush just thinking of the time I was in here with Leo.

"So," Dane says, "Leo pops Antonio in the face—BAM—and then what? Does Antonio get one in or—" Dane darts from side to side with his fists up like he's sparring.

"Argh. I've already told you. That's it. I jumped between them because I panicked that someone would get hurt—"

"Someone? You mean Leo," Josie says. "My brother hasn't been in a fight since high school."

"Leo's fist came out of nowhere. One minute they're both mouthy and next thing Antonio holding his nose. Leo was so fast and—"

"Leo must've caught him off-guard. That's all I can figure," Josie says.

"Go on, Harper. Josie hon. Let the girl finish her story." Dane raises both eyebrows.

Josie throws the foam ball at his head.

I sigh. "That's basically it. Then Antonio put his hands up in the air and his nose was bleeding and it was awful. I asked him to leave."

"Leo or Antonio?" Dane asks.

Josie throws a pen at him this time. "Antonio. Why would Leo leave? He lives there."

"So. Cool," Dane says. "You and Leo make up?"

"It's not that easy." I bend over and place my face in my hands. I peer up at Dane. "I need a stable guy. One I can trust with my heart, you know?" I stand so I can get back to my shift.

Dane makes a sad face and nods slowly. "So, you and this Antonio guy. You're seeing him now?"

Josie rolls her eyes. "Antonio doesn't want to date her. He's probably got his eye on my brother, not Harper."

"That guy? No way." Dane's brow furrows into deep lines.

"Told me himself." Josie says.

Dane grins and takes his feet off the desk. "There's never a dull moment with you two." He chucks my chin on the way out. "It'll turn out how it's supposed to turn out," he says over his shoulder.

"He's such a wise one," Josie says.

***

It's a Friday and I have the day off. Leo and I have passed each other in the hallway exactly two times this week. The first time, I pretended to read my cell phone while walking. The second, I held the phone to my ear and had a long conversation with myself.

It's beyond sad that the conversation was actually interesting. I'm so lonely for Leo in my life. Still, I'm not about to apologize for anything. What would I apologize for? I don't understand why he cares if Antonio walked me to the door.

Because even if Leo wasn't on a date that night, he was flirting with a girl—buying her

283

drinks, sitting next to her, letting her whisper sweet somethings in his ear. I get physically ill every time I picture the scene.

Antonio's just a nice guy who commiserated when I started blubbering like some sad baby over losing Leo and not wanting to let go.

I pocket my cell and walk downstairs to the bakery. Today, my landlord stands behind the counter in a purple apron.

"Hey pretty lady." Erik grabs a plate. "Let me guess. You look like you need one of my famous bear claws."

"That's exactly right. You are amazing."

"No charge." He hands me the pastry. "Let me get you a coffee."

"Yes, please. Listen. I have something really awkward to ask."

"Go for it. Awkward is my specialty."

"If I can find someone to take over my apartment, can I break my lease early?" I take the coffee mug from him.

He frowns and comes around the counter to my side. "Let's sit."

The place is empty since the early morning crowd has already been by for their breakfast. There's a spot in the front near the windows where I set up my breakfast and settle in.

Erik sits back and crosses his legs at the ankles. "Why do you want to move? Is the rent too much?"

"Well, no. I just…" I stare out the window. "The truth is that Leo and I don't get along. We had this thing and now we don't."

"And you hate him."

"No." I give Erik an exasperated look. "I wish I did. Then I could probably be okay living next door. But please don't tell him that."

"If you have to move, I understand. You can break the lease early. But we like renting to you. Don't do anything drastic. Sometimes, these things blow over."

After everything that's happened, I can't imagine not feeling something when I see him. Seeing him at Dastardly's is one thing. I can fake it and pretend he's any customer off the street. We don't have to be personal.

But some days when I stand in the hallway, I gaze at his door in hopes that he'll open it and say he's sorry. I want him to drag me inside and make me take a chance.

It's never going to happen. He changes his mind too much and he's too scared. I can't be brave for both of us.

Erik reaches across and lays his hand on mine. "I respect and understand whatever you need. James and I can always find another renter."

He rises and returns to the counter, throwing a sweet smile my way whenever I glance up.

My cell rings and I check the display. It's Grandma Lulu. She's a regular caller and I enjoy our chats, even though it's sometimes difficult to follow along with her.

"Harper?"

"Yes, Ma'am?"

"You're my guest at the senior citizens breakfast on Sunday morning. Be there or be square. Wear something cute. Do you have a mini-dress?"

A grin splits my face at her statement. "Oh, all right. I guess I can. And no, I do not have a mini-dress. Are you saying I need to dress up? Is there a service?"

"Yes. There's a pastor who comes and does a very brief sermon. I don't think I could stand anything more. But wear something short and fun. I need to remember what it's like to be young and thin. You can shake it up."

"I'll see what I can do." I smirk. Daddy would like Grandma Lulu in his congregation, even if she's demanding I show some skin.

After I end the call, I sit and drink more coffee. It's going to be time soon for me to get the next step of my life back together. Maybe Grandma Lulu and Josie would take a road trip to Texas with me.

It's time for the prodigal daughter to return home for a visit.

I'm whistling an old tune, Guns and Roses'

Welcome to the Jungle, as I walk up the outside stairs of the building.

I open the door and Leo walks out of his apartment and into the hallway. He points. "You." His mouth sets in a straight line, reminding me of a teacher catching a kid without a hall pass.

"What about me?" My heart beats faster.

"Do you know where my laptop is?"

"Why would I?" I'm alarmed by his tone, his body language, his accusing gaze.

"It's missing."

"Maybe you left it somewhere." This is a stupid comment. He has a laptop, but I've never actually seen him take it with him outside his apartment. It always sets in one place—that massive desk.

"No. I didn't." He turns away from me for a minute.

I'm unable to move a muscle. Blood is rushing in my ears and I cannot breathe. "Are you accusing me of something?"

He turns back to me and stares. "No."

It's all he says. One word. He doesn't say that I'm not a thief because he thinks I am. And well, I did take a postcard. My postcard.

"Why would I want it?" I shouldn't need to defend myself, but he's lying when he says he believes me innocent.

"The postcard files."

"What are you talking about? I shredded that card."

He leans his shoulders back against the wall. "Sorry. I'm going to have to report a theft. If…"

"I did not steal your laptop."

He turns to walk back to his door. "Sure. OK. You didn't even know I had the scan of the postcard."

"Stop. I did not steal a laptop. Are you kidding me? Scan? You have electronic images and you didn't tell me?"

He doesn't turn around which tells me he's thinking about my statement. Leo shakes his head and says, "I need to make a call. Forget it, Harper." Then he takes a step to his door.

I panic. "Don't walk away. We are talking—"

He ignores me and places his hand on his doorknob.

"Do not open that door."

He turns the knob without even slowing.

The fact that he's not listening to me burns me like a hot skillet. I should matter to him. My legs propel me forward and I jump him from behind. I jump like I'm shooting hoops—which I've never done but imagined—and straddle his back, hooking my arms around his neck and feet around his waist.

Leo wobbles from the unexpected impact

and then we are both going down. In slow motion, my brain registers the wood floor coming up to meet us. I don't have the reflexes nor time to react and let go.

Leo takes the brunt of the fall, going down with both hands slapping against the floor as he crouches with me on his back like a spider monkey. He loses his balance and goes to both knees with his hands on the floor.

"Get off! Trying to fucking break my legs."

I fall off his back and lower myself to the floor. He sits and then rolls back to look at the ceiling.

We lie side by side.

"What did you think you were doing?" he mutters in a dazed voice.

"Stopping you from walking away. Why couldn't you listen to me for a second? Who were you going to call?"

"I told you. The police. Is that why you stopped me? If you have the damned laptop, tell me. I won't file a report. Just give it back."

I smack him flat on the chest. "Oh. My. Gosh. I did not steal your laptop. I knew you were accusing me."

"No. I'm not. You said you don't have it. Do you think I'd really turn you in to the police?

I shrug. "Maybe. How would I know? You aren't speaking to me."

"I thought you were still mad that I hit that

guy."

"I am mad. But not crazy enough to steal your laptop to get back at you."

He snickers loud enough for me to hear. "Whatever you say."

"Did someone break-in?"

He turns his head to look at me. "Nope. And it's the only thing gone. I can buy another computer, but there's private stuff on there."

"Oh, don't tell me you have sex tapes."

He squeezes his eyes shut and my heart clunks to a stop. I don't want to imagine he's filmed himself with me, but even that vision is better than him filming another girl.

"Of course not," he says.

I sigh, relief rolling over my entire body.

I sit up on one elbow. Leo's silky hair falls over his eyes and I'd pay a hundred bucks I don't possess to run my fingers through it. I bite the inside of my mouth to distract me from the instinct to reach forward.

"I do the Mr. Expose blog with the understanding that some details will never be revealed. Plus, I don't want to be associated with it forever. Do you think I'll be taken seriously as a writer if people only think of me as Mr. Expose? It was only supposed to be something to make money until I'm able to sell my manuscripts."

"Oh. I've always taken you seriously." I

glance over at him.

"You haven't even read my writing." He turns his head and grins at me.

"Because you won't let me." I roll my eyes. "Speaking of the blog...I need the scan of my postcard."

"Why? Tell me what your obsession is with it."

"I object to you calling it an obsession."

He sighs, a low rumble that makes me smile, despite what's happened in the past minutes. "Please tell me about the postcard."

My belly whirls, making my skin tingle from the adrenaline. I brace myself for the leap of faith that he'll protect my secrets.

"If you printed the postcard, Wesley's daughter would find out the truth—that her father was a polygamist. I've suffered because of his lies, but I don't want to cause her more unhappiness. It's not right. If you printed the postcard, it would be news."

"I wouldn't have printed it. You only had to ask." He gets to his feet and gives me a hand up. The contact of his warm hand holding mine—if only for one instant—sends tingles along my body.

"I did ask. Remember? And then I decided to take it if you wouldn't hand it over to me. That was wrong, and I'm sorry." I take two steps to my door and put my key in the lock. "You don't know how someone got in to your apartment?" I turn to look at his face.

"Maybe I left it unlocked. I don't know."

I bite my lip and the bullet of shame. "It could've been locked. You still have the key under your mat?"

He throws me a sharp look. "I don't know. I used to hide one there a long time ago."

"Check it. That's how I got in when I looked for my postcard one day. Let me know if I can help look for your laptop."

With this confession, I let myself in and don't look back. New, honest beginnings.

Cover All the Bases

Leo

WHEN I WAS TEN, GRANDMA LULU spanked me for telling the guys that Josie didn't need a training bra 'because she didn't have any titties.' I'd made the vile comment to embarrass her because she stuck to me everywhere I went. It was a miracle she didn't insist on using the men's restroom.

Back then, I was angry over that spanking for a week and for many reasons. Reason one— it was no more than I would say to Josie's face. When I was a kid, I prayed for a brother. Repeatedly. One who didn't secretly blackmail me into playing dolls. Reason two—I was too old to be spanked. It was humiliating, which I guess was the point. Reason three—Grandma Lulu let Josie tell the boys I'd been disciplined for it and that each one would get the same if they ever disrespected any female again.

From the experience, I learned that I would be punished for taunting my sister and that Grandma Lulu and Josie stick together. Always.

So. Here I sit at the senior citizen facility facing a most uncomfortable situation. The semi-circle facing me feels like a firing squad. I'm positive Grandma Lulu or Josie intended it this way. They probably planned it together, giggling as they pictured my discomfort.

Grandma Lulu failed to mention anyone else would be attending breakfast. To my left is Josie, then Grandma Lulu, who sits in rapt attention to the person I'd hoped to never see again—Antonio. Harper sits quietly at his left and avoids my gaze.

"Well," I say. "Aren't I lucky to have lunch with *all* of you?" My stiff lips attempt a smile. "Antonio. That's an ugly black eye you have."

Antonio winks at me. "Perhaps it makes me look debonair." He turns and smiles at Grandma Lulu next to him.

"Nah. It doesn't." My hands ball into tight fists under the table. Is it wrong to deck a guy who is flirting with a woman four times his age?

Josie makes an Oscar the Grouch face at me. "I think it's hot."

Harper isn't saying a word. If she agrees, I may choke on the biscuit I've stuffed into my mouth so I'll stop speaking.

"Harper," Grandma Lulu says. "What are you and Antonio doing today?"

I flinch so hard I'll have whiplash. I'd thought maybe they were together only for the

294

breakfast.

They are actually dating. Harper is going to fall in love with this suave douchebag and I've let it happen. I practically forced her to get a life that doesn't involve me. My chest constricts and it's difficult to get a reasonable amount of air into my lungs.

Harper looks from Grandma Lulu to Antonio. She won't even make eye contact with me.

Perspiration pops up underneath the starched collar of my dress shirt. I loosen the knot of my tie. "Excuse me." I rise and my napkin falls from my lap onto the floor.

Josie picks it up. "Here."

I don't even say thank you. I fumble with it for a second before tossing it into my chair. "I can't stay. Sorry, Grandma Lulu. I'll call you later." I nod in the general direction of Harper and Antonio.

Then I'm striding away from the table as if the devil is on my heels.

I search around for a restroom and dart inside. It's empty and I lean back against the wall, studying the gray wallpaper. It blends with the gray tile floor. There's not a splash of color in the place. It's depressing and bleak.

Somebody needs to liven this place up a bit. Put a color on the walls. Stick a fake plant on the washbasin counter. It's a senior citizen's facility, for God's sake. It's like death in here.

I splash water onto my face and take my tie off. My face is pale, despite the heat I feel flushing my skin. Maybe I'm getting sick. That has to be the reason I feel so unbalanced. Plus, Josie and Grandma Lulu probably got together and decided to teach me a lesson with Antonio. Josie's unhappy that Harper and I broke up. That's it.

And Grandma Lulu loves Harper, too. It's evident from the way she brings her name up every time we speak.

It's a conspiracy between the females in my life. That's all it is. I force a smile to my lips. I've been fighting a battle against those two since I was a kid. I dry my face with a paper towel and study myself in the mirror.

My smile fades. Of all the things I love about Harper, it's her smile that I love most, and I don't think she smiled the entire time I sat across from her.

Antonio isn't making her happy. She was crying the last time I saw them together.

My pulse thumps louder, so loud I hear the undeniable truth in each beat. She's happy with me. I'm the one she's supposed to be with. If I don't stop allowing Tori to influence how I think about Harper, I'll end up like this gray bathroom—colorless and dead.

I know things can be different. My parents

were different. They loved each other madly until the day they parted this earth. Together. They're the ones who should color my view of love. Not Tori.

Get yourself together, man.

I leave the restroom a determined man. When I return to the dining hall, there's an empty chair where Harper was sitting. I glance around and hope she is okay.

Antonio stands before I can take a seat. "The ladies. They tell me there has been a misunderstanding."

That damned Italian accent. That's probably what lured Harper in. I may be a guy, but I know women love European accents.

"Oh?" I attempt to sound disinterested. If he's going to offer that we be friends or something, I'll have to inform him that I'm now officially the competition.

"I'm not trying to seduce Harper," he says.

Even Grandma Lulu has the decency to look embarrassed.

Antonio looks bashful. "Seduce is not what I meant. I'm saying that this is not a date. Josie invited me."

"Josie." I turn to my sister. "Where's Harper?"

Josie cocks her head. "She left. I tried to get her to stay, and she was upset. She didn't know we would be here."

"Are you happy now?" I shake my head at Josie and then glare at Grandma Lulu.

Grandma Lulu stands and places her hands on her wide hips. "You had this coming. Now go fix it."

I look at her, feeling like a school kid. She'd still chase me with a flyswatter if she could find one. "You're right."

Antonio gets to his feet. "Should I go find—"

"Casanova," I say, raising one eyebrow. "Don't even think about leaving this room."

He throws me a grin. "Catch her. Go."

I sprint to the parking lot and find she's already left. Damn she's fast. There's only one option for where she's going. I throw my car into reverse and peel out, heading home. Just in case I'm wrong, I try her number. It goes straight to voicemail.

When I pull into the apartment parking lot and see her car, I feel as though a giant weight has been lifted. I've been Atlas, carrying around a burden for weeks.

It takes all my self-control to slow down when I walk up the stairs. I've driven so fast that she was probably only minutes ahead.

When I finally unlock the outer door to the building and step inside, my heart stops. She's crouched over a box in front of my door with her hand covering her mouth.

"What's wrong?" I race to the door and pull

her up.

She's shaking her head frantically and backs away. "I know how bad this looks."

I don't release my hold on her shoulders. "Calm down." I glance down and look inside the box. It's a copy paper box filled with electronic parts and a smashed appliance. There's a disc drive and a motherboard. A small fan with cut wires.

Recognition settles in slowly. It's a destroyed laptop. On top sets a piece of paper with "XXOO, Harper" written on it.

"No. I did not do this." Harper takes a step back. "I'm so sorry. But you know I wouldn't. I couldn't."

I'm speechless. I look over my shoulder and down the hall. The heavy outer building door is firmly shut. Only someone with a key can enter.

"I know you wouldn't." I stare down into the box. I'd been trying to figure out the mystery of my missing laptop. Running over the events of Friday again and again, hoping to come up with something. I'd assumed that I'd left my apartment unlocked or that the culprit had found my key.

But I'd honestly forgotten about the new lock on the building's outer door. Until now.

She turns away from me. "I have no idea what's going on. I didn't steal it. And you say you believe me, but I have this awful feeling that deep down, you don't. I'm going to find a new place to live. You won't have to worry about running into me."

"I don't give a shit about this," I say, kicking the box. I kick it again for good measure. "And you aren't going to move."

She closes her eyes. "I saw your face when you walked into the dining hall this morning. You can't stand to be around me. And now when you see me here, you're going to picture this thing. This smashed up laptop you'll always associate with me. I have no way to prove I didn't do it." She steps away from me until her back hits her apartment door.

"Babe." I lower my voice and walk across the hall to be closer. "You didn't. I just know. Today at the senior facility? I wanted to jump over the table and beat Antonio's pretty face. I came back from the restroom to find you gone. I wanted to tell you that there was going to be trouble."

"What kind of trouble?"

"Antonio might have all the moves, but I have all the right words."

She stares at me. "There's nothing between me and Antonio," she whispers.

I grab her hand and press it to my chest over my heart. "Feel that? It's full of all these sappy words I haven't said. Emotions I couldn't handle. But I think it took realizing I could lose you. I'm not going to let fear win. I can't."

Harper's lips tremble and she looks away. "I want to believe in you. I do. But it's too big of a risk."

"Look at me, Harper. I'm crazy about you. I'm a sure bet. "

She gives me a half-hearted smile. "No. You're a high-stakes gamble. I did want to trust you before. Now, it's just too late."

She turns, enters her apartment, and leaves me standing in the hallway—my world turned gray.

***

I stretch my arms out above my head. It's still early, but the sounds of the bakery already drift up through the vents. Today, I begin my new life as a romantic. A hopeful. A believer in forever.

I pull on my clothes and walk downstairs. James is working the counter and Erik is in the back this morning. I examine my choices and my mouth waters.

"Morning. What'll you have?" James stands poised with a waxed paper ready.

"Cinnamon rolls. Four, please."

"Coming right up." He grabs the pastry and a white box. "Did Harper's friend find her?"

"I don't know," I say, getting my wallet out.

"I forget about the new lock. The girl came in saying she was supposed to meet Harper but couldn't get in. Sorry about that."

"No problem." I smile at him. "I'll let Harper know."

"Well, good. She said Harper would be really upset if she didn't get in." James waves off the bill I attempt to hand him.

I frown. Harper doesn't get mad at anyone. A tingle travels down my spine. "When was this?"

"Yesterday. The girl asked if she could borrow the key to get in for a few minutes."

"Did she have dark hair? Tall? Prissy?"

"Yeah," he says with a chuckle. "Prissy fits. She came back yesterday afternoon and said she'd forgotten to bring me the key back."

"Uh huh. We're going to have to get the lock changed."

"Problem?"

"Yeah. I'll pay for a locksmith. Are you cool with that? I'll get it done today and bring you new keys. Also if that girl comes back, call me. No one should be let in."

"Got it. Sorry if it was a mistake." James looks to the next person in line.

I eat one roll on the way upstairs. There are some things I need to remedy in my life and Tori is first on my list. I grab a red marker from my apartment and write on the white bakery bag—

'Sweets for the sweet.'

After showering, I tape the bag to Harper's door. Her words last night cut into my heart. I had expected a second chance. What if she never gives it to me?

I push the negative thoughts away. I have changes to make in my life, beginning now.

It takes forty-five minutes to drive to Tori's salon. Her doors aren't open yet, so I wait in a parking space. She's always late. It shouldn't surprise me when the front doors don't open on time.

When I walk inside, Tori sits in a styling chair. She flips through a magazine and doesn't notice me.

A receptionist greets me. "Good morning. What can we do to help you?"

"Tori," I say, pointing at her.

Her head pops up. "Leo. What a nice surprise." She looks around. Two stylists prep their stations. "We can talk privately in the back."

"No. That's all right. We can talk here."

She studies herself in the mirror and fidgets with her ring, spinning it around on her finger. It's her wedding set. She must wear it sometimes and certainly didn't expect me to show up today.

"I know you came by the apartment yesterday." I give her a hard look, my eyes narrowed.

"You're mistaken," Tori says.

The girl at the next station glances over curiously. I nod at her and return my attention to Tori.

"If you ever step foot in the building again, I'll do two things. I'll call the police, since you will be breaking and entering."

"I have no idea what you're talking about." She laughs, her lips tight in a fake smile.

"I'll also print a column about you and all your lies, every tiny deceitful thing you've done, on Mr. Expose. Have you heard of it? I'm Mr. Expose." I know she has heard of it. Even Good Morning America talked about the popularity of my blog, calling it the new generation of reality television.

I'm no longer ashamed of what I've been doing with my writing. It's print journalism that helps uncover the truth.

Her mouth drops and the other stylists stop what they're doing.

"So think about it," I say. "You'll be the talk of Nashville. Everyone will know what a bitch you are."

"You wouldn't." She takes a couple of steps forward.

"I would." I turn to the other stylists. "Have a nice day, ladies."

I turn my back on her and leave, betting she

won't stab me in the back with styling sheers since we have witnesses.

Eleventh Hour

Harper

"FRESH BAKED CINNAMON ROLLS. YUM." Josie munches on one and licks the sugar from her fingertips. "He wrote you a love note on the bag. Don't you think this is romantic?"

"Um...no. That's hardly a love note." I bite into my own pastry. "Sticking baked goods to my door doesn't change anything."

She lowers her chin and looks up at me with sad, puppy eyes. "Come on. Harper. I can vouch for him. He needs a second chance."

"Second?" I make a scoffing sound. "I appreciate that you love him and want us together, but I can't do it."

There's a deep, stabbing ache in my chest whenever I think about Leo. I look away from Josie so she won't see it in my eyes. The pastry suddenly tastes bitter and I throw it in the trash.

Josie glances at her cell phone. "What time is your flight?"

"At ten. Thanks for coming by. I guess I'd

better head that way." I grab my purse and suitcase.

Josie throws her arms around me. "Text me. Call me. Whatever."

"You know I will." I give her a too-bright smile. It feels odd to be leaving my little apartment and this life I've made, even if it's only for a visit home. "You don't want to come with me?"

She releases her hold on me and pulls back with a pout on her face. "I can't leave the bookstore. Or I would."

"I know. Thanks."

"For what?"

"For everything. For being a terrific friend."

***

I've been away from Austin, Texas for four and half years. In that time, nothing has really changed. I guess I expected my hometown to look different somehow.

I maneuver the rental car into a metered parking spot in front of Starbucks. My cell dings with an incoming text as I turn off the motor.

Josie: *Where r u now?*

Me: *Hey. Haven't even made it home yet. Supposed to meet a friend for a coffee first.*

Josie: *Can I get your parents address? In case I can get away from the store?*

Me: *Sure.*

I text the address before poking change into the parking meter. When I enter the coffee shop I'm glad to see it isn't crowded. There's an empty table near the windows. I order an iced coffee and head for it. This meeting has been coming for a while and I'm surprised at the excited, anxious feeling fluttering in my belly.

I've seen one photo of Isabella while researching online. I'm curious. I was surprised when I learned her age and Wesley's real age— both a decade older than myself.

I scan the cars as they pass on the street.

The café's door opens. A woman steps inside and holds the door.

A young girl with chestnut hair and chocolate-colored eyes in a wheelchair enters, her grin lopsided. She's young, female version of Wesley.

"Harper!" She wheels to the first table in her way and stops. I realize I should've chosen a better table and hop up to switch seats.

"Hey there. How did you recognize me?"

She tilts her head. "Your picture is attached to your email address. I asked Mom to show me since you guys are friends. Your picture is so old. You're much prettier in person."

"Oh. I don't ever go online." I glance up at Isabella. We'd agreed that she would tell Charley I'm a family friend. It's the truth.

Isabella is blonde and slim, with a heart-shaped face. Her coloring matches mine and it's startling that we sort of resemble one another. We could be sisters.

"Hi Harper. So nice to finally meet you," Isabella says.

I hold out my hand and she shakes her head. I'm confused, but then she takes the steps to close the distance and hugs me. When she draws back, she has tears in her eyes.

"Yes, finally." The hug feels nice, the kind from a long-lost friend. I'm intensely relieved that it isn't weird at all.

Charley attempts to move a chair to the side of the table. "Mom?"

"Got it. Don't be so impatient," Isabella says, arranging our table so Charley has plenty of room. She looks to me. "You two sit tight and I'll get some drinks."

She walks to the counter and I smile at Charley. "So. Tell me about your school. What's your favorite class?"

Charley launches into detailed explanation of her computer classes that she loves. "My dad taught me how to code, so I'm way ahead of all the other kids in the programming class." She pauses. "You knew my dad, right?"

"Yeah. I did." I keep my voice neutral even though the thought of Wesley and his secret double life still affects me. "He was a coder?"

Something sad flickers across her features

only for a moment. Then, it lifts. "Pft! He was the best one around. There's the guy in my programming class who looks exactly like Harry Styles."

"Who's that?" I grin at her.

"You don't know." Her lips quirk. "One Direction?" She grabs her phone and searches for something to show me.

Just like that, her focus changes from talking about her dad to a cute boy she has a crush on. When Isabella returns with the drinks for her and Charley, I can't stop smiling.

I've done the right thing. Revealing the truth would only hurt an innocent girl. Maybe someday, Isabella will tell her. I don't know. But I'm glad it's not for me to decide.

*****

I drive to my parents' house with the lightest feeling in ages. Pulling into the driveway is surreal. It's a modest neighborhood with houses lined in a straight row. It's the house I grew up in. A massive oak shades the front lawn and there's still a bare spot where the grass doesn't grow.

The curtains of the front window pull back and Mama's face appears. She waves and the curtain drops.

My belly does a nervous flip as I park the

car. I'd hoped she would run outside and greet me.

Although we've been cordial on the phone, I know they'll never forgive me for running off with Wesley and only leaving a note to explain.

I get out of the car. Baby steps.

Mama opens the door and waits for me. Her smile is huge. "Where have you been? We thought your flight landed at two-thirty."

I can't stop myself from running to the door and hugging her. "Mama, I've missed you so much."

I feel like I'm back with my best friend, my confidante, my mentor. I swallow the lump in my throat.

She hugs me back and pulls me inside. "It's so good to have you home."

The minute I walk inside, I glance around and my throat tightens. Maybe my homecoming isn't going to be easy after all. "Where's Daddy?"

I search my brain for all the reasons he'd be missing. Maybe he had a church function he couldn't miss. Or someone is in the hospital.

"He's in the kitchen." Mama takes me hand. "Come on. He's watching the oven. Cookies are almost done."

"Oh. OK." I walk with Mama through the house and into my favorite room. It's the one I've thought about the most when I missed home. The aromas of chocolate and vanilla hit me. And a different scent drifts through the air.

I turn the corner behind Mama and all I see are flowers. Flowers everywhere—on the table, on the counter beside the oven, on the rolling cart with the microwave. There are roses and lilies and sunflowers.

"Has someone died?" I mumble. There has to be a dozen arrangements scattered around the room.

She grins at me. "They're all for you."

"You didn't have to do that. This must've cost a fortune."

Daddy pulls a pan from the oven and tosses the mitt aside. He holds out his arms, waiting for me. "Sweet Angel. It's about time."

I fling myself into his arms. "Daddy." His arms close around me in a tight, comforting hug. He smells of the same aftershave he's worn since I was a kid. It's as though I never left.

"It's good to have you home," he says. He releases me slowly. "This young man sent all the flowers."

My head jerks up. "What?"

Daddy takes my shoulders and turns me. "Leo. He sent them."

Leo sits at the far end of the table. "Hi," he says softly.

My heart lodges in my throat. "You shouldn't be here."

"Yes. I know." His intense gaze studies me.

"I've been telling your father that you may throw me out. But I wanted to meet your parents in case you decide to forgive me. Actually, Josie scared me pretty bad. She didn't tell me you were only visiting. But that doesn't matter. I still would've come."

My mouth tips up at one corner. Oh, interfering Josie. You've gotta love her. "You need to do something about your sister."

"Yeah. I've been trying for years. There's no stopping her." He grins. "I'm going to a hotel room. You should spend time with your folks. But I have more to say to you. If you'll let me."

I only nod, overwhelmed and conflicted. Leo shakes Daddy's hand and Mama walks him to the door. Then, he's gone.

I sit at the table and scoot a vase of pink roses to the side so I can see my parents. "I...um...dated Leo, and we broke up. That's what all this is about." I wave my hand at the flowers.

"He seems like a very nice man." Mama smiles. "He told us he lives next door to you. He also told us about his parents and twin and his writing. Oh, and that online thing. Blog?"

My mouth drops. "He told you all that? How long was he here?"

Daddy takes the seat next to me. "Maybe half an hour."

I stare at Daddy. "And he just started giving

his whole life history?"

Daddy chuckles and shakes his head. "He said he wanted us to know everything about him. That boy sure is over the moon for you. I like him all right, and he's a talker. The gift of speech. Has he ever thought about the ministry?"

"No, Daddy. He's really not a talker. He's more the introverted type." A buried part of hope leaps out of my heart, screaming at me to see what he's done.

Daddy nods, thoughtful. There's a long silence. "You must be very important to him, then. Men like Leo don't just spill everything to strangers on a whim. He's committed to you."

I gulp, my skin hot and my nerves tingling. There's a reason I ran off with Wesley as an eighteen-year-old and didn't give my parents a chance to talk sense into me. Deep down, I'd known something was wrong. They would've known it and told me so.

They don't even hesitate with Leo. It's clear he's not hiding anything. When I was eighteen, I was sure they were always wrong. At twenty-two, I know they're right.

"Do you mind if I call Leo really quick? I know I just got here, but..."

Mama places her hand on top of mine. "Angel, he's on the front porch. He called a cab and he's waiting outside."

I rush to my feet so quickly, my head spins. In another two seconds, I'm out the door and running to the steps. I knock into Leo, who sits on a step. He catches my legs before I can tumble down.

"Whoa." He releases me.

I suck in air. "Why are you here?"

"Cab. I called—"

"No." I shake my head frantically. "I mean, tell me why you followed me."

"Can you sit?" He shifts over to make room on the brick step.

I sit next to him, sticking my shaky hands between my knees. Leo turns his indigo gaze on full force, dangerous as radiation. I feel myself melting.

"Because I can be as stubborn as you are." He grins. "I never wanted to get back together with Tori. But I wasn't letting her go either. I kept thinking about what she'd done to me and how it could happen again. And then you came along and wrecked all my intentions to stay unattached. I lied to myself, saying my life would be less complicated that way. But it was just that. A lie."

He reaches across and takes my hand in his, linking our fingers. "If I thought I could forget about you, I would. It's what you've asked me to do. Leave you alone. But I can't."

Leo brings my knuckles to his lips and

kisses them. "So, I sent flowers and tried to win over your parents and I've written a post on Mr. Expose about my identity. About not hiding behind a facade with the people who are important in my life. I'm playing all my cards. That's why."

The cab pulls to the curb. I unlace my fingers from Leo's. "So you're saying you're not a quitter," I whisper. My heartbeat thrums in my head.

"That's it. Basically. And that I'm in love with you."

My breath catches at this simple phrase, one I know he doesn't take lightly. "That reason works for me." I grab his shirt. "Now shut up and kiss me."

Daddy opens the door and sends the cab away.

Leo lowers his head. "Whatever the woman wants."

The End

the
Fiction of Forever

BRINDA BERRY

About the book:

He has a second chance at the one who got away—but it's on national television, and she's calling the shots.

Kiley Vanderbilt wasn't just fuel for Gunner's teenage dreams about the curvy pageant queen. She was the one who got away.

Until now.

When Gunner returns to Nashville, his high school fantasy in heels challenges him to accept a spot on the dating reality show Forever. And although she's the show hostess and off-limits, he's going to prove once and for all that she wants more.

Fourteen days of filming. Six camera crews. And a minefield of hidden cameras. This time, no one's getting away.

Forever and a Day

High School, Sophomore Year

Gunner

I GET SWEATY HANDS when I look at Kiley Vanderbilt. Another part of me notices as well, but I fight to ignore that awkward fact as much as possible when in public.

In private, I worship the photos on my phone. Worship might sound a little creepy. Actually, it sounds a lot creepy. I prefer to think of my photo collection as our pre-dating album.

Kiley is every guy's dream girl.

In my favorite photo, she wears a tiny pink bikini. I snapped it at her sixteenth birthday party last summer. She'd been standing by the edge of her outdoor pool talking to my friend Aiden, an all-right guy, when he isn't hitting on the girl who should be with me.

I conveniently cropped him out of the photo.

The photo isn't my favorite because she's almost naked. I appreciate all her curves, but mostly I like the shot because she looks happy.

319

Her eyes dance with the pleasure of having all her friends around, or maybe of turning sixteen so she can drive the SUV her daddy bought her. Whatever it is, I want to know what gives her this feeling so I can make her look at me like that all the time.

Tonight is the night I'm going to make my move. I've just played the best game of the football season and everybody's been congratulating me on winning the game.

Kiley sneaks looks from beneath her dark lashes whenever I'm in her line of sight. She smiles that smile where she holds back a little.

Shy. It's not like her and the chatterbox that she is, which tells me a lot. She likes me. Maybe she has a photo of me on her phone.

A hand touches my back.

"Hey, Gunner. Nice pass in the fourth quarter," Jenna says.

"Thanks." I sip from my red plastic cup and hope she'll leave. I like Jenna but Kiley's moving closer to the bonfire. It's my chance to get her alone.

Jenna takes a couple of steps to stand in front of me, blocking my view of Kiley. "I was wondering something."

"What's that?" I crane my head to the left to make sure Kiley's still alone. Dang. Now some douchebag from another school is moving in on her and handing over his football jacket.

"Well, I don't have a date for the dance next Friday."

"Hm." I take another sip.

"Gunner?"

"Yeah?"

"I thought maybe we could go together."

"That's really nice of you. But...um...I was going to ask someone else tonight."

Jenna follows my gaze to the bonfire and Kiley. Kiley who takes the jacket from the guy I don't know.

"I hope you don't mind if I give you some advice." Jenna's voice is low, as if she's giving me top-secret info.

"What's that?"

"Kiley's nice. And she's my friend. But..."

"But what?" I narrow my eyes. It's hard to switch between focusing on what Jenna has to say and making sure Kiley doesn't get away before I can talk to her.

She shrugs. "She doesn't date anyone for long. I don't want you to get hurt."

Jenna places her hand on my arm, as if she's offering me consolation.

"Well, thanks Jenna, but I've known Kiley all my life. I'm not too worried about it." I lift my plastic cup to take a gulp. She drops her too-friendly hold on my arm.

"I'll see you later. All out of drink," I say, holding up my cup to give some kind of reason to get away from her.

"Sure," she says and looks over at the bonfire where Kiley stands.

I guess I'm not very subtle, but I'm limited on time. It's the first time in a while since I've gone out after a game. Mom's cancer diagnosis moved everything else in my life to the unimportant list.

In minutes, I'm across the field and standing before the most beautiful girl in Tennessee. It's been documented. Pageant judges put a crown on this girl every time she steps on a stage.

"Hi." Kiley says. "You were fantastic tonight. You were generous to pass so much. I know you could've run that ball down the field every time."

I shrug and an embarrassing heat floods my face. I'm not good with compliments. Other guys may need them, but I don't. I'm a team player, not a glory hound.

My gut churns with anxiety all of a sudden. Why does she make me so nervous? I've planned everything I want to say and if the douchebag to her left will get out of the way, I can.

Kiley removes said douchebag's jacket and hands it to him. "I'm warm now. Here you go."

He takes it from her reluctantly. "Are you sure?"

"Yeah. Gunner, can you walk me to my car?

I need to get something."

"I guess I can do that." Slap my stupid mouth. Of course I'll walk with her. I'd walk to the moon and back if she asked. Hopefully, I'll only have to master talking to her without saying something stupid.

She leads the way to the area of the field where she's parked. Kiley's dad always lets us set up the field parties on his land. He's the coolest dad I ever heard of.

I walk beside her and look straight ahead, rehearsing my speech about how we should go to the dance together. We're a couple hundred yards from the bonfire when I know it's the right time.

"Kiley—" I say.

"Hey, I—" she says at the same time.

We both laugh. Hopefully, mine didn't sound as nerdish as I feel like it did.

"You first," I say. Look at her. I turn my head and damn if the girl doesn't take my breath away. It's sappy and true and terrifying.

Only the moon and stars illuminate her face, but it still shines with a beauty like nothing else.

She twists her hands in front of her and then turns to look at me, hopping a little as she walks. It's cute because she seems excited.

I glance at her again. She messes with straightening the bottom of her mini-dress.

She's so hot with that mid-thigh dress and cowboy boots. My brain sends an emergency alert message to my dick every time I look at her.

God, I hope she doesn't bend over in that. I have enough problems without adding an aneurism or blue balls to the list.

"Want to sit in my vehicle and talk?" she asks. "It's chilly tonight."

"Yeah," I say in a near croak. Calm down, calm down, calm down. You'd think she asked me to party naked with her.

Is that really what she's asking?

My gut churns. Shit. One aneurism, order up.

We get to her SUV and she clicks the key fob to unlock the doors. Her vehicle's parked behind a thicket of tall brush. Once I'm sitting in the passenger seat and looking at the front windshield, I exhale rather noisily. We're practically hidden from seeing what's going yards away at the bonfire. Even the music sounds dim and faraway.

"So," she says and shivers. "Are you excited about the state fair?"

"Not really." I turn to her. Oh, shit. That was a stupid thing to say. Does she want me to take her? Now I'll be the dumbass who says he doesn't like fairs and then asks her.

I try to think of something to say. Anything

that will help me get past the usual talking-to-Kiley panic.

"I haven't seen you around much. Now that we don't have classes together this year…"

"I've been busy." I could tell her my mom's been so sick that I don't have time to think about much else. If I wanted to put a downer into this conversation, the topic of Mom's cancer would certainly do it.

"Classes are killing me this year," I say.

"Oh."

"I wish we did have classes together. You still doing the pageant thing?" I search my brain for something—anything else to talk about. I don't want to talk about how my home life sucks.

"Yes. I was in one last weekend." She pauses. "I was wondering… Are you dating anybody?" she asks.

"No." Her question surprises me and heat creeps into my face. I inhale and try to stay cool. I don't want to say that I'm not interested in anyone but her. Even I'm smart enough to know that's coming on too strong. Or is it?

"Oh. That surprises me." She gives me that smile I've been waiting for. The one from the photo where all her happy vibes point at me, as if I'm the one who made it happen.

Be honest. That's what I need to do. Make this moment count. "I want it to be the right girl,

325

not just any girl." Great. Now I'm the emo douchebag.

Her grin continues and loosens the worry in my gut. She likes that thought.

"Me, too," she says. "Not the right girl, but the right guy...you know what I mean."

"Yeah. I know."

We sit in silence and look at the front glass. A layer of condensation films across it, hiding the rest of the party.

"Want to kiss me?" she asks.

My heart rams into my throat. "I...um...who wouldn't?"

She straightens the edge of her skirt. "Funny," she says.

But I'm not joking. Doesn't she know how I've wanted to ask her out all year?

"Maybe you don't." She runs fingers through her dark hair, lifting it off her face. "You're in a secluded car with me and you haven't tried anything. So, I'm not sure."

I will certainly die at any moment.

Happy.

Maybe not totally happy, because I'd like more than a kiss.

She's waiting for a response from me and I'm not sure if I should yell, "Hell yes," or go for it.

"But I understand if you only want to be friends," she says, but doesn't move. "It might be weird since we've known each other forever."

I lean over the top of the console and I'm not sure what to do with my hands. Feeling her up will probably be more than she's bargained for tonight.

Her breathing is shallow, her gaze locked to mine. She smells like the most delicious thing I've ever smelled—something flowery and heady.

Pretty and perfect.

She stares at my mouth as I come closer. The car's console digs against my waist. I can't control my hands.

Without my permission, they move to slide against her neck and pull her closer, linking in her silky hair and capturing the back of her head in my hold.

She licks those full, pink lips.

I slant my mouth to touch hers in a light kiss, then pull back and look at her with our noses barely touching. "You feel like the right girl."

Kiley's eyes dance at my words. She grabs the sides of my jacket and kisses me, her tongue sweeping across the inside of my lips. I move one hand from her neck to snake down her back, her sweater soft as a rabbit's fur.

I press her close to my chest. She skates her hands into my open jacket and around my back. The tension shooting through me rivals running down the football field with somebody on my ass. Our mouths move hungrily against each other's. I graze my teeth along her full bottom lip and there's nothing I'd like more than to eat her up.

Her fingers tighten their grasp on my shirt, her fingernails barely skimming my back. She feels better than I imagined. The console prevents me from pulling more of her body against mine.

We break apart panting, our air mingling.

"We'd have more room in the backseat." I regret my words when her brow furrows. Shit! Now she thinks I'm expecting to get laid. "Only kissing. Promise."

She gulps so loud I hear it. "OK."

I open my door and run around to the driver's side to open hers. She steps out and gives me a shy smile.

Both of us are shaking from the cold by the time we're in the backseat. I take off my jacket and wrap it around her.

She leans against me, her teeth clicking together from the chill. "This is nice."

"Yeah."

"I've always had a crush on you, Gunner Parrish."

I smile with my head above hers and out of sight. "I've always had a thing for you, too."

"Good," she says. She turns into me, her

hands running over my chest and her lips meeting mine.

Our kiss escalates with my tongue darting into her sweet mouth and my hands skating up and down her back, over her sides so near the swell of her breasts.

Her hands find the bottom of my untucked shirt and skim higher on my bare skin.

My heart's beating so hard it's sure to explode at any moment. A kiss was all I wanted, but I think she loves this as much as I do.

More might happen. My life sucks lately, but this night might redeem all the suckage and make it bearable.

Kiley moves a hand to the front of my chest to rest over my pounding heart. She pulls her lips back. "I don't want you to think that I do this—"

"Shush," I say and stroke her hair back from her face. "I don't make out with just any girl. Unless it's the right girl. And this is the beginning, not a one-time thing."

I don't tell her that I'm a virgin. That I'm scared shitless that we'll go too far or not far enough. That I'm scared this thing between us will slip through my fingers and I'll wake from a dream.

"God, you're so beautiful." I whisper the words as I lean forward and kiss the edge of her jaw, the crook of her neck, the base of her throat.

She unbuttons the top buttons of my shirt and stares at the open V of my shirt collar. "Your skin is so warm."

I tentatively touch the top button of her sweater. My gaze flicks from the button, up to her eyes. She nods without me having to ask. I unbutton three buttons of her cardigan painfully slow. If I don't stay slow and steady, she'll see how much I want to race down her buttons and shove the sweater down off her shoulders. Her white lace bra peeks from the top of the opening and my dick gets even harder, if that's possible.

Our eyes lock on one another. Daring each other because our heartbeats match rhythm in time. Ba boom. Ba boom. Ba boom. Then my mouth crashes onto hers and I'm wrestling with her buttons and she threads her fingers through my hair.

Kiley falls back against the seat and I slide on top of her, pressing my erection against her thigh and not caring that she'll know.

We're beyond being coy.

Meeep. Meeeep. Meeep.

It takes more than a second to realize it's my ringtone—the one that sounds like a weather alert warning. Reserved for only one person in my contacts, the sound causes my heart rate to jump for a different reason.

"Just a sec," I gasp.

We break apart and I struggle to pull the phone from my pocket.

"Hello," I answer. She never calls unless it's important.

"Um...Gunner? Sorry to bother you while you're out."

"Mom. What is it?"

"I'm sick and think I should probably go to the emergency room. That last round of chemo really did a number on me. I can't quit vomiting."

A wave of pure panic washes over me. "I'm coming."

"Don't speed," she says. Her weak voice scares the hell out of me.

Kiley's wide eyes are sympathetic, but I don't have time to explain. "Is everything OK? Do you need me—"

"No. Gotta go." I leave Kiley in the backseat without explanation and run faster than I ever have on the football field. I run because I shouldn't have left Mom alone in the house.

She'd begged me to go and let her have some time to rest. Read a book. Watch a movie without me hovering. But I was wrong to leave. I don't have time for high school or Kiley Vanderbilt.

I run because Mom wouldn't call me unless it was bad.

Animosity

Current Day

Kiley

THE FITTING ROOM OF VISIONS BRIDAL smells like designer perfume, new fabric, and old money. I fidget in front of the three-way mirror and my wedding gown of silk and lace whispers against my skin. I've dreamed about this moment most my life.

Except, a woozy feeling swirls in my gut. Things are very wrong with this picture of happily-ever-after.

Perhaps my wooziness is only because I'm sweating more than a hardcore dieter in an ice cream shop. Lately, I've drowned my nerves in tubs of mocha chocolate chip, as evidenced by the snug fit of my wedding dress that I naively bought a size too small.

I wave my hand in front of my face to circulate air and ironically crave more ice cream.

The overly cheerful woman working at Visions kneels behind me, fluffing the elaborate train. The gilded mirror of the empty shop reveals my every angle. My fiancé, Mason, ignores me in favor of checking email or texting while he sits in a small velvet chair. Why did he insist on coming if he isn't going to pay attention?

The Visions' store clerk, an attractive middle-aged woman, finally stands, walks around in front of me, then stares at my chest. "Kiley, I think it's gorgeous. Breathtaking. Does it feel all right? I don't think we can take out the bosom anymore. We don't want to ruin the drape of the Leavers lace. We couldn't take the risk."

"Mm hm." I can't say more because I need to conserve my energy for sucking in and shallow breathing.

The pearl encrusted lace bodice itches like a fiberglass bra, and I rub two fingers inside the fabric encasing my cleavage. If I weren't waiting for Mason to look up from his phone, I'd be changing. Pronto.

"Mason? Remind me again why you insisted on coming to this fitting? You're not even looking."

He swipes a finger across his cell phone display. "Oh, of course I am." He lifts his head and eyes me approvingly with small nods of his head.

I attempt to calm down. The last thing I want is to start another fight with him. Unclenching my fists and my jaw, I inhale and exhale and inhale again. I examine the bodice for any signs that one more inhale will bust a seam. Who knew breathing could be dangerous?

Pre-Wedding Disappointment #1: Not sticking to tradition where the groom doesn't see the bride until she walks down the aisle, one of those old-fashioned ideas I had about weddings.

We're the new-age, non-sentimental couple. No secrets between us, he'd said. I'm a little sad that he won't be surprised to see my gorgeous gown.

Disappointment #2, that led to fights one through three of the week: Him telling me how to wear my hair for the wedding, which jewelry is acceptable—a pearl choker he gave me for a wedding gift that's uglier than a hairless cat, and last, his arrangement for us to spend our wedding night at his parents' home in Dallas before we leave on our honeymoon. He's crazy if he thinks I want to spend a night of passion with his parents twenty feet down the hallway.

Disappointment #3: He's taken to buying me gifts instead of apologizing when he is clearly in the wrong. A second wedding gift of lingerie, white sheer panties that will give me a wedgie before I make it to the altar and won't make me forget our huge argument about a prenup.

He clears his throat. "My mother said she's going to have to add fifty people to the wedding list. They're friends of my father's," he says. "It's so late now, they'll know they were forgotten from the original list. You won't mind if she tells them you forgot to send their invitations..."

He keeps talking, but I shift my attention to my reflection. His mother. He's already agreed to what she wants without asking what I thought.

He gives the store clerk a dazzling smile reserved for pretty female witnesses in the courtroom. "Miss, I'd bet you've heard every word I've said." He adds a wink. "But my future bride seems distracted. Do you mind stepping out for one minute so I can talk with her in private?"

The woman flushes and returns an approving smile. "Of course."

He stares at me in the mirror. "You see my point?"

"Oh. Sorry. What were you saying?"

He offers me an impatient smile, so tight his lips disappear. "We have to talk about your dad's show."

"Now? We've been over this." I tug at the confining bodice. He's not going to like it when I strip down naked in the middle of the store.

He smiles again. "I think we need to clear the air before I leave for New York. My flight leaves in a couple of hours."

"You're leaving early?"

"I must've forgotten to tell you." He finally puts the flipping phone in his pocket. "I know you're slated to star in Forever this season, but it's ludicrous. You don't need a career. Being my wife will be a full-time job."

Mason crosses one leg across the other to rest an ankle on his knee. He's not wearing socks with his cream summer suit, and I focus on his tan skin—courtesy of a "work" trip he took alone to the Bahamas last month.

"I can't believe we're going to talk about this again. I'm tired of arguing with you."

"I don't want my wife working instead of concentrating on our family. I've ordered credit cards for you. You'll have an allowance."

"An allowance?" I frown into the three-way mirror. "I'm not a teenager."

"You're acting like one."

I pull the bodice from my skin to give me some relief. Deep breath. "I have wanted to be on the show ever since the first season. This is very important to me."

"For Christ's sake, it's a reality show."

Mason rolls his eyes. "You know I won't be stingy with you when it comes to money. You're accustomed to your father's bank account. I understand."

"I don't care about the money. It's something I want to do with my degree. I know Forever isn't broadcast journalism, but I have a knack for this. I've been matching up my friends with the right guys since high school. I'm good at matchmaking and this will get me noticed. It could open the door to all kinds of opportunities." His expression says he doesn't understand.

Money makes sense to him. I should stick to mentioning what I'll get paid.

He sighs and narrows his gaze. It's a hard look, one I'm not used to seeing from him. "You're not single anymore. You think it sounds exciting to be on television. I get that. But can you think about me for once? What about my needs?"

He gets to his feet and strolls toward the mirror without breaking eye contact. Placing his hands on my shoulders, he leans in and kisses the back of my neck in a brief, perfunctory way.

When he lifts his head, his face is corporate serious. "I'm going to be honest. I should've stated this earlier. There is no fucking way my wife can be on a reality show. It's a bad idea. I'll be the laughing stock of the firm. If you ever

337

want me to make it past junior partner—"

"I can't believe you're asking me to sit at home and wait for you to come home every day." My voice cracks. I stand straighter so I can get some air into my lungs. I can't look at him, with his concerned look, as if I'm the one ruining some perfect plan he has for our life.

He moves both hands to my upper arms and squeezes lightly, the pressure making me look at him again in the mirror.

"I didn't realize you put this reality show over our marriage. I've never kept my career goals a secret. But when I put that ring on your finger, you agreed to a partnership," he says.

"Giving up everything I want sure sounds like a dictatorship."

He caresses my shoulders. The three-way-reflection doesn't lie, portraying how nice we look together—he in the tailored suit, me in the pearl and gossamer, albeit itchy, gown.

Walking around me so we're face-to-face, he grabs my chin and tugs my face upward. "My sweet girl. I love your ambition. I do. But what happens when we have children? Will your wants and needs come before them? Maybe you'll send them off to summer camps and miss their recitals because you were busy."

I'm suddenly a little girl again, hundreds of miles away at a summer camp with strangers. Looking into the dark audience at the ballet recital hall, pretending my dad is out there watching, only to discover my nanny at the end of the performance.

Too many years of being homesick and heartsick. For too long the need to talk louder, be prettier, and basically perform a freaking tap dance overcame me whenever Dad entered a room.

I struggle to control the quiver in my voice. "That's not fair and you know it."

"You're right. It wasn't." He folds me into his arms. "I know you aren't your father."

Mason doesn't even mention my mother— he knows better than to go that far. I nod, unable to speak past the need to rant, but knowing I won't. He's a trial lawyer. Strategy is his game, not mine.

He kisses me gently and steps back. "I want you to know I have a plan for a financially successful family life. I don't want my wife trying to juggle a career and the people she loves. I don't want you to have to choose."

"Women today don't have to choose."

"And who told you that? Your feminist friends?" He shakes his head. "We can talk about it later. I can't miss this flight. I'll see you back in Nashville."

I look at myself in the mirror and pretend to adjust the bodice of my dress. If I don't keep my hands busy, I may succumb to punching him in the throat for the feminist remark.

How have I missed this small yet important attitude about women?

"Don't pout," he says. "Where's my future bride I love so much?"

"Not pouting." I allow one corner of my mouth to lift in a half-hearted smile. I'm overreacting. He's parroting his father and the handful of partners I've met at the firm. All male.

He'll learn I'm my own person and plan to have a career.

"Oh," he says and looks at his cell. "I almost forgot. We have to host a dinner party on Friday night. It's very important that we make a good impression. We can use your father's house since he's on that cruise. My apartment isn't right for this."

"This Friday? As in a few days from today?"

"Plenty of time. Three couples from the firm. And you'll do a fantastic job because you are my incredible Kiley." He tweaks my nose, something I hate but I'm not fast enough to step back and avoid. He walks toward the door of the shop.

I pick up the yards of gossamer fabric circling my legs and twirl to watch him go. "But that's not enough notice. No one can arrange a dinner party of that size this quickly."

He smiles at me with the confidence of a

newly promoted junior partner of Ellison, Montgomery, and Caldwell, LLP. "Of course you can. But if you don't feel up to it, call my mother. She'd love to help."

I bet. She'd love to prove I can't do it alone.

He checks his phone. "I'll talk to you tomorrow. I hope you won't be upset with me. I know you. I know where your heart is and what will make you happy. And see? You thought you could handle the stress of a television show and you're getting stressed out over a meal."

I hear the chime of the door as he leaves the bridal shop. I close my eyes and exhale in a long shuddering breath. Pre-wedding jitters dance around my brain, taunting me. I've known what kind of man Mason is. I wanted a man who wants to be involved in every part of his partner's life.

A family man.

Not a man who wants everything to revolve around him.

I rub the hollow between my breasts, wishing I could tear this gown off. Everything about it chokes me. "Ma'am?" I call out in a choked voice. What was her name?

She doesn't appear.

I grab the silk fabric of the train and tiptoe into the dressing room to close the door. I reach around with one hand to locate the tiny hooks above the hidden zipper. Must break out of the dress before I hyperventilate. If I can cool off, I can think. I skate my fingers along the back of the dress, searching futilely. No need to panic.

I continue my pat-down of the dress back until my arms hurt from contorting. I'm welded into this dress forever. A woman who had too much mocha chocolate ice cream last week and is paying the price now.

But that's silly. It's not only the tight dress. It's the vice-like grip of Mason's words. Does he realize I don't want to bend to everything he wants? Let me pick out my own freaking underwear, even if it's basic cotton panties.

I sit on the padded chair in the corner of the private dressing room. The fabric pinches my waistline in protest. "I need out of this dress!"

END OF PREVIEW

Find out what happens when Gunner comes back into Kiley's life in *The Fiction of Forever.*

Visit www.brindaberry.com for more information.

Also by Brinda Berry

Adult Novels
Chasing Luck (A Serendipity Novel, #1)
Tempting Fate (A Serendipity Novel, #2)
Seducing Fortune (A Serendipity Novel, #3)
Serendipity Boxed Set (Books 1-3)
The Beauty of Lies (A Stand By Me Novel #1)
The Fiction of Forever (A Stand By Me Novel #2)
Fit for Love (A Stand By Me Novel #3)
And Then He Kissed Her: A Contemporary Romance Boxed Set (Sweet Romance)

Young Adult Novels
The Waiting Booth (Whispering Woods #1)
Whisper of Memory (Whispering Woods #2)
Watcher of Worlds (Whispering Woods #3)
The Waiting Booth Boxed Set (Books 1-3)
Wild at Heart II (An Anthology)
Lore: Tales of Myth and Legend Retold (An Anthology)

Twitter: @Brinda_Berry
Facebook: BrindaBerryAuthor
Website: www.brindaberry.com

www.ingramcontent.com/pod-product-compliance
Lightning Source LLC
Chambersburg PA
CBHW020226180626
46810CB00006B/2062